Snow on the Danube

FRANCIS GILBERT

This edition first published in 2017 by Blue Door Press:
https://bluedoorpress.co.uk
Copyright © 2019 Francis Gilbert
Blue Door Press, London UK, bluedoorpress@gmail.com
British Library Cataloguing-in-Publications Data
A catalogue record for this book is available from the British
Library.
ISBN: 978-1-9164754-0-3

Dedication
Michael Whyte, great friend, colleague & most perceptive reader.
Acknowledgments
Erica Wagner for all her help.
Pam Johnson and Jane Kirwan at Blue Door Press for their support
and wonderful, creative advice.
Clare Alexander, Jason Cowley, Jane Harris, Nicolas Soames &
George Szirtes for reading earlier versions and providing helpful,
incisive comments.
Cover design by Sam Sullivan:
https://bluedoorpress.co.uk/associates/associate-2/

Also by Francis Gilbert
I'm A Teacher, Get Me Out of Here (2004)
Teacher on The Run (2005)
Yob Nation (2006)
Parent Power (2007)
Working the System (2011)
The Last Day of Term (2012)
How to get a great English Degree (2013)
Who Do You Love (2017)
The Mindful English Teacher (2018)

CONTENTS

Prologue

23RD JANUARY 6.30AM

Phone message.

Hi, Karolina, it's me, Béla. Why aren't you picking up? I'm standing on the Chain Bridge right now. It's freezing. And I'm looking down at the water. I can see the snow falling into its iciness.

I know it's early, but normally you're up, aren't you?

I'm going to do it.

I'm going to jump.

Did you know my one of my relatives did exactly the same thing, right here, in this spot?

Jumped into the Danube.

Suicide runs in the family, you see.

There's no way out.

You led me to believe that we'd be together forever, and now I'm in a living hell.

You know that I don't know anyone else in Budapest, I don't speak the language. I'm not going to try again. This is it. You did this to me, Karolina. I'm going…

From: BelaPongracz9@gmail.com
To: KarolinaTarr99@outlook.com

Hi Karolina,

You'll have noticed from this email that I didn't do it. An old lady in a shawl stopped me.

I was standing on the railings and she was shuffling by and she dropped her sack of onions and carrots and just pulled me off, shouting at me in Hungarian.

I've no idea what she said, and then she took my hand in her big gloves and pulled me over here to this café and said something to the owner who gave me a large coffee and a pancake. He speaks a little English. He said, 'I'm keeping an eye on you! You call a friend to come and get you before I let you go!'

And so I called you, and of course there was no answer, so he gave me the wi-fi code and I'm writing this email to you on my bust-up old MacBook, which was going to disappear with me into the Danube.

I feel a bit better. The old lady made me laugh, ranting and raving at me, and I like the big café owner. He's so Hungarian! He has a great big black moustache, he's unshaven, and walks around in a dirty apron like he's king of the world. The *palacsinte* is really nice, great smotherings of jam, and the coffee tastes bitter but good.

I'll call you a bit later on, I think. You're going to need to come and get me, because this guy is definitely not going to let me go unless someone comes. And that comforts me too. It doesn't mean I haven't given up on the idea. I'm going to do it at some point. I definitely am if…

And since I am, I have nothing to lose.

You see, the truth is Karolina I don't have a great job as a CGI visual effects programmer in London, and I'm not here working for a film production company. That's bullshit. I'm unemployed, and I've spent all my money coming here.

No, the real reason I came to Budapest is more sordid, more complex. It hurts me to talk about it. You see, there's a lot I haven't told you. And I think, before I go, I'd like to explain.

It really started a few months ago, back in October. It was late in the afternoon. I had just got up and was playing GTA on the PS4; that's how sad I am. I'm nearly thirty and all I fucking do all day is play computer games in my mother's flat. She's always going on at me how I need to get my act together; there was a spell when I did, but I tried hard, and I didn't get anywhere. But that's another story.

The main thing for you to know is that I don't have a fancy loft apartment in Shoreditch. I live with my mum in a council flat in Bethnal Green – a kind of different area. It's near to Shoreditch though and we have quite a few trendy tossers moving in near us.

Until October, I lived with my great-uncle. He's the one I've told you a little about. It's true he was a Count, but he's not alive.

I don't know whether I told you he was alive.

Perhaps it was to give you the impression that I am going to inherit a lot of money. You're a very artistic, intelligent woman Karolina, and being with you was the one of the most beautiful things that's happened to me.

I'm sorry I lied so much.

But I'm telling the truth now.

It was the late afternoon on Wednesday, and I'd just killed some prostitutes and was just jacking a fancy camper caravan when my great-uncle, who was sitting beside me, made these massive gesticulations with his arm. At first, I didn't take off my headphones because I was used to him doing things like this. He could be very dramatic.

I shared a room with him and every night, he would listen to Radio 3, conducting with his arms as he lay in bed.

I found it very irritating but I now I wish I could have him there in the bed next to me making all those crazy movements in the darkness and saying in that great Hungarian accent of his, 'Ah yes, Béla, my dear grand-nephew, just feel the sublimity of Ravel's *Gaspard de la nuit*, the shimmering crepuscular cadences entering your veins as you drift into sleep...'

That's how he talked. You'll see in a minute.

The terrible thing was, I took him for granted.

But I need to tell you this. I was sitting there playing GTA and the Count (that's what we called him) was watching this documentary about Hungary during the Second World War. I caught a glimpse of the Chain Bridge – the one I was just standing on – all blown up, and the Count uttered, 'Oh János, oh Anna, oh Imre!'

These were names I didn't understand.

And then he stood up, which was unusual for him -- he was nearly a hundred years old -- and staggered towards the TV and collapsed.

I ripped off my headphones and shouted to mum, and then saw his white face lying on the carpet. There was a tear in the corner of his eye.

And then he stopped moving. It was eerie his body so still.

Mum got up from the table where she was on her phone and lit a cigarette and puffed smoke over the Count's white hair. 'Hmmnn...doesn't look good!'

'You can say that again!' I yelled and called an ambulance. The medics took a while to come. And I didn't know what to do. I really wanted to carry on playing GTA, but mum wouldn't let me.

'Your great-uncle is probably dead! You can't play a computer game in front of his dead body!'

That made me feel terrible. I stopped and together we looked at his body and then at the documentary which now had the sound turned down.

There were images of Nazi and Soviet soldiers, bombs going off, piles of bodies being burnt in Auschwitz. It made me want to watch the programme but I knew mum would shout at me again, so I switched it off. This seemed the respectful thing to do.

And all sorts of difficult thoughts travelled through me as we waited. I was thinking: 'God, now I get my own bedroom at last!' I've had the Count sleeping in my room since I was young. He came to stay with us because he really needed looking after.

And although we didn't do a great job, at least we made sure he was fed, and he listened to Radio 3. During the summer, until a few years ago, he'd always go to the Proms, queuing up for the cheap tickets. Sometimes I went with him, but never enjoyed the music as much as he did.

And so the ambulance guys came and took us all to the hospital, where there was loads of waiting around. We had to leave him overnight so that there can be a post-mortem. When we returned in the morning, we were given the death certificate and the cause of death, which was a heart attack. I asked the doctor whether a shock could have triggered it.

'It's possible, but he was very old, and his heart was weak so it could have happened any time. Don't feel guilty.'

I asked mum whether she thought seeing that documentary could have killed him.

'Yes, maybe. I heard from my father that he was a bad boy during the war...'

'What do you mean bad boy?'

Mum lit a cigarette, puffing out smoke wearily. 'One thing you should learn, Béla, is that you don't ask Hungarians about the Second World War. Especially not at this time.'

That was – and is -- typical of her. Mum gives you a little tantalising clue about something and then shuts you down. I suspect that's because she doesn't know anything anyway.

My mum is a very bitter and frustrated woman. Her Dad, who was also born in Hungary, was a good scientist but a terrible father. Divorced my English grandmother after some dreadful bust-ups. I think it made Mum very angry inside – I used to see a counsellor, and I worked that one out. But she doesn't ever talk about it except to curse her father every now and then. He's dead now. Another heart-attack. But he was much unhealthier than the Count, his uncle; a very fat, chain-smoking man, loved his Hungarian pastries and goulash too much.

I guess this important to know because it meant that apart from Mum there's no one really I can ask about what actually happened.

Mum and I were totally broke, and we couldn't afford an expensive send-off. Although we are technically Jewish, we're not believers and so we opted for a secular, no-frills funeral. Mum moaned like mad because it cost over a thousand pounds! And even then, his Excellency had to be housed in a plywood coffin!

Still, our undertaker, Mr Hitchcock, was very understanding: he looked like the film director, fat and Cockney, but his manner was much nicer; it felt like he understood the pain of grief somehow. He was very good about collecting the body from the morgue and dealing with everything. We couldn't have done it all without him.

My only real job was to find some suitable clothes. With trembling fingers, I took the Count's powder-blue suit off its hanger in the wardrobe in our shared room and walked down the Bethnal Green Road with it in polythene bag, and I gave it to Mr Hitchcock, who made the Count look very aristocratic and Hungarian, putting a blood-red rose in his button-hole and delicately making him look almost alive with make-up. The eye shadow suited my uncle! There was always something artificial about him which the make-up highlighted. He was a distinctive-looking man, with large melancholic eyes and sculpted cheek-bones. Some people say I have his nose.

When I watched him roll into the incinerator, I was surprised to find myself sobbing. I never realised that I cared that much for him until that moment. It was as if I discovered there was this deep crater inside me, like coming home and finding your house has had a bomb dropped on it. That sense of absence hasn't gone away. And I'm not sure why because he really annoyed me when he was alive. There was no one there, but ourselves. Everyone he knew had died long ago. Sad, eh?

The day after we collected his ashes, mum dug around in his most private stuff and found his will. Suddenly she had this completely crazy hope that maybe he'd left us loads of money. We both knew that this was impossible -- because why would he have come to live with us if he had money? But then when she unearthed the will at the bottom of a drawer in a sealed envelope saying, 'To be opened in the event of Count Zoltan Pongrácz's death' and opened it, a mad hope seized us because there was a safe deposit box for us to open with a key in an envelope.

'And he's written that you are to have all the contents of it!' Mum gasped.

This knocked her sideways. 'God, after all I did for him!' she grumbled as we went into the City to the bank. 'It's all right Mum, I'll share it with you, don't worry!'

Since we found the envelope, we had been dreaming that we would never have to worry about money again; that we've have inherited some big estate in Hungary or something.

But of course, it didn't turn out that way at all. The deposit box just contained a manuscript and a letter addressed to me.

I scanned everything a while back into my Apple Mac, so you can read it too:

Dear Béla,

My dear anxious boy, I am writing to you now to introduce a piece of writing of mine which I was most anxious not to share with you while I was alive.

I would like to thank you for allowing me to sleep in your room for all these years; I hope you have learnt a modicum about the indescribable marvels and mystery of classical music.

I am aware that things have been difficult for you, as they have been for me. My health and nerves have never been respectable, and I suspect you too have inherited my disposition. I see you have your computer games to assist you with passing the time on this earth, as I have had my pálinka and music. They, at least, make things a little bearable.

Curiously, it was you that prompted me to write what you are about to read when you were a young boy at secondary school.

You were a lovely little thing then, always full of questions about me and my past, which sadly, you may have noticed, I was not keen to dredge up. You may not remember but you were required to conduct a project about a country that interested you, and initially you chose Hungary.

I am ashamed to say that I rebuffed all your questions about my past with improbably bad manners -- not the 'done thing' for a Count -- but perhaps, as you read, this you will understand why. But the questions did make me think, ah yes, 'The poor little mite might not be ready right now for the truth but at some point he will be!' And so, while you were out at school, and your mother at work, I wrote the following narrative. It took me a profoundly long time; some four years, writing a little at each day. But as I wrote, I became increasingly determined to finish my story.

I both hate and love my story. I am proud that I completed it. This must be said.

I did a terrible thing, Bela, and saw terrible things. My eyes are full of tears as I think about Anna and Imre. It has been the most torturous travail of my life to pen my account of what occurred, and I know I could endure no questions about it.

It's better that I am dead. But I also think you should know of these events, these travails of my past – and so, in a sense, of yours.

Your ever humble servant,

Count Zoltan Pongrácz, your great-uncle.

Quite a letter, eh? Mum was furious about there being no money, and had no interest in reading the manuscript.

'Believe me, you don't want to read it! His self-serving justifications won't ever convince me!' she said.

'What do you mean?'

'He was a traitor, Béla! I put up with him in my house because he was family, but make no mistake about it! He betrayed my grandparents.'

'What do you mean?'

'My father never forgave him. That's all you need to know. Throw away the manuscript and let's get a drink!'

But I didn't. Instead, over the next day and night, I read it.

I want you to read it, Karolina. You're Hungarian -- and 48 hours ago you said you loved me. Can you read it and then we can talk about it? Can we meet again? Call me. I'm still in the café. I'll send you the first part of the story now, and then show you some more later? Here you go. I hope we'll speak soon.

Part One: First Moves

1: THE LION BRIDGE

Hungary wore black on the day of my birth. Street vendors tied black ribbons around bouquets of flowers; archdukes donned their darkest garb and thrummed their fingers on gold-tasselled armrests. Tram-drivers left their trolley buses in the depot and sat with their children in their tiny flats. Priests and civil servants hoisted black flags and watched them flutter in the air. The streets were empty. Church bells rang. Gamekeepers cancelled their early morning walks; they slumped in their chairs, hounds at their feet. Maids failed to make their daily trips to the grocers and lay on camp beds in their cubby-holes; bakers neglected to light their ovens and open their shutters. The keeper at the City Zoo threw a few thin slabs of meat to the lions and slouched home.

It was a day of national mourning. In Paris, a treaty was signed that butchered Hungary. Two-thirds of the kingdom was turned over to Romania, Czechoslovakia, and Yugoslavia. Hungary had supported the losing side in the First World War.

My father had two reasons to wear black on June 4, 1920. Not only had he lost the family's monumental Transylvanian castle in the unceremonious carve-up of the Treaty of Trianon but he had also, on the very same day, to endure the birth of his son.

My memories from those very early years are vague. I don't remember much about the family's life at our chateau in Villány. I can recall my father's imperious voice barking orders at the workmen who toiled all day at the bottom of our ornamental garden. 'Down there! Careful now. Easy with those girders!'

His shirt sleeves were rolled up and his bald head seemed to glow as he twirled his silver-topped cane. Seething below his polished hunting boots was a mass of perspiring muscles, mushrooming dust and heaving bricks. I had no idea what was going on but I guessed it was of the utmost importance.

My first memory of my sister is of her informing me about those mysterious, grunting proceedings. Her black hair brushed my cheek as she leaned towards me and whispered: 'They're building a bridge. Papa says it's very important that the lions have tongues.'

Trying to connect the idea of the bridge with lions was very difficult for me. I imagined that Papa would place real ones on the bridge and this was the whole purpose of the exercise: to give the lions a decent home.

This supposition was no more ridiculous than what he was attempting to do. My father, being fanatical about bridges, thought that he could somehow rectify the dire financial problems afflicting his vineyards by building a replica of Budapest's Chain Bridge at the bottom of his garden. He persisted in believing in this illusion for a long time, even after the construction of the imitation bridge had bankrupted him, forced him to sell the chateau and move permanently back to Budapest.

Many years later, when I would stroll with my father on the actual bridge in the Budapest twilight, he would sigh and point to the monumental but tongueless lions, commenting regretfully: 'People were coming from miles around to see my Chain Bridge at Villány. The archduke Frederick himself greatly admired it. That bridge was the only thing that wretched estate had going for it: it was a rotten, dry, wizened sort of place. We never grew a single decent grape there.'

After the Count's death, I discovered that this was an outright lie. Although my father sold the chateau, he continued to own vast tracts of the vineyards. He had the good sense to appoint an honest and practical Magyar supervisor to run them all. This doughty chap wasn't even discouraged by the lack of any venue to make the wine in and converted some abandoned cellars on the estate for that purpose. The fantastic Hungarian wines that this chateauless estate produced was the only real source of income that my family had.

But, of course, I knew none of this as a tiny child gazing on all those workmen toiling away at the banks of the small river that babbled at the bottom of our garden. At the grand opening of the bridge, which most of the neighbouring villages attended, my father held me up proudly before the stone lions.

'My lions have tongues that definitively exist -- unlike the lions on the Chain Bridge in Budapest. They'll be seeing my lions' tongues for miles around! Just look at them!' the Count roared as he held me aloft before the curled manes of those sandstone felines. To be honest, I don't remember this but the anecdote was recounted with such regularity in the following years that it has almost become a genuine memory.

Certain smells awaken glimmerings of the chateau at Villány in my mind. The sharp, rich tang of fermenting wine transports me to the time when Anna gave me an illicit sip: I can still see her dimpled fingers wrapped around the glass. The cool dampness of mould compels me to recall the wooden barrels in the wine cellars. The baked warmth of the hard earth makes me see those dry vineyards tapering off into the horizon. And the delicious whisk of a breeze sends me back to the moments when I would stand in the middle of the bridge, watch the water ripple underneath and feel the airy draught against my cheeks. Ah yes, I'm never far from those sensations.

My sister told me that we used to play a lot of games around the bridge's building site. Her favourite pastime was a game that she had invented after reading Molnár's *The Paul Street Boys*. This was a classic Hungarian children's story about a group of boys who engage in a fierce battle with a nasty gang to claim ownership of some derelict but treasured land in the slums of Budapest. I'm not sure that our massive garden in Villány, with its circular ponds and cherub-infested fountain, topiary hedges and lichened griffins, replicated those conditions but apparently Anna managed to persuade the servants' children and myself that it did.

According to my sister, we all had a marvellous time throwing sand and bricks at each other and hiding behind wheelbarrows until I received a vicious crack on the head. Anna had to scoop me up in her arms and run with me into the drawing room where my mother was reading. Mama said there was so much blood spurting out of my head that Anna's white frock turned red. Because there was no hospital nearby, they had to take me to a gypsy healer who waved some leaves over my battered skull and curtailed the bleeding.

My only memory of the event is of a warm stickiness sprouting out of my scalp and wondering whether cocoa and other hot beverages were extracted from people's heads. Push back my hair and you can still see the long, white scar.

* * *

Yes, yes, yes: there are black and white photos from this time. There's my father, the Count, standing in his hunting gear and deerstalker hat with his Purdey shotgun in front of the fat-tongued lions. There's my mother, sitting under a parasol in her white, floral dress, reading *Pride and Prejudice* and looking like the fair English maiden that she was before we moved to Budapest. There's me, as a baby, wearing a long, cotton dress with frilly edges and long sleeves being carried by my mother in the road leading to the Archduke Frederick's farm – his wine cellars and hunting grounds were close to us and we used to visit them regularly. What big round eyes I have! But you can certainly see in my pale, agitated face the first inklings of the illnesses that would plague me for the rest of my life.

* * *

And there's Anna. Doesn't she look naughty with her dark, inquiring eyes, her cheeky grin, her thick black hair, and her high, Pongrácz cheekbones, all dolled up in that ridiculous harlequin's costume and hat? She always loved dressing up, even in the days when she became a hardened communist.

And here we all are together in our stately horse-drawn carriage, setting off for Mass in our Sunday best: my father is dressed in sober black with a top hat and my mother entirely obscured by the huge, netted hat she's decided to model. And there we are behind them: me, in an absolutely tiny shirt and tie, and Anna looking distinctly grumpy in a Transylvanian frock. She never liked acting the role of a Magyar. But my goodness, she looks so slim and young!

2: BEETROOT MEDICINE

It's a shame that I remember so little from that time, but I was only five years old when my sister and I left Villány. My memory only revives when we moved to Budapest. And those first days and weeks I can recollect so vividly that I can shut my eyes and replay them with the same ease that a projectionist can pop a film into his whirring machine and shine it in Technicolor onto the darkened cinema screen.

Her warm breath smells of that curd, *zsendice*, made from sheep's milk. She's been nibbling in the kitchen again. Naughty girl. She's whispering something in my ear. 'Look what I've got for you, Zoltán!'

I lift my head off the pillow, trying to banish my dreamy sleep, and look at her rosy hand holding out a large, ripe peach. The sunlight filters through the nursery window and dapples the fruit. Anna presses its downy flesh against my cheek and I savour its coolness while sinking back into the bed and shutting my eyes. I'm so sleepy.

'Come on sleepyhead, get up!' Anna insists. 'Take a bite.'

She stuffs the peach into my mouth and I find that I'm sinking my teeth into its sweet flesh. Juice dribbles out of my mouth and I can feel Anna's hands cupping the flow of it and wiping away the stickiness with the sides of her hands. Her small fingers are warm.

'Get up. You're dribbling, Zoltika,' she says, tickling me under the bed clothes. 'I'll give you a piggy back.'

I open my eyes and kick away the blankets, wheezing slightly as I stand up suddenly on the bed. I sniffle. A little bubble of snot blinks out of my nose and I feel my passageways clearing. I can breathe properly. I smile and leap onto Anna's back.

(Why are these happy memories the most painful? I could tell you the nasty stuff without a tear in my eye but this memory makes me want to dissolve into the earth.)

I immerse my cheeks in the silky texture of her thick, black hair. I listen to her vibrant breathing as she carries me out of the nursery and into the hallway. I'm already panting but her breath is steady and true. I can hear the pendulum clock ticking behind us in its ebony case as Anna thumps across the shiny floor and bashes through a door studded with milky glass. We flap through and laugh at the sight of the empty kitchen. Not a maid in sight! Where are they?

A large cast-iron cauldron, a *bogrács*, is bubbling on the big, white stove. From the vantage-point of my sister's back I can see what's going on inside it. It's disgusting. There are lots of eggs shells tussling around in a scummy, brown froth. Little bits of carrots and celery, and other vegetables that I haven't learnt the names of yet, keep bobbing up to the surface.

'Yuk. What is that, Annuska?' I ask.

'Don't look at that,' my sister says. She hitches me up higher on her back and takes a final run towards the window, letting me drop down onto the wide brim of the sill. She undoes the catch and opens the window. We can hear our maids screeching down below. But it's very odd because there's nothing to be seen; it's as if invisible people are causing a commotion in the courtyard.

Anna hitches me up on her back again and she rushes through a small door in the kitchen. We pass through a cramped room that has two mattresses lying on the floor, another small room, and then find ourselves at the top of a flight of stairs that look nothing like the main staircase of the apartment building. They are very narrow and dingy, the banisters don't have the fancy ornaments that adorn the other stairs, and there's a horrid smell of mould and bird droppings.

'Look,' Anna says, pointing down at the dark courtyard.

I peer over her shoulders, down through the maze of the t banisters and gnarled steps but I can't see anything. But when I screw up my eyes, I can make out what is happening. At the base of the stairs, Teresa and Margaret, our two waddling maids, are beating the hell out of a pretty rug with their cane carpet beaters. Dust billows up out of the shadows and dances when it hits the slanted sunbeams that are pouring into the stairwell from the courtyard.

It's difficult to hear what the two maids are saying but I can see they are enjoying hitting the carpet with their *prakkers* and they seem to be laughing. I've never heard them laugh. The idea that they're not wearing their usual morose, silent faces seems inconceivable to me.

I lean further over the banisters and catch their words echoing up the stairwell.

'And this one's for the old crow! And this one's for his son, mewling, puling thing!' I hear Teresa saying.

Her greying, thinning hair is tied up in a knot. Margaret is hooting so much that she has to blow her nose on her ragged handkerchief. Before I can listen to anymore, Anna's hands press against my ears and yank me away from the stairs, back through the tiny room and into the kitchen.

'Don't listen to them,' Anna says. 'They're just big hens.'

I gasp. Calling a woman a 'big hen' is a great insult in Hungarian. It makes me think that perhaps the maids were referring to me when they were thrashing the carpet. When Anna squeezes my hand and whispers, 'I'll protect you,' my confusion only deepens.

I never feel entirely safe with Teresa and Margaret again after that. I won't even let them give me my nightly medicine. Only Anna can do that.

My sister grips my wrist. The spirit lamp throws billowing shadows against the roses climbing up the wallpaper. Darkness enfolds the big dolls' house that stands tall on the mahogany table: its tower, gingerbread trimming, jutting balconies and gothic windows cast spiky silhouettes onto the icy floor. I can hear the ebony clock ticking in the hallway and the hum of air in Anna's throat as she lets go of my wrist and pours the red liquid from a moulded brown bottle onto the tablespoon. She tells me to open wide. I shut my eyes as I swallow the horrid medicine, which tastes of old beetroot, and try to absorb the warmth of her body and smell the apricot scent that always seems to linger on her, and forget the wretched medicine.

'It will make you sleep better, Zoltika,' she always said as she placed the brown bottle on my bedside cabinet and then climbed into her own bed that situated in the far corner of the nursery. 'Do you know the story of the beetroot medicine? I will tell it to you, if you like. It is a unique cure made many hundreds of years ago for the Pongráczes. In those days, the Counts lived a huge castle in the mountains and owned forests, lakes and land as far as the eye could see. But although they were very rich, they weren't happy -- because they were afflicted by terrible stomach, head and bone aches. Their guts roiled, they felt as if their skulls were pierced by daggers, their shins and elbows felt as if they would crumble to dust. They paid for the best doctors in the world to visit them and provide a cure for their ailments, but to no avail, until one day, a beggar woman and her beautiful daughter with long flowing hair visited the kitchen to sell the cook some beetroots. Now -- it so happened that the young Count was in the yard near the kitchen... he was, in fact, being sick, vomiting copiously, thinking he was not in sight of anyone. The beggar woman and her daughter saw him as they turned the corner into the yard and rushed to his aid. The Count was very embarrassed but then, when the daughter stroked the back of his neck to soothe him, he explained his problem. The beggar woman promised she would cure him -- but he had to grant her one wish if she did. Because the Count felt so ill, he hastily agreed. That night, the beggar woman locked herself in the kitchen making a medicine out of her beetroots, boiling them up in a big pot and add lots other herbs and spices. Only her daughter observed her making the potion. In the morning, she gave the elixir to the Count. After only a few minutes, he began to feel better. He was so overjoyed that he asked the woman to tell him her wish. His face fell when he heard what it was: he had to marry her daughter. However, he'd been so sick the morning before that he hadn't noticed her beauty so when she entered the room and he saw her flashing eyes and golden skin and tumbling hair, he smiled, and said he would agree. And so, the Count married the beggar woman's daughter, and, as a result, the secret of the medicine has stayed in the family ever since, with the female line showing trusted servants how to make it. The maids and our butler are the only people currently able to create the potion, and I have been given the recipe in father's will. Do you know what the name was of that beggar woman's daughter Zoltika?'

'No,' I gulped, feeling the magic of my sister's story filter through my bones.

'Anna!'

If I hadn't been fully convinced of the medicinal powers of that beetroot medicine, I was now. Before hearing this story, I thought that the elixir made it even harder for me to sleep, as it gurgled through my addled passageways and settled in my gut, making me belch and fart all night long. But now I didn't worry. I always knew that I would sleep because I had the beetroot medicine and Anna was in the room with me. When I heard her deep inhalations, I knew that it was safe to shut my eyes.

3: JÁNOS AND THE ZOO

Our parents did not hurry to move with us to Budapest. They went motoring around Europe and judged us too young to go with them. As if to compensate for such negligence they left express instructions that we shouldn't be allowed outside of our huge, elevated apartment unless accompanied by our butler, János.

Although I was not inclined to venture abroad if Anna entertained me in the nursery, she was endlessly curious about the vast, golden avenue that sang outside our window. She was just tall enough to peep over the windowsill and peer down at the treetops that lined it. Every now and then she would heave me onto her back -- against the wishes of Teresa and Margaret who were obviously worried I might fall through the glass -- and show me the street below. The rich green leaves of the treetops obscured my view but I did see the occasional bonnet of an automobile or a horse's bridle flashing in the sun.

These fleeting glimpses of a totally alien world were enough for me -- after my fateful trip to the kitchen even the shortest of piggyback rides tended to exhaust me – but Anna was not content. I would hear her arguing with Teresa and Margaret that she wanted to go to the zoo, that papa had promised to take her there, and that he would have them beaten with their own *prakkers* if they didn't escort her.

'His Excellency told us that you must not go out until János comes back,' Teresa would reply in a meek voice -- so unlike the vicious screech she had hurled at the Persian rug that I wondered whether there were two separate Teresas.

After receiving this patient reply a few times, Anna would slam the nursery door behind her and return to playing doctors and nurses with me – our main recreation. You see, we had a wonderful dolls' house and several beautifully attired dolls to play with. Unknown to me at the time, the house was a valuable antique that Anna had retrieved, against our mother's express orders, from the library. It was an incredible object; I can see it as vividly as daylight even now. It was three storeys high, and had windows projecting from its sloping roof that allowed the light to flood into the attic where several black-suited servants slept in iron-framed beds. There were four narrow chimneys and something that Anna explained to me was a belvedere, or lookout tower.

'The belvedere makes this more than a dolls' house, it makes it actually a castle,' she confided to me once. 'This is a very important dolls' house.'

The tower provided the model with a simultaneously monumental and mystical aura. But the carved gingerbread trimming around the windows, balconies and the roof offset the haughty severity of the belvedere wonderfully well, evoking a contrasting cosy atmosphere.

Each window was pointed, smaller than a child's hand and held patterned glass, making access into the house nearly impossible from the outside. However, it was easy to open it because it was divided in half by hinges and was mounted on wheels so that it swung open when you unhooked it at the sides. The interior was a real revelation. Despite its Gothic exterior, it was decked out like a proper English country house inside. There were five main rooms: a dining-room, a parlour, two bedrooms and a music room, all of which contained scaled-down furniture, including a tiny grand piano and brass handrails.

The dolls themselves, who were all girls apart from the dull-coloured servants, were dressed in colours of sugared almonds: primrose, lilac, pistachio and white. Each of their silk dresses was draped in transparent muslin, bustled and looped and trained. This meant that one of the servants had to double up as a doctor while the white dressed doll posed as a nurse when we played our interminable medical games. Usually, the format of these games was very simple. One of the dolls would fall out of the tower after being chased by a *prakker*-wielding servant. Then the doctor and nurse would arrive and take the injured person to the parlour for a major operation.

I had absolutely no idea where my parents were and I didn't care. I didn't understand the concept of having parents. I automatically assumed that every boy had a sister who played with him and gave him medicine, two friendly maids who fed them and two sinister maids, looking just like the friendly ones, who beat rugs with their *prakkers* down in the stairwell in the early morning.

But I suppose my butler was much more of a parent to me than my actual ones. When I first encountered him, I felt that I had never seen such a fine man as János before. His polished shoes pattered across the varnished floor of the nursery with a crisp rhythm that seemed utterly thrilling when I compared his perfect tread to the irregular waddle of the maids. Only Anna's twinkling, feathery steps were more refined than János's walk. But I've never come across a more musical male gait than János's.

Those shiny shoes halted before me. He didn't deign to look at Anna but addressed me by bowing decorously. Then he straightened his tail-coat, took my hand in his strong, weathered palm and kissed the back of my fingers. I can still remember the sensation of his whiskery moustache bristling against my hand, the smell of his freshly laundered shirt and the slight tang of his sweat.

(Sometimes I wonder whether I was as sick as Anna claimed I was then. She was always telling me that I suffered from a terrible head cold for most of my childhood but the most vivid memories of my childhood are of smells: her sugary warmth, János's sweat, the maid's goulash, the coffee breath of Andrássy.)

* * *

'Your Excellency, noble son of the Count Pongrácz, I am for this one day, entirely at your disposal. I will serve you in any way that you see fit,' the butler said, and then with another shorter, more peremptory bow departed.

Anna stopped pushing the nose of the rocking horse with the same aggression that she had been when János had entered and ran over to me, giving me a big hug.

'But don't you see what this means, Zoltika? We can go to the zoo!' she said.

I remained limp within her grasp because I had been thinking that I would like to enlist János in the doctors and nurses game that we had been playing; he would make the perfect patient. So far, we could only play the game on lifeless dolls, the effect of which was beginning to wear thin. We could operate upon his moustache and see what was underneath that white shirt. When I explained this to Anna, her eyes grew wide with disbelief and then she started to laugh.

'You can't do that. He didn't mean that.'

'He said he was entirely at my disposal,' I whined, my eyes brimming with tears at the thought that we wouldn't be playing doctors and nurses after all and that we would be forced to visit the zoo which sounded more frightening than Bluebeard's castle with all its wild animals. (When my sister lovingly explained the whole concept of the zoo to me, she omitted to mention that the animals were kept behind bars and so I had the impression that we might be attacked by lions and tigers, bitten by snakes and stampeded by elephants.)

When it became clear that I was determined to ask the butler to play doctors and nurses, Anna leaned closer to me and whispered in my ear: 'If we don't go to the zoo, I'll carry you down to the stairwell in the morning and you can get beaten with the rugs, you little monkey.'

It was the first time Anna ever threatened me. Her words had a sobering effect and I stopped crying. A little undulation of fear shot through my sickly frame: here was the person I most trusted in the world saying that she would make the necessary arrangements to hurt me. I didn't entirely give credence to her warning but I believed her enough to be thrilled by the fright.

Although it was directly outside our window, I had no idea just how majestic Andrássy Avenue was until I stood on its pavement. Standing in it for the first time felt like meeting a mighty king all bedecked in his royal finery. The tree-lined promenade islands seemed like the huge coils of jewels that hung around his neck, the great curling arches of its buildings formed his vast forehead, and the sunlit expanse of its roadway was his splendid smile.

I looked back at our apartment and gazed up, open-mouthed, at the enormous sculptures of Hercules that supported the pillars underneath the balconies of our apartment and thought how lucky it was that we lived in a place that was protected by such strong men. I almost wouldn't have believed that we lived in such a well-protected domain but I recognised the royal red of the curtains and I could see the tip of the rocking horse's head poking through the gap.

János escorted me, with due decorum, off the pavement and into the automobile that was waiting underneath the shade of a big tree. Anna still lingered on the pavement, looking like a wind-blown rhododendron in her starched pink pinafore. I stood on the leather seat of the car, leaned over its rim and yanked at one of Anna's pink shoulder straps.

'Do we really live there, Annuska?' I asked.

'Of course, we do, you silly sparrow. We're important,' Anna said, taking my hand away from her dress and squeezing it. 'And you're the most important person of all because right now you are the master of the house. You don't know what that means, do you?'

I contemplated this and realised that those huge strongmen with stone drapery wrapped around their naughty bits somehow indicated that we were not just anybody. Anna still hadn't got into the car despite János's best efforts.

'That means you can do anything. Even go on the metro if you want to,' she continued. Anna wanted to ride on the underground railway that ran underneath Andrá↔ssy Avenue. She was always making little tunnels underneath my bed and telling me that metro trains take you to the zoo.

'I'm afraid that the Count has forbidden for the young lady to go there,' János said sternly, waiting for the awkward girl to hop into the car.

'But the Count isn't in charge today,' Anna said with a wicked smile. And then pointing at my tiny figure, my head dwarfed by the big door of the car, she said: 'The master is. And he commands us to go on the metro, don't you Zoltika?'

Ever mindful of her whispered threat about sending me down to the courtyard and leaving me to the mercy of those horrid *prakkers*, I said weakly, without really knowing what I was letting myself in for, 'Yes, I command that.'

János deposited us back in the apartment without a murmur of complaint. He stowed the automobile back in the garage where it had mouldered, unused, for over a year, and then took us both by the hand and led us down to the metro.

What a miserable place that metro was. Yes, I know it is supposed to be one of the nicest underground railways in the world – indeed it is the oldest in mainland Europe – but I hated it as much as my sister loved it. Before we boarded, she sniffed the singed air -- caused by the ozone of the direct current electricity -- and ran up and down the empty platform. János watched her with weary patience and held my hand. His fingers felt warm and solid.

When the train arrived, she pushed her way through the crowded carriage and squeezed onto the wooden bench next to a ragged old lady. Anna banged into her as she swivelled round and knelt facing the window. The old lady was about to complain but she saw János glaring at her and lowered her eyes as if ashamed. Utterly oblivious to this exchange, Anna pressed her nose against the trembling windowpanes as we rattled through the darkness. She begged me to do it as well.

'You get such a funny feeling in your ears,' she said brightly.

I clung to János. I had never seen so many people. I didn't know that so many people lived underground. Anna kept calling me to look at the tunnel but I couldn't face it. I already wanted to go home and play doctors and nurses with the dolls. Dolls were so much easier to control than all these huge people with their flapping dresses, tatty trousers and scuffed shoes. I even saw several people whose feet were bundled up in newspaper. I wondered why their servants didn't polish their shoes. I shut my eyes and buried my head in János's black coat. It smelt clean and not frowzy like these chewed-up people.

Eventually we emerged from that long hole in the ground and strode into the sunlight. High above us, materialising out of the blue sky like the genie in the Arabian Nights, appeared lots of beautiful sea-green minarets, glittering in the sun. I was so engrossed in watching the interplay of the clouds on their effervescent surface that I didn't notice that a ring of frozen polar bears were peering at me from the top of a large archway. But I leapt back in fright when I did.

'Careful János, they might eat us!' I screamed.

Anna giggled as János reassured me in his quiet, indefatigable fashion that there was nothing to be scared of because those bears weren't alive. Nevertheless, I remained a little nervous of them and the two large, stone elephants who were poking their trunks at me as János bought our tickets.

We lost Anna as soon as János had bought her some candyfloss. She ran laughing – her cheeks all smeared with sticky, pink crystals -- into the Elephant House and vanished. János didn't seem overly concerned, but I fretted. Firstly, I wondered if she would get trampled by the elephants or eaten by the lions. Then when János entered the elephant house and I saw the huge concrete ditch that separated us from those thundering feet and snorting trunks, I realised the idea of a zoo without bars I'd got from Anna was wrong. I suddenly began to think Anna knew nothing about zoos and had, contrary to her assertions, never visited one before. She was like one of those silly girls who entered Bluebeard's castle – running off into a place that was totally unknown to her.

By the time we had hurried past the animals and reached the Reptile House, even János seemed a little concerned that we hadn't seen a peek of that pink dress. The muggy air of the Reptile House oppressed me and the sight of lots of dead white mice lying at the bottom of the cages seemed foreboding. Their little eyes oozed blood. I gazed at their crushed carcasses, pondering what horrible creatures could harm such innocence. And then the ground seemed to move beside them and a large black snake rose out of the brown undergrowth. I jumped away from the glass and ran out into the yard.

Wheezing from these unexpected exertions, I spent a moment catching my breath and stared up at a knot of children twisted around what I believed to be a tall, misshapen, shaggy-haired man with a big mouth and nostrilless nose. Anna was at the front of these children and was feeding this monstrous humanoid twists of her pink candyfloss. When this 'person' opened his mouth, I realised to my horror that it wasn't a man at all but a terrible monster with a long neck and a scrubby hump on its back. When I saw its big yellow teeth, I automatically assumed that it was intent upon swallowing my sister and storing her inside its hump.

I ran through the crowd, yelling at the top of my voice: 'No, you mustn't touch Anna, you humpy monster!'

My protestations clearly had an effect because the crowd parted and Anna dropped her candyfloss as she turned around to face me. However, as I approached, her shock at my outcry quickly turned into mirth.

'Zoltika, come here my little sparrow! It's not a humpy monster, it's just a camel!'

Even when she held me up to the railings and showed me the camel benignly chewing on some straw in the dusty corner of its pen, I still wasn't convinced: I already had a sense that the friendliest-looking creatures were the most dangerous. They lured you into a false sense of security. Ultimately, I was perfectly content to accept that I lived in the same world as vicious animals like snakes, lions, tigers, and tarantulas, but I was very reluctant to tolerate the existence of the camel. I couldn't believe it was harmless.

I hooked my hand into Anna's and didn't let go of her until we left the zoo and were settled down on the horses of the merry-go-round in the fair. I was never happier than sitting on what I assumed would be a stationary black and white horse. Unfortunately, I hadn't reckoned on it moving forward as well as jolting up and down. I screamed for the second time that day and let go of the supporting pole in a desperate effort to reach out for Anna's hand. But the awful waltzing music was too loud for my yells to be heard and besides, she was too busy trying to stand on the saddle of her horse to notice my pleas. I remained stranded. Behind me, angels blew their horns on the front of jingling sleighs and boats rocked about on stormy seas. I covered my ears and shut my eyes, trying to blot out this erupting world of movement and fear.

Eventually, the ride came to a stop and I climbed off, begging János to take me home. However this became difficult when Anna ran off yet again. The butler was compelled to take me in his arms and chase after her. He caught up with her in the courtyard of the Vajdahunyad – the amazing replica of a Transylvanian castle that is situated by the City Park's boating lake. Anna was gazing up in awe at its myriads of needle-point turrets and rows of arrow-slitted fortifications. Her small pink pinafore was so engulfed by that morass of arching stone and sloping brown towers that she looked like a little puff of candyfloss about to be gobbled up by its dragon's teeth.

Fortunately, János was far too tired to entertain her desire to look around the castle, and he dragged her away as she said to me in confidence: 'I think that's where Bluebeard lives, you know. János does not want to take us there, because his ancestors were related to Bluebeard's great-grandfather!'

I laugh to remember this comment now, but at the time it terrified me; could János be fully trusted if he had some of Bluebeard's blood in his veins, even if it was very diluted? As with everything Anna said, there was an infinitesimal grain of truth in it, because I was to learn from my father some years later about János's lineage: his ancestors had been servants to the Pongráczes for centuries – and how they came to work for my family is a fascinating tale.

My father told me that one of the Count Pongráczes in the 15th century had been sent on a diplomatic mission to Brittany to meet with a powerful lord. The lord was called Gilles de Rais, and the talk concerned Joan of Arc, the Maid of Orléans. Was an alliance with Joan a sensible option for the Hungarians? She was in the ascendancy at the time, conquering France with her army. Gilles de Rais was one of the female warrior's strongest allies. But the negotiations were not successful; the Count was wary of allying the nation with such a rebellious faction.

Yet eeven though things had gone badly, the Count accepted de Rais's offer of hospitality and sojourned for a night in the Breton's castle. That night, with a full moon flooding through an arched window, the Count found himself shaken rudely awake. Before him stood a frightened boy dressed in rags. At first the little thing was quite incoherent, but when the Count could muster some sense from the chattering wreck, he learnt that the Breton was planning to poison him at breakfast and send an imposter, a lookalike, in his place back to the Hungarian court and claim that an alliance was entirely suitable. Although puzzled as to why he was being told this by a member of the household, the Count believed the boy and departed with his men almost immediately. The retinue were leaving the castle as quietly as they could when they were surprised by someone running towards their carriage in the dark; to their relief it was the young boy and not Gilles de Rais's guards. The boy begged them to take him with them because he believed he was going to be murdered shortly as well. 'None of the children survive in this castle,' he said. Grateful for the tip-off, the Count agreed and asked the boy's name, which was John, at which point, the Count gave him his Hungarian name, János.

This pathetic little thing grew up to be a fine man who was trained by the Count personally to be his bodyguard and butler. He married a servant who worked in the kitchen, and had twelve sons, all of whom served the Count in different ways, and all of whom had sons themselves. And so, the custom was established that the eldest son of the eldest János would learn to be the Count's most trusted servant. Remarkably, this tradition continued through the succeeding centuries: there was always a János to help the Pongráczes cope with whatever history threw at them: the nightmare of Ottoman invasions, ridiculous Austro-Hapsburgian bureaucracy and political infighting, and numerous wars, famines and revolutions. Each generation distinguished itself by unremitting, unquestioning loyalty, brilliant organisational skills and absolute discretion. And now, these most of loyal of servants were sticking by the family as they dealt with the worst blow of all, the Treaty of Trianon.

Of course, at this point in our lives neither Anna or I knew the history of János, or were remotely aware that Gilles de Rais is considered by some to be the model for Bluebeard. Anna had only picked up silly, inaccurate rumours, and did not know that actually both his and our own ancestors had helped each other to escape the monster's clutches. Oh, the silliness of childish gossip!

However, I think both of us were aware that if we were going to trust anyone with our lives it was János. As if to prove our unshakeable faith in our butler, we smiled at each other and held hands as János summoned a cab after that eventful trip to the zoo. And we continued intertwining our fingers in the back of the carriage, as we trotted through Heroes Square with its giant statues, chariots and columns and down the glorious smile of Andrássy Avenue. Ah, the warmth of Anna's fingers! If only I had them to bring life to my chilly digits now!

4: THE DOLL'S HOUSE

After that trip to the zoo, our games in the nursery changed drastically. Anna found some clay from God knows where and we spent some time attempting to make different animals. In reality, they didn't resemble beasts at all but I believed they did because Anna said so. These misshapen blobs looked a bit more convincing when we painted them. Even so, we were both disappointed with our efforts and decided that we needed to make an impressive zoo in order to compensate for the models' deficiencies. We puzzled over how we might do this for ages. And then Anna was struck by a marvellous thought.

'We can make a zoo which is like Bluebeard's castle. We can use the dolls' house. It's got a tower like the castle and its windows are similar.'

To an adult this might seem an illogical idea but I remember thinking at the time it was a brilliant notion that solved the intractable problem of where to keep our animals at one fell swoop, and it made the zoo much more than a zoo. It made it a place of mystery, darkness and murder. Although I didn't enjoy being confronted with the real horrors of actual camels, I was very happy to deal with them on an imaginary basis.

And so, Anna set about 'renovating' the dolls' house with gusto. We endeavoured to make the outside like the Vajdahunyad's by sloshing black paint over the creamy grey exterior. At the time, it seemed like we were successful; when we had finished, the belvedere and balconies looked very menacing indeed, glinting darkly underneath the electric light. We opened the house and ripped out much of the furniture from the delicate rooms, pulled down some of the walls and poked our black paintbrushes against the cardboard walls.

We decided to make the dolls look more realistic. We tore off the transparent muslin, cut each silk dress into shreds and dirtied their chests and legs with grey paint and scuffed their faces a little. I took off the twinkling shoes from one of the dolls and stuck tiny shreds of newspaper on her feet.

'You can't go to the zoo with newspaper on your feet,' Anna said indignantly.

But Anna was impressed when I explained that I had seen someone on the train with their feet wrapped in newspaper. Because the metro had always been situated underneath Anna's bed, she decided that we had to move the zoo-castle next to her bedside table so that we could have the metro running next to the zoo. Anna neatly placed the newspaper doll beside the old steam train that always resided in the chasm between the varnished floor and her bed.

Finally, we were set. Our endless games with the zoo-castle began. They would last whole days, although I forget exactly what they involved. But I do remember that we managed to combine both doctors and nurses and elements from Bluebeard's castle into the game. Invariably Bluebeard would capture my doll – the newspaper doll. His punishment was always to lock my doll up in a dark room, usually the attic, in the turreted zoo-castle that used to be the dolls' house. At some point in the fantasy, Anna's favourite animal, the camel, would always rescue me. It's a measure of the love that I felt for her that I allowed the camel to liberate me; I didn't like the thought of riding on the camel's back at all. Luckily, the clay animal who posed as the camel did not look remotely like the creature I had seen in the zoo and I could imagine that it was a tiger that I was riding home on and not that nasty humpy monster.

When we were not playing the Bluebeard game, Anna would entertain me by showing me pictures of our 'real life' castle. It looked like the most extraordinary place. It was situated high up on a mountain top and it had lots of boulders surrounding it, five turrets sprouting out of it, two towers guarding its portcullis and one big courtyard which contained no less than three wells. I knew all of this because we spent some time counting the various items in the shadowy engravings of the castle.

'This is where all the Counts Pongrácz used to live. We lived there for centuries,' she would say, stabbing her finger angrily at the pictures. 'Until the stinky French and Romanians took it away from us. That's our castle. We used to have 50 servants. We lived in the mountains and we had two very big carriages that were drawn by horses and sometimes we would go down to the village and they all would bow when Papa passed them.'

She would proceed to tell me about the various parts of the castle. There was the Gutenberg Tower where the Pongrácz's library was housed, the Count's Hall where wild boar was served in front of a big fire, and Medallion Hall where the family coat of arms and armoury was kept.

'But did you ever live there, Annuska?' I asked once.

Anna mused upon this for a second and then pronounced: 'I think so, I feel like I did. But you didn't. You were born on the day when the bad things happened. Papa said that you will probably have bad luck in your life because of it.'

I was not as concerned by this last comment as you might expect because I already had a dim sense, possibly because of my constant poor health, that I would always be dogged by bad luck. At the age of six, I had pretty much come to terms with the fact that I was an ill-starred child.

One day the heavy oak door of the nursery clicked behind us and a tall, thin figure stood before us. I nearly screamed because this tweedy shadow had entered the room so quietly that I had no idea he was there until the door shut behind him. A veined hand scooped a gold watch out of a waistcoat pocket and let the coils of the chain rest in its palm. A big thumb deftly flicked open the lid of the watch and tapped the glass surface.

'What on earth is going on here, my dear?' a hoarse voice said.

I stuck down a ragged newspaper doll carefully on a spike of the belvedere and gazed up at the skinny figure before me. I took some time to recognise his bald pate, his high-arched cheekbones, his piercing black eyes, his clean-shaven face, his long nose and full lips. But Anna had no such problem. She dropped her humpy camel and rushed towards the figure's long socks and brown brogues. She hugged his plus-fours.

'Papa, papa, you must come and see what we've built! We renovated the dolls' house specially for you. A whole castle which is also a zoo. I don't think anyone else has ever, ever built such a thing before.'

I watched the Count's red lips curl into a smile and then observed his lantern face bend down to kiss Anna's black hair. There was a bustling behind him and a plump woman wearing a felt hat and a long linen jacket trimmed with braid approached my father. Anna turned to her and repeated herself with the same fervent urgency.

The Count's smile quickly vanished when he saw the look of sullen discontent that was rapidly creeping over his wife's face. She took off her hat and patted her hair as she surveyed the nursery.

'Louis, what on earth have these children been doing to this room?'

Now I can enjoy the privilege of scrutinising that room with her eyes and I can understand her expression of horror. She saw a room strewn with bits of newspaper, blobs of clay and paint pots. Most horrifyingly, she must have spotted that the beautiful gothic tower, balconies and walls of her antique dolls' house were crudely daubed in black, and the silk dresses of her lovely dolls had been cut into shreds.

My mother pushed Anna away and turned to her husband. The Count coughed and rang the bell that was resting on the dresser.

'Yes, I suppose it does look a bit unfortunate,' he said.

'Unfortunate! That dolls' house is a prize antique! My grandmother played with it in Sandringham. Look at it now, it's ruined, totally ruined,' she exclaimed.

Anna retreated backwards, away from our arguing parents. I could see that she was swallowing hard and her eyes were narrowing malevolently at my mother. But before my sister could give full vent to her anger, Margaret and Teresa had scuttled into the room and, at the furious command of my mother, desperately tried to pick up the bits and pieces off the floor.

'What on earth have you two being doing all this time? We can't leave you for a minute, can we? These children have run amok. This room contains some very valuable furniture and some of it looks like it's been ravaged,' my mother moaned. 'I want to see that this room is spotless in half an hour.'

With that she flounced out of the room, leaving her children and her husband staring in her wake. My father frowned a little and then gave us an impish smile. He tousled Anna's black hair as he said: 'You are a little vixen, aren't you?'

He peered down at our zoo-castle and winced.

'My dear, surely you could have done better than this. You should have attempted to build a bridge,' he said, waving a contemptuous hand at our magical domain. With this dismissive comment, he left.

I don't think Anna would have reacted so badly if he hadn't made this last remark but she always found our father's gentle, ironic contempt far more cutting than our mother's predictable bluster. She waited a moment before he shut the nursery door quietly and then she stared ominously at the defaced dolls' house with her hands on her hips, mimicking a gesture of our mother's. She gritted her teeth, then lifted the dolls' house by grabbing the belvedere like a club and imperiously commanded me to open the door, which I obediently, if apprehensively, proceeded to do. As soon as I opened the door, Anna ran through it, along the hallway, through the butler's pantry – which wasn't a pantry at all but a small room where János kept his tools locked away in an eagle-winged cupboard – and into the Red Room, which was the long reception room of the apartment. She tottered past the fluted carved columns and ornamental niches that were interspersed between the French windows, and asked me to open the glass doors. Once I had carried out her orders, she could climb onto the balcony that overlooked the courtyard.

Below us, the blossom from a cherry tree was fluttering down onto the silky heads of two naked wood nymphs that were frolicking in a sparkling fountain. I remember leaning over the iron railings and thinking that they seemed much happier than I felt. But they soon wouldn't be -- Anna hurled the dolls' house over the balcony and it landed on their heads with an unceremonious thud. Little bits of the wood nymphs' faces broke off and fell into the water. The belvedere snapped off the roof and fell into a nymph's lap. The hinges pinged and the rest of the model broke in two. Oblivious to the massacre that had occurred in its basin, the fountain sprinkled droplets merrily over its crumpled walls.

Anna didn't even bother to look down at the havoc she had wrought in the courtyard. She dusted her hands and marched back inside.

5: THE DEADLY TREATY

Over the next few days the apartment seemed to grow. It felt a bit like watching Anna untying the tight knot of her black hair and letting her luxuriant locks fall free across her shoulders: you would never know she had so much hair when it was pinned up. Likewise, I had no idea that there were quite so many rooms in the apartment or that it could produce so many unfamiliar sounds and smells. Until then I had only thought of it consisting of the nursery, the kitchen, the Red Room, the butler's pantry and the hallway.

Anna and I had always eaten at the big wooden kitchen table. The vast dining room, with its cut-glass decanters, butter dishes, floral crockery, fat gleaming silverware, cream-coloured curtains and the landscape painting of the Great Hungarian plain, was as foreign to me as the metro had been. Its shiny, circular table which reflected the carved, stuccoed ceiling and the diamond drops of the chandelier seemed more like a dark lake than a table. I would touch its cold surface, half-expecting to be putting my hand into water. Its solidity was a great disappointment.

The nursery was completely rearranged. Most of my toys – the teddy bears, the dolls, the steam train, my paints and brushes – were removed and replaced with a large army of little red-coated, metal Hussars who sat on the dresser pointing their swords at me. A portrait of one of my ancestors, apparently, the original Count Pongrácz, was hung high over my bed. In the gloomy picture, his shoulders were draped in a jewel-bedecked and gold-chained short fur cape and a magnificent fur cap plumed by white feathers topped off his waxen head. The feathers created an unfortunate effect because the Count looked a bit like a royal-robed chicken.

I had a great deal of time to study the portrait in the ensuing months because Anna's bed was shipped out of the nursery. She was funnelled off to one of the numerous, oaken rooms that seemed to have magically appeared with my parents' arrival. Early the next morning, Margaret told me in hushed tones that I shouldn't ask for anything and should stay in my quarters. From behind the door, I pressed my eye to the keyhole and saw my mother, in a dark blue dress and with her hair put up in a bun, gesturing at ragged men carrying big tea chests into the hallway. She kept barking orders at them, and screeching at them to be careful of the ebony clock.

'That clock was a present to my father from the Prince of Wales. I don't want the slightest suggestion that you are even going to go near it with your boxes or your filthy hands,' she would shout.

My mother's dictates and the sound of scuffling, marching feet and creaking walls and furniture made the apartment sound like it was a ship in choppy waters looking for safe harbour. Eventually it docked. And the familiar hum and lilting calm that had existed before returned.

However, life was different. This was the time of mama's great ascendancy. She demanded that English was always spoken when we were in her presence and forced even Margaret and Teresa, who were very poor linguists, to talk to her in Anglo-Saxon grunts. With everyone else this wasn't a problem, because the Count spoke English superbly and his butler was perfectly competent; János would even translate for us if we didn't understand a word. Anna and I, of course, spoke fluently because of our mother. Paradoxically though, she decreed that we weren't allowed to speak at all during dinner, and dictated that we must always wear our best clothes when we left our own rooms and that we must salute the photograph of George V.

Mama used to hold court in the Music Room, reclining in a great wooden easy chair with scrolled legs and angels' heads for armrests.

Anna and I would sit timidly beside her, close to the shuttered harmonium and listen to her endless tales of her English upbringing. Generally, they were rather incomplete. Nothing of great moment happened in them, but my mother had a knack for conjuring up visual images of great echoing stone halls and windswept, rainy hunts, of her diminutive father on his gigantic white horse, of her bitchy sisters and their obsessive desire to marry a English duke or lord.

'I went one better than all of them,' she said, setting aside a copy of *Northanger Abbey*. 'I married a Count with his own castle in the Carpathian Mountains, masses of vineyards and this amazing apartment in the most fashionable European capital of the time, Budapest.'

She met my father at a diplomatic function in St James's Palace in London and was immediately struck by his impeccable manners and the dangerous lustre in his eye. 'Your father was so much more interesting than all of those tedious fat lords. I loved his accent at once. He rolls his 'r's' so beautifully. He was slim, alert, fit and full of stories about his castle and the amazing bridge that he was building that would link his castle with the village on the neighbouring mountain. Your sister has seen it. I wonder if she can remember it. It's quite remarkable, isn't it Anna?'

This was the only point in the conversation at which Anna would become animated. She still hadn't entirely forgiven my mother for the dolls' house incident and tended to remain silent when listening to Mama's stories. But she was very happy to elaborate upon our mother's tales of the Pongrácz castle.

'Yes, Zoltán, it was the biggest bridge you can imagine. When you looked down you went dizzy it was so high and there was a river running at the very bottom and lots and lots and lots of dark trees. And the villagers would always bow when they saw Papa approaching, and kiss his hands.'

'Oh dear, yes!' my mother would exclaim. Then lowering her voice, she said: 'All that kissing of hands, wasn't it jolly odd? János still does it when he's given the chance.'

'I saw him do it to Zoltán once,' Anna said, giggling and then tickling my skinny frame with her strong fingers. I tried my best to join in with their mirth but I sensed that somehow I was betraying my father – and ultimately my countrymen – by laughing at something that I regarded as a perfectly acceptable custom. Why shouldn't inferior people kiss the hands of their superiors?

Sometimes these conversations could continue for a whole day, sometimes for only a few minutes, depending upon my mother's mood. She was extremely erratic in this regard. On a good day, she would expound at great length about the Pongrácz castle library and all the books it contained from the Middle Ages, or speak of the ghosts that were said to haunt the Raven Tower, or provide mouth-watering details of the great feasts that were held in the Medallion Hall when some foreign dignitary came to stay. But often she was peevish and would scarcely give her children a second glance, preferring to bury herself in *Northanger Abbey* or *Emma* instead.

We hardly ever saw our father except at meal-times. According to Anna he was hiding away in his workshop which could only be accessed through a secret door in his study.

'But what's he doing there?' I asked.

Anna shrugged her shoulders.

We found out one lunch-time when János was ladling out soup with liver dumplings from a silver tureen into our china soup bowls. My father was slumped in his customary fashion at the head of the table, gazing disconsolately down at the wreaths of painted flowers that garlanded the edge of his bowl when my mother suddenly rushed from the room, begging to be excused. I'm not sure what was the matter with her but I suspect that when she caught sight of those horrid dumplings swimming in that greyish soup, she felt compelled to leave the room.

The minutes ticked away and still she didn't re-appear. Gradually my father's face began to brighten when it became clear that my mother's absence was going to be a prolonged one. He slurped vigorously at his soup and then, having finished it and dabbed his mouth with his embroidered napkin, he turned his attention to us and began to tell us of the amazing model bridge he was currently constructing.

'It's going to be an exact replica of the old London Bridge, complete with houses on top of it. It's all part of my master plan to construct models of every single bridge that has ever been constructed in London. I'm starting with the oldest and working my way through the centuries to the most modern.'

I didn't know what to say but Anna's response was immediate.

'Can we play with them when you've finished?' she asked.

The Count considered this with a very stern expression on his face and then, like the bright shining moon emerging from clouds, a smile slowly unfolded on his lips. He gave Anna one of his wicked eye-glints: 'If you let me play with you too!'

Anna's joy was too much to contain. She leapt out of her chair and rushed up to my father and hugged him, saying: 'We're going to play lots and lots of games with Papa.'

Unfortunately, my mother re-entered the room just at this juncture and was alarmed to find that, despite her only having left the table for a few minutes, mayhem had already been unloosed. She ordered Anna to return to her seat at once and then shot my father a wrathful look.

Before he could offer any kind of defence, Anna had piped up and was explaining, oblivious to the anguish she was causing in equal measure to both her parents, that Papa was going to play bridges with us in the nursery.

'I think your father has had enough of playing bridges with anybody else except himself,' my mother said. 'I'm not having him infecting anyone else with his nonsense. It's got all of us into enough trouble already.'

My father tried to protest: 'Oh Ellen, can't you see bridges are beyond the realms of economics? People will be visiting the Chain Bridge in Villány for years to come.'

My mother pushed away her bowl of liver dumpling soup.

'Yes, I've no doubt they'll visit it to laugh at the sheer, brazen folly of its creator.'

This sour observation made my father buckle in his seat and retire to his workshop without eating his soup. We did not see him for many weeks afterwards. Sometimes though, a chiming doorbell tolled in the hallway in the morning and silvery men would give their silken black hats and long overcoats to Margaret and file into the Count's study. Anna would assure me that they were very important people who were asking my father's advice on running the country; he was an advisor to the District Council and sometimes took his inherited seat in the Upper House of Parliament. Cigar smoke would leak out of his room and occasionally deep-throated laughter could be heard.

Not that I had much opportunity to concentrate upon the noises that so fascinated me. Shortly after the liver dumpling soup incident, a very fat man stood wobbling by the ebony clock and greeted me with a kiss on the hand. His double chin flopped over my tiny fingers and his wet mouth left a little dribble of spittle on my fingernails. It occurred to me that hand kissing was only a pleasant experience when János performed it. When the tubby man stood up, his belly threatened to break out of his green waistcoat.

Margaret guided us into the library where leather-bound books grew like fungi out of the walls. We sat down at the large red reading table and I listened to the gilt-edged chair groaning under the weight of the man's big bottom. He told me proudly that his name was Mr Wenceslas and then, leaning towards me, he whispered in my ear that he was my private tutor. His breath smelt of soggy biscuits dipped in coffee.

He delved into the large suitcase that he was carrying and produced a little bell, two exercise books, a pen, a red book and a big chart. He pointed to the chart and sniffed proudly, 'Now you will see that I have allocated a time for everything. Every lesson has been timed precisely. At the end of each lesson I will ring the bell, like so!'

He then pinched the small bell between his podgy fingers and shook it. A sweet, high-pitched note trembled through the air like a fragment of birdsong. I had never heard such a beautiful sound. It felt as if I were about to embark upon a long adventure.

Unfortunately, the tingling promise of this initial bell was not realised. Lessons with Wenceslas were unspeakably tedious. He tried to teach me how to read using a book called *The Deadly Treaty* that was a densely worded diatribe against the Treaty of Trianon. I do not remember much about my failed attempts to come to grips with the text except I do recall reading the word 'No!' which was printed in large capitals underneath a map of Hungary being cut up by a large pair of scissors.

Hungarian is an entirely phonetic language and it is relatively easy to read if you learn its alphabet. But Wenceslas didn't have the good sense to teach me even that. He read for me and I repeated the words after him. I unearthed the book quite recently and found that it was full of sentences like this: 'The Peace Treaty of Trianon is therefore a violation of the Peoples' Right to Self-determination. Consequently, the Treaty of Trianon has no moral value.'

Together Wenceslas and I both laboured under the illusion that I could read.

6: LESSONS OF PAIN AND PLEASURE

With the arrival of Wenceslas, a new routine established itself. I rose early and Margaret would serve my tutor a continental breakfast of milky coffee and a buttered roll. I've never enjoyed breakfast and, pushing my roll to one side, I would sip at some hot chocolate.

We would then retire to the library and I would follow the fat man's finger through the labyrinthine forests of text that filled the Latin primer, *Euclid's Geometry* and *The Deadly Treaty*. By elevenses, I was utterly lost and usually suffering from a ghastly headache. However, Wenceslas was always chipper when food was served. He would snap his napkin with gusto at the sight of the little dish of sausages Teresa placed before him and then would wash down the execrable gristly things with a glass of beer. I would do my best not to feel sick and would nibble at one of the thick cheese sandwiches that Teresa made. Usually, seeing that I wasn't hungry, Wenceslas would ask in a concerned tone of voice, 'Are you quite well, Master Zoltán?'

When I said that I felt ill, he would shake his head and tut, saying: 'Oh deary me. Oh, dear.'

But his chagrin at my poor health never stopped him from eating my sandwich as well as his, and calling for another glass of beer to wash it down.

Thankfully, Wenceslas's over-indulgence at elevenses meant that he stopped ringing his stupid little bell – this divine sound had now become a signal for torture – and proclaimed officiously that it was time for my own private reading. I would bury my nose in the nearest book to hand and pretend to read while watching his fat features begin to droop and drowse. More often than not he was snoring loudly on one of the library's red leather reading chairs ten minutes into the lesson.

I would wander round the library enjoying my freedom for a few minutes and then begin to miss Anna. I only really saw her, tight-lipped and pouting, at luncheon, and the rest of the time she disappeared behind one of the numerous bulky doors of the apartment. Sometimes I would hear the fragile notes of a piano tinkling in the Music Room and I would wonder if it were her practising. I don't know what pieces she was playing but in my mind I've come to associate them with Ravel's *Gaspard de la nuit*: glittering melodies tiptoeing through the aether. I still can't listen to *Gaspard* without a lump rising in my throat: the fairy fluff of the notes makes me remember Anna as she was then, hidden from me and yet so close.

I would contemplate running out of the library and racing to the place where the music emanated from but I never dared. The thought of opening the door frightened me: I preferred Wenceslas asleep to Wenceslas awake. I knew that he would never slumber during my lessons again if my mother caught me meandering around the apartment. And so I chose the safe but unsatisfactory option; roving around the library, bored but feeling secure.

Our main meal was served at 2 o'clock when Anna's governess and my private tutor would join forces underneath the dining room chandelier. We would plough our way through three courses that usually consisted of Jókai bean soup, stuffed cabbage and cottage cheese squares for pudding. Again, I would eat very little. I'm yet to be convinced by the wonders of Hungarian cuisine. It seems guaranteed to give one constipation. Likewise, Anna seemed so disgruntled that she hardly had an appetite, although she ate more than I did. However, Wenceslas and Miss Virág tucked in with alarming relish. Unlike Wenceslas, Miss Virág was a thin, stick-like woman with grey skin that looked like cracked porcelain but, for such a little lady, she had a hearty appetite.

My incredulity at their appetites goes to show how little conception I had of what life was like outside the apartment. I had no idea that most Hungarians rarely enjoyed food of the quality I scorned every day.

After the main meal Wenceslas and Miss Virág departed, leaving me to complete the exercises that Wenceslas had supposedly set me. I was banished to the library to do this and, I was to learn when I tried to escape, locked in by my mother. Meanwhile Anna was allowed to muck around on the piano in the Music Room. I would hear her playing and feel my hands buzzing with frustration. Even at that young age, I knew that I was destined to make music. I could feel it in the way the marrow of my bones would harmonise with the beautiful noises in the world, I knew it by the prickling trajectory of the hairs on my back when I heard some pleasing cadence, I could discern it in the fantastical pictures that some music conjured up in my mind. But I had to content myself with dozing in the crushed trough of Wenceslas's reading chair and humming to myself.

At night Teresa and Margaret would serve us a platter of cold meats and some weak tea and then pack us off to bed. In the morning, the dreary routine would begin again.

* * *

We saw very little of our parents. I think that there must have been a rapprochement between them because, on the rare occasions when we did see them, usually at meal-times, they seemed to be on speaking terms. Together they would talk fondly and nostalgically about the Pongrácz Castle: its servants, the neighbouring village, the wonderful bridge, its ghosts and the great banquets. My father now amplified all the stories that I had heard before from my mother. Sometimes he would discuss its history: apparently several hundred Turkish prisoners were interned in the dungeons during the time when the Hungarians were at war with the Ottoman Empire.

'There was even a Sultan amongst them whom the Count at the time was ordered to execute, much to his dismay,' my father would say, recounting his favourite anecdote. 'He begged Corvinus, who was king of Hungary at the time, to have mercy on this chap. You see, Count Pongrácz, like the others that followed him, was a cultured man. He had invited the Sultan to look around the library and had even shown him a copy of an illuminated Bible hand-written by monks. The Sultan had spent many hours perusing it and after reading it in the original Latin asked to be converted to Christianity. It was a day after this request that Corvinus's order came through. It was incontrovertible. Corvinus did not become the most successful leader that Hungary has ever had because he was a merciful man. For all his Renaissance trappings, he was ruthless. And so the Sultan was executed, but not until he had been converted to the Catholic faith. Unfortunately, the priest who performed the conversion was a drunk – he was the only one that the Count could get at such short notice – and the conversion was not conducted in the proper fashion. The Sultan, it transpired after his death, was only half a Catholic. This was to cause a terrible commotion because the Sultan's ghost came back to haunt the Count and the castle, unleashing all sorts of trouble. The castle was sacked by the Turks and nearly burnt to the ground. Finally, the Count asked a good priest to exorcise the ghost. The priest spoke to the Sultan and discovered that the ghost would not vacate the premises until the Count's first born son changed his name to his own. This request was carried out almost immediately and the Count's teenage son was re-christened Sultan -- Zoltán -- in honour of the ghost. The haunting stopped after that. And that is also why you were given your name.'

My mother would always laugh after the Count finished this story, which was often embellished with tales of the Great Turkish Sacking of the Castle and the Count's correspondence and dealings with Corvinus.

'It's all a lot of nonsense, of course,' my mother would say, but it was clear from the sparkle in her eyes that she never loved her husband more than when he talked about the Pongrácz's magnificent castle in the Carpathian Mountains.

7: THE RESCUE

Apart from dinner times, I didn't see much of the Count. But my knowledge of my father was to change one snowy evening in November. As usual, I was languishing in bed. I had caught the beginnings of a bad cold and my little frame was agitated with coughs and snuffles. In the purplish dusk, I watched the snowflakes flutter in between the bare branches of the black horse chestnut lurking outside my window. I listened to the sound of the cabs clip-clopping down the avenue and the occasional put-put of a car's engine. I imagined Anna was in the room and that it was still called a nursery and we still had our Bluebeard's castle to play with and that she was climbing into my bed and was cuddling me into warmth.

I was cold. I drew the covers about me and tried to draw some heat from the blankets. A loud rap on the door interrupted me. I tumbled out of the bed because I recognised the unmistakable tread of János. What did he want? Now that the Count was at home, he didn't pay me much attention.

I sunk my frozen toes into slippers and pattered over to the door. János greeted me with a bow and kissed my hand – a gesture he reserved for the most formal of circumstances. I shivered at the touch of his whiskery moustache and felt grateful for the little jet of warmth provided by his breath.

'Your father requests your presence in the library,' János said, nodding sagely.

'My father?' I said incredulously. I never, ever saw my father except at meal-times.

János helped me divest myself of my dressing gown and the multiple layers of my pyjamas, and plucked a silver key from his pocket. He opened the whale-like, creaky wardrobe that not even Margaret and Teresa went near – they retrieved most of my clothes from the walnut chest of drawers near my bed. His arms reached inside and produced a large coat hanger. He peeled off the covers and held up a small black suit.

I put on a freshly laundered, ironed shirt and then the suit. The most enjoyable part of the whole evening was the sensation of János's firm fingers helping me to nip and tuck in the jacket and trousers that were just a teeny-weeny bit too big for me. But with some expert discreet tacking, it looked perfect.

I donned my buffed black leather shoes and strode into the hallway looking like a miniature civil servant. In the library, János introduced me to the back of the large, red reading chair. I wouldn't have detected that anyone was present if there hadn't been a shining, fleshy dome poking over one of the brass studs that lined the chair's headrest. A disembodied arm waved away János, who bowed – even though he couldn't be seen – and retreated with a quick, backwards step out of the library. The door clicked shut and my heart began to thump. I was alone for the very first time in my life with my father.

A soft but jolly voice hailed me: 'Ah yes, Zoltán. I'd like you to come and sit with me by the fire.'

As I tiptoed past the splayed red arms of the reading chair, one of János's pins, which he had used to shorten my trousers, pricked my skin. But I didn't yell out -- I would have done if I were with anyone but my father. I sat down on a pouf by the flaming grate. The blood trickled down my ankle. I tried to warm myself by the fire. I rubbed my hands, feeling the soothing light flood into my cold bones. For a moment, I entirely forgot that there was anyone else in the room.

When I turned around, the Count had taken a silver case out from the table next to him and was snipping off the end of cigar. He struck a match and puffed, creating a veil of smoke that temporarily hid his face. When the haze cleared, I found his two eyes, shiny and black, staring down a long nose and observing my fidgeting fingers with playful haughtiness.

The Count's skin seemed even whiter and tighter than before, making his high cheekbones protrude like the overhanging ridges of cliffs where the sea has eaten away the limestone down below.

There was silence. I didn't know what to say or even if I was supposed to say anything. The Count rested his cigar in a cut-glass ashtray, cradled a large snifter in his hands and swigged at the chestnut liquid that sloshed around at its base. Then he rubbed the stem of the glass between his two fingers.

'So -- what has Wenceslas been teaching you?' he asked with forced merriment. His question was as unforeseen as receiving an elbow in the stomach.

He smiled very briefly and suddenly his face attained life; fissures sizzled through the tall cliffs of his cheeks and his eyes seemed to sink even further into a whirlpool of wrinkles. His face fascinated me. I wanted to feel it to see if it had the same texture as crumbly rock.

I nodded, trying to imitate his smile and finding myself unable to speak. What could I say? What had Wenceslas been teaching me? I didn't know.

'Yes,' I eventually mustered, realising that this was an utterly inadequate response.

My reticence seemed to disconcert him and he sucked irritably on his cigar.

'I hear that he's been teaching you about the Treaty of Trianon. That was on my express instructions. It is perhaps the single most important thing you will learn about in the next few years. It is what has nearly ruined me -- and Hungary. Deprived the Pongrácz of their castle and much of their wealth. I don't like to talk about it too much in front of your mother because it upsets her so but now, man to man, we can discuss it and get to grips with the horror of the situation. You do know how much territory Hungary lost because of that Treaty, don't you?'

I repeated my imbecilic nodding smile and didn't answer; I had no idea what he was talking about. He repeated the question and again I failed to answer. He stabbed his cigar into the ashtray, drained his glass and leant forward. The alcohol on his breath made him smell a bit like Teresa. This surprised me. How could someone as important as my father – who was also his Excellency and the Count – smell the same as a maid?

The ensuing smell of the cigar reassured me a little. Teresa never smelt smoky. I realised that the two smells in combination somehow meant you were important. I still can't smell the interwoven smells of brandy and cigar smoke without thinking of my father.

He frowned. Evidently, he had been expecting to have a prolonged chat about the whole issue but my total ignorance meant that I was unable to engage in any meaningful discussion about it. My father was not a patient man. He didn't like explaining complicated things -- despite his predilection for telling stories.

'How much territory did we lose?' he asked, hissing irritation infecting his words.

A hot, molten rock rose in my throat.

'Yes, yes,' I said, still trying to smile. But it was useless. I was crying.

The Count rang the bell loudly, mumbling to himself: 'This is useless. Useless.' Within a minute János whisked into the library and was guiding me outside. As the kindly butler shut the door, I could see my father shaking his head with melancholic exasperation.

* * *

The next day, I did not endure the sight of my portly tutor dipping his thickly buttered bread roll into his coffee. When Wenceslas tottered into the library, he did not greet me with a kindly smile, nor did he join me at the writing desk where I was waiting patiently with my sharpened pencil. Instead he collapsed into the reading chair where my father had been stationed the night before. He was sweating profusely; the smell of rotting onions seemed to waft from his face; there were damp patches under the arms of his faded, green waistcoat.

He caught his breath and lifted his shuddering weight out of the chair. Then with a false smile, he pulled his teaching chair right up to where I was sitting and placed his filmy hand on my bare knee – I was wearing dull grey schoolboy shorts for my lessons even though it was winter. I suppose that horrid podgy hand did heat up my chilly skin quite a bit, but I began to resent the intrusion when he pushed his wriggling fingers underneath the hem of my shorts.

'Now then, how much territory did Hungary lose in the Treaty of Trianon?' he asked desperately.

When I was unable to furnish him with an answer, he pinched me. I tried to scream out in pain but he quickly smothered my mouth with his hand. 'Today, you will learn the hard way, since my kinder methods do not seem to have had any effect.'

If I had dreaded my lessons before, now they became terrifying. Wenceslas obviously felt that he could teach me to read by pinching my upper leg every time I made a mistake. This novel educational technique has probably never been employed elsewhere and justifiably so since it did not render beneficial results.

This misery continued throughout the rest of November. The snow fell in whirling torrents throughout that bleak month and filled Andrássy Avenue with a perfect blanket of pure whiteness that was transformed into a black, oozing sludge by the end of the day. Each morning I awoke praying that Wenceslas would cease his pinching lessons but by the end of the day I felt as dirty and contaminated as the snow that was sprayed into the gutter by the wheels of the vehicles that raced down the Avenue.

My dreams became poisoned with visions of camels. Their bulbous heads and ragged humps would surge out of the floorboards of the nursery and smash through the walls of the dolls' house, asking between masticating chomps: 'How much territory did Hungary lose in the Treaty of Trianon?'

I would awake and find myself unable to breathe; it felt like I had grown a camel's head and body in the night. But my terror of becoming a humpy monster was such that I couldn't talk about it. When you're frightened of something, you don't discuss it for fear that your very articulation of your terror might bring it back to you again the very moment you are speaking about it.

The situation deteriorated so much that one night I woke up screaming: 'Trianon, Trianon!'

My words rebounded against the dark walls and were absorbed by the stucco ceiling which seemed to be snarling in the dimness. Once again, I felt the camels squirming inside my chest. I sat up and went through my customary procedure of feeling my back to see if I had grown any humps.

But I heard a quiet knocking on the door and a concerned voice calling my name. It was Anna. I couldn't believe it. Her presence outside my door was an impossibility because I knew that since the dolls' house incident my mother had decreed that both of our bedroom doors should be locked. We weren't supposed to see each other.

I ran over to the door, forgetting that I might have been turned into a camel, and tried to yank it open. Unfortunately, it was still locked. I asked: 'How much territory did Hungary lose in the Treaty of Trianon?'

There was a pause and a rummaging at the lock. I stooped down and jumped back because I saw an eye staring through the keyhole.

'Stand back, I'm going to open the door,' her intrepid voice said. (I can still hear her saying those words even now. The words that were destined to change everything. Brave Anna! Immortal Anna! You are the only one. There will never be another. When I die, I hope I see your face smiling down upon me as I breathe my last.)

But I am jumping ahead of myself. I stood aside and the door swung open. A ghostly red light fell through the fanlight in the hallway tingeing Anna's night-dress with a reddish hue and revealing her body underneath. I perceived that she was changing. The girlish form that I remembered seeing in the nursery seemed to have vanished and had been magically enclosed by an even greater marvel; her breasts were beginning to bud, her long hair was abundant and lustrous, and her hips seemed to have widened.

But don't misinterpret me, my obsession for Anna was never sexual. I noticed these changes dispassionately. Our love was always pure. The thing that I most prized was the pad of her feet on the parquet floor. Her footsteps always set a metronome tick-tocking in my heart.

I flung my arms around her. Now that she had come to find me, I was unashamed to reveal my misery. She carried me back to the bed and sat down beside me. Her hair fell over my face and I could feel her curls caressing my throat, and the light touch of her breath.

'We lost three quarters of our territory in the Treaty and three million of our population,' she said.

I couldn't speak such was my relief and shock at her presence. Being a self-pitying wretch, I started to blub. And blub. And blub. What a miserable specimen of manhood I was and still am! History would prove again and again that I am obviously quite incapable of behaving in a noble and courageous fashion. However, that may be the reason that I am still here today, and many who were far braver and greater than I, are lying in their graves. And then she told me a story: 'There was a little boy and a little girl and they lived in a snow palace and went skating on the frozen lakes…They were so happy because they were together forever.'

I don't know how long Anna comforted me because the moment she took me in her arms, I promptly fell asleep with images of the falling snow at the window tumbling through my dreams. When I woke the next morning, she had gone.

Snow had fallen in the night and the filthy Avenue seemed to have been absolved of all its previous sins; its stony grandeur lay sparkling white in the winter sun. The virgin snow encouraged me to think that the pinching leg lessons were not going to happen.

However, the sight of a fat finger dipping a roll plastered with butter into a cup of coffee obliged me to confront the reality of the situation: Wenceslas was here to stay. Anna hadn't surfaced and nor had Miss Virág. My greedy tutor had me all to himself – even at the breakfast table. I nibbled my bread roll, desperately hoping that Anna would appear. She didn't.

I followed Wenceslas into the library. The sweaty fear that dominated his demeanour just a few weeks before had departed and was replaced by a wobbly swagger. Such was his confidence, he took a pile of biscuits into the library. Evidently, he felt that his new teaching technique was a success.

He was just about to reach over and pinch me for the fifth time when the moulded brass handle of the library door began to rattle. Anna swept into the room in a white pinafore. Her hair was tied up a large knot but with a few strands left to fly free as she sailed up to me. Wenceslas hastily withdrew his hand from my thigh and gazed open-mouthed at my sister as she pulled me out of my chair. I remember seeing a few crumbs of biscuit drop onto his chin as I was escorted out of the room.

By the time we reached the door to my father's study both Miss Virág and Wenceslas were pursuing us, calling out to their respective charges to return to their lessons at once. But Anna had flung open the door to the study before they could grab us. She pushed me over the threshold and I found myself in a room that I had only dreamed about entering.

An enormous writing bureau and tall lampshade towered before me. The room smelt of fresh paint and glue. Cigar smoke billowed in a cloud above the bald figure of my father. He was evidently putting the finishing touches to his model of London Bridge by attaching three mullion windows to the upper stories of his gate-house. His tongue was poking out of his mouth as he squeezed some glue with one hand and held a smoking cigar with the other. His golden ring glinted in the electric light and the black hairs on his arms, which were revealed to me for the first time because his shirt sleeves were rolled up, shone. My mother was sitting with her feet up on a pouf in the corner of the room reading a book. I was to learn from Anna later on that day that it was called *Dracula* and was a naughty book to read. My father dropped his tube of glue and my mother hastily hid her book under her reading chair.

'Mama, Papa, I have something to show you. You must see this now!' she shouted, wagging her finger at the shiny rim of the mahogany desk where London Bridge was perched. My mother stood up and took off her reading glasses. Her long dress rustled loudly as she shuffled awkwardly towards her daughter. My father smiled broadly, as he was wont to do when he was challenged by an entirely unfamiliar situation, but my mother frowned. She grabbed Anna by the shoulders.

'Anna, what are you doing? This is entirely improper. You must leave here at once. You know you are not allowed in your father's study,' she said, blushing a little. I can see now that she was embarrassed because she didn't like being caught with her feet up reading an aberrant book in the presence of her husband who was doing something that she had hinted to us was an entirely unsuitable occupation for a grown man. She had shown us that she was more tolerant of her husband's hobby-horse than she would have liked us to think.

After briefly glancing disdainfully at the grinning Count, Anna proclaimed: 'Mama, Papa, I want you to see what that horrible man has been doing to your son.'

With this, Anna wrenched down my grey shorts and revealed the hideous bruising that a whole month's worth of pinching had inflicted upon my legs.

My father's grin turned into mortified laughter, but my mother's eyes were suddenly fired with horror. The Count's abashed merriment soon stopped when he realised the full extent of my injuries.

'My God, Louis,' my mother ejaculated – it was the first time I had ever heard her call my father by his Christian name. 'What has that tutor being doing to the child?'

I was conscious that behind all her severe remonstrations, my mother cared for my welfare. Her chin wrinkled in concern and her eyes narrowed in horror as she scanned the abuse my legs had suffered.

8: THE HAPPY GYPSY

After that, I never saw Wenceslas again. Instead I was taught by Miss Virág. I joined her, with Anna, in the parlour. To begin with, she gave Anna some exercises from the Latin primer to get on with, and devoted all her energies to me. Although she had no little bell or a time-table, she was far better teacher than Wenceslas. I grew to love her bird-like frame, her beaky nose, her dove-like arms which became so animated when she explained a point, her cracked porcelain skin, the vague smell of camphor that emanated from her white frilly dress and her wrinkled fingers with their long, yellowish fingernails pointing to the words on the page.

Within a few weeks I was reading Hungarian; a couple of months later I was writing it. By my eleventh year, under her tutelage, I was reading and writing English, German and Latin and I had mastered the basics of arithmetic and geometry. She was an inspired teacher. She took us out, as 'our weekly treat' as she termed it, to see some site in Budapest: usually a museum or, if the weather was nice and we had worked hard, the great City Park which was the home to the zoo, the circus and the fabulous Vajdahunyad Castle which I will forever associate with Bluebeard's Castle. Miss Virág was evangelical about Budapest. Her enthusiasm made me entirely forget my apprehension about going outdoors. Her lectures enabled me to regard most of the city as my friend and confidante, not my enemy.

Thus, Anna and I became acquainted with the cocooned centre of Hungary's capital city. I suppose we were given what now might be termed the classic tour of the city. The tree-lined boulevard of Andrássy Avenue led to a plethora of delights. I seemed to have recovered from my asthma and walking became a joy. The Sphinxes that rest their ample breasts on the plinths outside the Opera House would wink at me through the rain and the sunshine as we descended the steps of the metro and travelled towards our 'weekly treat'. Although I continued to suffer from claustrophobia underground, somehow Miss Virág's presence managed to calm my fears.

We tramped the echoing halls of the Hungarian National Museum learning about the nation's struggle for independence. We sipped hot chocolate amidst the Viennese pastries of Gerbeaud's. We crossed the Chain Bridge and took the funicular railway up to Castle Hill and felt dwarfed by the statues of Buda Palace, and, above all, we haunted the environs of Kossuth Square.

Like many Hungarians, Miss Virág was obsessed by Kossuth. His was the story that she most loved to tell and she usually positioned us before the newly erected statue, which was stationed in front of the Houses of Parliament, before she recounted the story. Unlike the one that is there now, which depicts a dynamic statesman and leader of a fight that proved victorious in spirit, the monument that we were shown was a miserable affair. It showed a despairing leader with his head bowed who is obviously thinking that nothing has turned out as he would have wished. Eight very gloomy ministers flanked him on either side.

'He looks like he's stepped in some dog droppings, doesn't he?' Miss Virág would chirp – she was always making a gentle joke about something or other. 'Now what I want you to do is take a few steps back and look at his real monument: the Houses of Parliament! He was the man who led the fight for the independence of Hungary. He fought and lost but he brought a spirit to the Magyar people that will never be crushed.'

I would take a few steps back and realise the true enormity of the Parliament building because I would see that there was layer upon layer to the building, rising high into the sky. The large, purple domes and roofs seemed to be floating upon the mountain range of the spires and turrets. In the spring, the smell of violets would drift past us; in summer the pleasure boats on the Danube would bob past the back of the Parliament; and in autumn and winter, dead leaves and snow would swirl around our ears as Anna and I listened to our tutor.

We truly travelled across the centuries with her. She took us back to classical times as we wandered around the Roman remains at Aquincum. We galloped into the Carpathian basin with the Magyars and observed the great, barbaric courts of the Árpád dynasties. We watched Stephen being crowned as a Christian king in the year 1000. We fought bravely but were defeated by the Ottoman Turks in the 14th century and then suffered the further indignity of the tyrannical Austro-Hapsburgian rule from the 17th century -- until Kossuth tried to establish independence in 1849. In particular, we were made to learn the poems of Sándor Petőfi, János Arany, Endre Ady, and Mihály Vörösmarty off by heart. These poets were all great nationalists who had an almost mystical love of the Magyars. It makes me slightly sick to think of those poems now because the great Hungarian nation that Miss Virág took such pride in was to let her down so badly. I suppose it wasn't any of those poets' faults – but I do think that they're implicated in some way. I can't help finding the memory of Miss Virág talking about Petőfi's passionate participation in the Battle of Segesvár profoundly moving. She cried for that poet who was fighting for Hungarian independence. And what did the valiant country do for her?

But I had no inkling then of the catastrophe that was to come. Miss Virág would always make us recite Petőfi's poem *'Talpa magyar'* – *Rise, Hungarian* – and then would proceed to expostulate about her true hero.

'Kossuth represents all that is best about Hungarians. He set up one of its main papers, the *Pesti Hírlap*, he led the insurrection of 1849. When he was exiled from his beloved homeland and he arrived in New York, he received an enormous parade. He wanted equal rights for everyone,' Miss Virág would always begin and then would continue more solemnly: 'Sadly, his death, like the death of so many Hungarians, was an ignominious affair. He died a very lonely and bitter man in near poverty with none of his dreams realised. It is the curse of our nation that everything ends badly for us. But that doesn't mean we shouldn't have the right to dream of a better world. No matter what the world throws at us that is what we will do. Perhaps there is a better day for the Hungarians just around the corner, who knows?'

Judging from the lugubrious grimace that she always pulled at this juncture, Miss Virág didn't have high hopes for the Magyar people. But to tell you the truth I've never met a Hungarian who did.

Miss Virág's other great love was Shakespeare. She would often say that we should be proud that we were half English because we had been born into the tongue of the great Bard. This seemed to delight our mother, but it puzzled Anna and I as much as the poet's language did. Why should we proud of the words that we spoke? It seemed an odd notion because, unlike statues and buildings and flags, words were only breath or markings on a page. They didn't seem substantial enough to take pride in.

At that time, Miss Virág's favourite play must have been *The Tempest* because we read it countless times. I think she was in love with Prospero. With tears in her eyes, she would read that famous speech: 'We are such stuff/As dreams are made on, and our little life/ Is rounded with a sleep.'

I could never quite understand her hatred for Caliban though. She would always speak in furious, outraged tones about the bestial slave but would never reveal what his crime was.

'I'm afraid his crime was so horrific that it is not for your ears, Zoltán and Anna,' she would say darkly.

Naturally Anna would pester her and this would result in our tutor getting into a terrible flap. 'Oh dear, oh my, I should never have read the play to you. Whatever will your parents say?' Miss Virág would fret. This usually resulted in my sister reassuring her that her question wasn't important and that we both loved reading Shakespeare.

One day, when we had both proved ourselves to be fully conversant with Kossuth's involvement with the Revolution in 1849, his brilliant speeches and writings, Miss Virág announced that she had a special surprise for us. We were standing underneath his mournful statue; it was a beautiful but blustery spring day. Lemony sunlight illuminated black-suited men who were flapping in and out of the doors to the Parliament. There was a smell of dumplings and goulash on the wind and the noise of dignified chatter all around us.

I shielded my eyes against the sun and saw a handsome young man bounding towards us, dressed a bit like a gypsy or a pirate in baggy trousers, a bright red shirt and a rakish bandanna wrapped around his forehead. His grin seemed as wide as Andrássy Avenue. Miss Virág patted her tightly knotted white hair and looked at Anna. A blush glazed her white skin. She pronounced proudly: 'That is my brother!'

Neither Anna nor I could believe that this youthful, vigorous stranger, with his sun-tanned face, aquiline features and glowing Bohemian clothes was related to Miss Virág.

'But he doesn't look anything like you. He looks more like Ferdinand,' Anna said, her pupils dilating at the sight of this gypsy-clad Adonis. Miss Virág chuckled at this Shakespearean reference and said: 'I suppose you could say he represents beauteous mankind! And he's part of the brave new world -- I am sadly of the less courageous, older one.'

Anna was too preoccupied with goggling at the handsome man to pay attention to her tutor's comment but I found that it stirred something in me. I glanced at her. She was touching a golden locket that hung around her neck. It was a keepsake. I still didn't know what was inside it but wondered whether she once had a young man that she was in love with. Anna's enthusiasm for her brother seemed to sadden Miss Virág in an unusual fashion, perhaps reminding her of happier, more romantic days. There was always something slightly melancholic and mysterious about Miss Virág, even in those trouble-free years.

Imre Virág greeted us warmly, kissing us both on the cheeks. At Mr Virág's suggestion, we all retired to Ruszwurm Confectioners where he bought us apple strudel slices and frothy coffee in glasses, which we ate over the old cherrywood counter. I loved the sugary, woody, caffeine-scented atmosphere of the place.

'Now then children, can you guess what my brother does for a living?' Miss Virág said after wolfing down her apple strudel.

'He's a Bohemian. He roams the whole of Europe and he plays the violin to his gypsy friends and they all sit round a fire and tell ghost stories,' Anna blurted out immediately, adding with a simper that was entirely uncharacteristic, 'and maybe he has a dancing girl who is his friend and they sing and drink pálinka in the woods…'

Suddenly Imre burst out laughing, evidently charmed by the wild vision of himself that this strange, intense black-haired girl with aristocratic cheekbones had. But Miss Virág seemed a little disconcerted and asked me less confidently what I thought his profession was.

'I think he's a tramp,' I said bluntly, feeling jealous of the gushing praise he had drawn from my sister.

Imre chuckled again and then explained: 'Well, you're both wrong. I'm an actor; that's why I'm wearing this silly gypsy costume. At the moment I am, at least. I would like to go to university but I'm not allowed to.'

'Yes, well, we won't go into that now,' Miss Virág said, pushing my apple strudel closer to me. I still hadn't touched it.

But it was too late. Anna wanted to know everything about him and demanded answers. Miss Virág looked disgruntled as Imre accounted for himself. 'My sister and I are both Jewish. Jews are not allowed to go to university here. A law was passed in that very Parliament over there excluding me and thousands of people like me from going. Your father is a good man because he employs my sister when many people of his class won't. Nevertheless, he was a member of the Upper House when that law was passed.'

I ruminated upon his words. I had never known that Miss Virág was Jewish. My mother had talked about Jews dismissively on odd occasions, complaining that she saw far too many of them -- with their long noses and swarthy faces walking around Budapest -- when she went shopping. I had naturally assumed that Miss Virág was Hungarian because she had porcelain skin and talked with such passion about Kossuth. But my father must have known who he was employing to educate his children: I decided to follow his example rather than my mother's. There was nothing wrong with Jews.

'That's enough now, Imre!' Miss Virág expostulated. 'We came here to talk about your play, not all of that.'

'But it's not fair,' Anna said, wielding her fork like a spear and then banging it down on the table. 'Everyone should be allowed to go to university if they're clever enough.'

'My sentiments entirely,' Imre agreed and then, with a merry wink, added: 'Perhaps we should talk about my role in *The Happy Gypsy* – it's being put on very near you. I've got the starring role...'

Imre proceeded to entrance us with the story of this play. He was a natural storyteller and when we went to see the production at the National Theatre with our parents, I was assured by my mother, who knew about such things because she used to frequent the London theatres, that he was also a very fine actor. After the performance, my parents chatted about whether he would make a good tutor for both of us now that we were getting older. Miss Virág had asserted that he was a very knowledgeable historian and scientist as well as a patient teacher.

Their fatal mistake was discussing this in front of Anna who rose out of her seat in the Mercedes and grabbed my mother, saying: 'Oh yes, yes please. He would make the best teacher in the world. I just know it. You've got to ask him.'

My mother screeched at Anna to sit down again – we were just turning around a corner and the whole car lurched so that Anna fell on her lap as she was pleading. Anna wouldn't sit down unless she was given some reassurance.

'We'll see, Anna, we'll see,' my father said, wearing his customary dismissive smile.

9: THE DYNAMITED TRAIN

At first, Miss Virág taught me the piano on the upright Steinway in the Music Room, but she relinquished these duties within a year, proclaiming that I could play Mozart better than she could. One Saturday morning, when I was eight years old, Miss Virág spent some time examining herself in the mirror and then suddenly gripped my hand. Together we tiptoed into my father's study.

He peered up from behind a large skeletal model of Southwark Bridge that he had just begun. He took off his gold-rimmed glasses, waiting for us to speak. Our shoes scraped over the parquet floor. There was a smell of beeswax, and little flecks of rain garnished the windowpane. Miss Virág patted her hair, cleared her throat and launched into a hymn to my musical abilities. Eventually, she ground to a halt and awaited my father's reply.

He stood up and sat down on the edge of the desk in an entirely untypical pose.

'Although you haven't quite formulated your point, I think I can guess its purpose. You have come to suggest that Zoltán here should take lessons from some professional musicians because he has shown great aptitude in this area? Am I right?'

Now he pulled a smile. This was very unusual; my father very rarely smiled at his social inferiors. Miss Virág quivered and blushed -- something I didn't know she was capable of.

'That is entirely correct, your Excellency,' she said hesitantly.

My father still seemed a little uneasy and shifted back to his place behind his desk.

'But must future gentleman like my son study music with such diligence?' he barked, appearing somewhat rattled by the forthright tutor.

Miss Virág touched her golden locket again. She always did so when she was threatened or a little sad.

'*The man that hath no music in himself,*
Nor is not moved with concord of sweet sounds,
Is fit for treasons, stratagems, and spoils,' she recited.

This Shakespearean defence seemed to both hearten and vex my father. I'm sure he didn't know what play it came from, but he did know that the Bard was generally to be deferred to in matters of culture. He returned to the sanctuary behind his desk and gazed wearily at his papers. 'I have no objections,' he said. 'I trust you will make all the necessary arrangements, Miss Virág. Only let's make sure he studies proper music: Mozart, Beethoven and such like. I would be most unhappy to hear that he was learning the music of my more dissolute compatriots. He should learn good, manly, uplifting music. Nothing decadent.'

Miss Virág nodded and added pointedly, perhaps even a little sarcastically, 'Of course, there will be nothing decadent. I wouldn't allow the slightest trace of immorality to affect your child.'

She knew that my father was referring to Béla Bartók who, despite being Hungary's greatest living composer, was regarded with suspicion by the conservative regime of which my father was such a pillar. I didn't know anything about Bartók then but I would soon, despite my father's express instructions. The languid man who Miss Virág recruited to be my violin and piano teacher was a student at the Liszt Academy of Music where Bartók taught.

I remember Peter Lazár's chronic acne and his constant sniffing more vividly than his actual lessons, but he must have taught me something because by the time he had finished with me I easily passed the entrance exam for the Academy. He was a very sleepy person: he would lie down on the chesterfield sofa as soon as Miss Virág closed the door and would press his runny nose with a damp handkerchief. Sometimes he would shut his eyes but mostly he would stare at the ceiling and would comment upon my tonal and rhythmic expression.

He took very little interest in my technique and as a result, although I am a very competent performer, I have always lacked the technique to be a really fine one. I think I have Lazár's sleepy sniffiness to thank for that. Still, he gave my playing an emotional sensibility, a delicacy, a refinement that it has never lost.

He only became animated when he talked about life at the Academy. He obviously hadn't heard of my father's injunction not to talk about the more dissolute elements of the Hungarian musical scene – or if he had, he chose to ignore it.

'There are very exciting things happening now!' he would say, swinging his long legs off the sofa and onto the ground. I would stare at his faded trousers and the holes in his socks, wondering why his servants didn't mend his clothes. 'Hungary is leading the world in developing a new kind of music. You see, Bartók and Kodály are doing something that no one else has ever thought of. They're going out into the countryside and recording all the traditional folk songs of the Hungarian people and using the melodies in their own compositions. One day, the world will look back on this time as the golden age of Hungarian music, lit up by two geniuses.'

It was my teacher's words that first made me aware that I was living in a historical era as opposed to some mythical fairy tale time. Under Lazár's dreamy but impassioned tutelage I became aware of the different musical ages: Bach and the Baroque, Mozart and the Classical, Beethoven and the Romantic, Bartók and the Modern.

All summer Miss Virág had been complaining about the strikes and shortages that had been afflicting the area where she lived. She moaned that the shops in her neighbourhood were empty and it was difficult to get food. I comprehended that although I lived in the timeless arena of the apartment, the rest of the world was subject to the tides of history. It was September 1931 and those violent currents were about to affect my own life – and bring me closer to my own father.

Late one evening, after supper, János knocked on the door in his customary sedate fashion and summoned me to the library. When I entered, I saw a cloud of cigar smoke rising out of an opened newspaper. Immediately, my heart began to beat faster because I had never actually seen my father read a newspaper in the library before, although I had seen them neatly folded by the side of his study desk on the odd occasion.

The Count's waxen face rose above the rim of the paper as I approached. His arched, shrunken cheeks were dappled with tears and his eyes were bloodshot. He hastily mopped his face with the white wad of his of folded, monogramed handkerchief and picked up his cigar.

I kissed his hand and sat down on the leather chair next to the fireplace. The weather was still warm and the fire hadn't been lit. I studied the lumps of black coal with great interest, trying not to think about my father's tears. My first thought was that he was crying because Miss Virág was not happy with my composition and reading.

The Count folded the newspaper, rose and picked up the photograph of the Prince of Wales that always rested on the mantelpiece.

'I can only hope that the English help us when our hour of need arrives. I certainly fear the worst,' he said, putting Edward and his horse back on the marble lip of the mantelpiece and picking up the paper again. Hurriedly, he thrust the paper into my lap.

'Soon you will be a man and you must deal, like me, with these things,' he said, pointing to the headline of the paper. I read: VIENNA EXPRESS DYNAMITED OUTSIDE BUDAPEST – 63 DEAD.

'The Baron Káldy was on that train. He was the good man who assisted me with my inaugural speech in the Upper House many, many years ago,' my father said with a high quiver. He retrieved his cigar from the ashtray on the bureau and lit it. 'It's the communists, you know. They very nearly ruined everything back in 1919 and they're trying to do it again. Mark my words, Moscow dynamited that train. They think that their chance has come.'

Oh dear, why did I never understand what he was talking about? I felt fraudulent as I endeavoured to nod sagely at his words. He tailed off and puffed thoughtfully on his cigar. Clouds of smoke wafted above the fireplace.

I remained silent, still not fully comprehending his words or his sentiments, but sensing that change was in the air. When I left the library, the world seemed both a blacker and a warmer place. I had never imagined that my father had emotions before but now that I had seen his tears, I knew that he wasn't the stoic, stern Count that I had always taken him for. He was a cry-baby like me! I was always crying; the slightest criticism of my piano and violin playing usually set me off in floods of tears.

I found Anna waiting for me when I returned to my room. She was desperately curious to know what our father had said to me. She sprung off my bed and grabbed me by the shoulders, her black eyes sparkling. Outside, the first yellowed leaves of autumn fell in the twilight.

'Well, what did he say? Did he tell you anything about Imre? Is he going to be our next tutor?'

I was reluctant to tell her about our father's melancholia. I shrugged my shoulders and tried to change the subject, suggesting that we went to the Music Room and played a duet on the piano.

'Oh don't be so boring!' Anna said, pushing me playfully. 'Just tell me what he said.'

I was silent for a moment and then said: 'I can't.'

Anna was incredulous. She pushed one of her black curls out of her eyes and tucked it behind her ears.

'You can't? What are you talking about? We always tell each other everything. You know that. No secrets.'

I considered this for some time and played both sides of the arguments like the two opposing and complementary melodies in a Bach cantata. I realised that I had a responsibility to my sister to inform her of everything that she needed to know, but I was also aware that she was female. Despite being surrounded by the opposite sex for most of my waking hours, I was beginning to learn that certain topics were not suitable for women's ears.

'We were talking man to man,' I said finally and emphatically, proud that I had come to what I regarded as a decent decision.

Anna's reaction was instantaneous. She tossed her head dismissively at me and walked out of the room, slamming the door behind her.

'You're a fine man then,' she said with a sneer as she left.

* * *

I couldn't sleep that night, such was my distress at incurring Anna's displeasure, but I knew that I couldn't succumb to the urge to tell everything because I was certain that I would be betraying my father. I longed to leap out of my bed and pad into her room, which was now unlocked, and climb into bed with her, and whisper the truth into her ear. The thought of her soft, warm body and her enfolding arms assailed me throughout the night, but I managed to resist.

She didn't speak to me for a month after that. And when eventually her stony-eyed sulking broke me down and I offered to tell all, she pretended not to want to hear.

'I know already. The boring Baron Káldy, who no one liked anyway and my father never went to see, died in that train bomb thing. So what?' she said with studied nonchalance.

Stung by her coldness of heart, I hastened back to my piano practice.

In the meantime, as if rewarding me for my silence, the Count would invite me with greater regularity into the library for our manly evening chats. Gradually, I began to understand little snippets of what he was talking about but generally I would find myself completely lost in the rambling thickets of his sentences. He never demanded that I responded verbally and, although I knew that I wasn't required to answer, butterflies always hovered in my stomach during these sessions. One day, I might have to say something. Over the months I learnt there was one major topic that he returned to: bridges. His conversation always became more animated when he spoke of their construction, their maintenance, their strategic importance in war and their metaphorical significance.

'It was the English who first realised that crucial role of bridges. With the construction of London Bridge they showed that a whole society could be built on the water and then, much later, during the industrial revolution, they saw that bridges were the key to economic success. If you build a bridge, you can carry things over it: people, coal, steel, sugar, soldiers and royalty. The success of the British empire was built on their bridges. They saw that bridges are the way to connect alien cultures and warring peoples and bring them together.'

And so it would go on. And on. His digressions about bridges could detain me in the library well into the night unless my mother discovered us and insisted that I was sent to bed.

10: IMRE AND DRACULA

Shortly after our trip to see *The Happy Prince* at the theatre, my mother, charmed by Imre's performance, suggested that we employed him as our tutor. Miss Virág had been saying for some time that we were both rapidly outpacing her in our scientific and mathematical knowledge and that we would need a specialist tutor to coach us through the exams that every Hungarian child had to take at the end of the academic year. She had mentioned that her brother might be suitable but had not liked to press the point. Now my mother – either casting aside her anti-Semitism or preferring not to think of the Virágs as Jews – did Imre's bidding for her. My father took up references and then employed him, proclaiming that he was obviously a very intelligent chap because he had passed his science exams with distinction without studying at a university.

I loved Imre's tutorials. He was such a brilliant, handsome man with his magnificent jaw, his wavy black hair and his shining eyes. He smelt of eau de Cologne and of Turkish cigarettes. Everything about him seemed to be modern: he wore a cotton shirt, a silk tie with a matching pocket handkerchief and a lovely blue three-piece suit which included a double-breasted waistcoat, a jacket with flap pockets and wide trousers. I can see now that he must have spent every pengő he had on such a marvellous suit but back then I thought this suit came with him in the same way his luxuriant hair did.

From the moment, he entered the flat and we heard his strides bounding through the hallway, Anna and I would jerk our heads from our Latin primers and look at each other and smile.

His appearance in the library was always dramatic because he would grip both the handles of the twin doors and push on them suddenly, tilting his head forward. He seemed to break through into the room like the archangel Gabriel dropping out of a cloud. Miss Virág would try her best to settle us back to work but it was impossible: I think her brother made even her wrinkled old heart flutter.

Once his sister had left the room and he had drawn his chair up to ours – he sat next to us and not opposite us – he would say with sparkling eyes: 'Now are you ready for your first lesson, comrades?'

He always called us 'comrades'. Not pupils, not children, not Anna, not Zoltán or your Excellencies, but 'comrades'. We nodded our heads enthusiastically and moved our chairs conspiratorially towards him, so that our knees were touching, as he pulled his books out of his bag and rested them on his lap.

'Now, as you know by now, you must swear yourselves to the utmost secrecy today because what I am going to teach you is the truth. The truth is highly dangerous so nothing must leave this room,' he would breathe urgently.

Anna was always the first to pledge herself. 'I swear by the words of Marx, Lenin and Trotsky that I will say nothing!' she would say gleefully, putting her hand on his knee as she did so.

I would repeat Anna's words and the lesson would begin. Imre was charged with teaching us history, chemistry, physics and English. He was an inspired teacher because he taught everything in context. For example, he would lecture about the Industrial Revolution and then he would tell us about the physics of the steam engine, using Newton's laws to elucidate how it worked.

Unfortunately, having no head for the sciences, I don't remember much about most of his lessons except that he talked a great deal about the oppressed and the proletariat. He often told us how the workers would soon rise up, have a revolution, take over the means of production and achieve a Utopia. He explained how it had already happened in Russia and very nearly happened in Hungary, just before I was born: there had been a communist government for 123 days.

My brain was far too shallow to absorb much. I already believed, because of my talks with my father, that Counts, Barons, Dukes, Kings and Regents generally knew best and that it was foolish to disagree with them. I also knew that my father hated communists because they had blown the Baron Káldy to smithereens. But I kept my mouth shut because I could see Anna was enchanted and, to my amazement, seemed to understand all Imre's talk of dialectics and divisions of land and labour.

The only thing that I can remember now are the English novels he used to read to us at the end of his lessons. He was an impassioned, energetic reader who would put on all sorts of different voices. He loved Dickens and I still can hear his crackly imitation of Miss Havisham – he made her sound like his sister. But it wasn't Dickens that ultimately caught our imaginations but his reading of Bram Stoker's *Dracula*.

I don't know why we loved the book so much; perhaps it was because the vampire was a Transylvanian Count – like our father. Perhaps it was because I had seen my mother furtively reading it on the day that Anna had pulled my pants down in the Count's study. Or perhaps it was because Imre wickedly imitated the voice of our father when he read Dracula's lines, or perhaps it was the descriptions of the evil one's lair that seemed to be a hideous, ghostly parody of our own long lost Castle. I think Imre loved it because the whole novel seemed unconsciously to mock the pretensions of the Hungarian nobility with its portrayal of the blood-sucking Count. Sometimes he would break away from reading the text and say with an enigmatic grin: 'Remember that comrades, that's what they all are: blood-suckers!'

I was too young to understand that Imre was insulting my father. I giggled with Anna at this repeated comment; it seemed to make her happy. She would prod Imre on the knee and lean forward and whisper in his ear: 'He's a blood-sucker, isn't he?'

I was too busy watching the way Anna's long, curling black hair obscured her high Pongrácz cheekbones and the swell of her breasts underneath her blouse to work out what the two of them were joking about. I assumed that they were talking about *Dracula*.

Once we had finished reading the book, Imre announced at the end of the lesson that he had bought some tickets to see *Dracula* at the cinema. 'It's a talkie,' he said, 'And it stars a Hungarian who I used to know.'

Under the watchful supervision of our mother, who made sure that we never saw anything unsuitable, both of us had seen, and had loved, a few silent movies. *The Thief of Baghdad,* which starred a beautifully-buttocked, lithe and leaping Douglas Fairbanks, was my favourite: I loved the flying carpet, the incense-bearing trees and the turreted, domed city with its fire-eaters, dervishes and beautiful maidens. But most of all, I loved the music. The Corvin cinema had its own in-house orchestra and organ that played a version of Rimsky-Korsakov's *Scheherazade* in accompaniment to the film. This perfect marriage of music and pictures awakened a kaleidoscope of sounds and images in my head and, for a few days afterwards, I could shut my eyes and feel myself floating away on a magic carpet, drifting through emerald skies, buoyed by the strains of Rimsky-Korsakov's divine music.

But we had never seen a talkie before, despite our continual protestations to our mother that we should be allowed to do so. Our mother believed that there was something very sinister about the talkies. Once, playing a game of hide and seek in the study, concealed inside my father's huge but empty wooden filing cabinet, I had heard her talking to the Count in low, urgent tones. After complaining about the way her children were pestering her to go to see *The Jazz Singer*, she said: 'I've heard that these talkies can hypnotise young children into doing the things that are actually happening on the screen. I think it's a new version of mesmerism!'

I could see through a crack in the cabinet that my father was too busy putting the finishing touches to his model of the Hammersmith Bridge to listen to her: he was tightening and straightening the suspension cables – a very tricky and delicate operation. 'Mesmerism is very interesting,' he said abstractedly, his pliers twiddling with a bolt.

Mama wrinkled her nose at this somewhat tangential comment and said irritably: 'It's not interesting, it's dangerous. I'm convinced that the talkies have a mesmeric effect on impressionable minds.'

My mother's superstitious disapproval of the talkies only served to stiffen Anna's resolve -- but it considerably dampened mine. However, once Anna proclaimed herself game to sneak out of the apartment on Saturday afternoon to see the horror movie, I quickly mimicked her enthusiasm, not wanting to be deprived of her company for that length of time.

'This is a top-secret sortie, comrades,' Imre said, putting his finger to his mouth. 'No one must know about this. Do you swear by Marx, Lenin and Trotsky not to breathe a word?'

Although I promised myself to silence, my mother's words began to haunt me throughout the week. What if we were all actually hypnotised and turned into vampires after watching the movie, where would we all be then? We wouldn't be able to get up during the day and enjoy our lessons, or go boating in the City Park on Sunday afternoons, or drink hot chocolate in Gerbeaud. We'd have to get up at night and search for blood to suck. It may have been fine for Dracula in Transylvania but it would be an entirely unsatisfactory for someone of noble birth who lived in Budapest.

By the time Saturday rolled around and Anna and I had slunk out of the library where we were supposed to be completing our homework, I was in quite an agitated state and I blurted out my fears to my sister. Her response didn't reassure me. 'But we'll live forever!' she laughed. 'And we can turn into bats when we want and no one will be able to see us in the mirror.'

'But I don't want to turn into a bat,' I moaned. Yet the thought of staying alive forever did seem appealing; maybe then I'd be able to learn Latin grammar and difficult chemical formulae.

Following Anna, I sneaked out of the apartment by running down the servants' staircase. As I fled, my heart walloped against my chest: this was the first time I had ever consciously transgressed. I knew that Mama and Papa would be jolly cross if they found out what we were doing. Much as I didn't want to offend them, I was more frightened of disappointing Anna. Although we had drifted apart since the Wenceslas episode, I knew that I was eternally in her debt. She had saved me from unendurable suffering.

We waited for Imre on a wooden bench underneath the dappled shade of a lime tree, a couple of blocks from our apartment. It was a fine spring day and the sculptured garlands of fruit and nymphs that adorned the Opera House smirked at us in the sunlight -- though the statues of Erkel and Lizst seemed to be frowning. Imre emerged out of the subway station and ran over to us with a lighted cigarette smoking in his fingers. He looked frightfully dashing, though his suit and tie were slightly shabby in the sharp light. Imre was a man who was in the prime of life: he was vigorous, bold and inexhaustibly curious about the world around him. He blew out smoke at the dour statues and grinned at us. 'Are you ready, comrades?'

Anna assented enthusiastically but I only offered a weak nod of the head. As we walked up to the Octogon Square, Anna told her tutor about my anxieties. Imre laughed and patted me on the back. 'Don't you worry, comrade, we'll look after you!'

This exhortation comforted me and made me, for the first time, appreciate what communism was: it was about everyone pulling together, the strong supporting the weak.

We caught a tram at the Octogon and travelled sedately along the Grand Boulevard, the Nagykörút. I stared up at the unfamiliar angels, cherubims and naked strong men who plastered the walls of the apartment buildings. They all seemed to be much smaller and more insignificant than the gigantic statues, caryatids and verdant adornments of my own avenue. It was as if the Nagykörút was the sickly brother of the regal Andrássy.

It was the first time that I had ever travelled on a tram. What a revelation it was. Here, at last, was a mode of transport that I enjoyed. I loved the charming, dawdling pace, the melodious ringing of the bell, the elevated, stately view of the world outside and the folding, disappearing doors. It felt as if I was riding on the back of a benevolent, yellow-breasted elephant, plodding majestically through the streets, nosing through the traffic and gesturing people out of the way with its white trunk.

My sudden affection for the tram quite melted my fears about seeing *Dracula*. I passed by the bas-relief sculptured stone panels of the great Matthias Corvinus that decorated the Corvin cinema without so much a flicker of fear. However, once we had passed through the cavernous lobby and entered the glimmering theatre, and the venue darkened as some shimmering, spooky music seeped out of the air like ectoplasm, I began to tremble.

I tried my best to keep my terror to myself but when the cadaverous Count wafted onto the screen, I gripped Anna in fright and noticed that she, too, was holding Imre's hand and pressing her cheek against his shoulder. The film was absolutely terrifying. A deathly quietude suffused it. The Count's luminous, mist-blown eyes appalled me. (It's odd how the memory works because superimposed upon those evil eyes is the image of the last time I saw Imre. He was staring at me in a similar fashion. Except that his stare was the absolute inverse of Dracula's – petrified, not petrifying – but curiously akin.)

Béla Lugosi's Dracula didn't have fangs, he didn't leap out claw at his victims, he didn't leave puncture marks on their necks. Instead he crept towards them, slowly stalking them, hypnotising them with his dark Hungarian features. It seemed to me that this was exactly the mesmeric phenomenon that my mother had been worried about.

Even the simplest of Dracula's phrases were imbued with menace. When Dracula offers the madman Renfield a drink, he says: 'This is…very…old …wine.' Why did I find these words so sinister? Was it because I vaguely remembered my father saying something similar about our ancient vintages from Villány?

When I left the cinema, I found that I was blinded by the blast of the afternoon sunlight. My anxiety that I had been transformed into a vampire was already quite considerable, but my bedazzlement was final proof: I could no longer tolerate daylight. Before I collapsed, my heart was ringing against my chest like the tolling of the huge bell in St Stephen's Basilica as I shouted: 'I am a vampire!'

I awoke to the sensation of a damp cloth dabbing my cheeks. I caught a glimpse of Margaret's puce face and sunshine playing with the naked cherubs on the ceiling. 'Is it still day?' I croaked.

When the maid answered in the affirmative, I clamped my eyes shut again. The flurry of my mother's unstrung voice woke me a while later. Again, I asked what time of day it was. When Margaret, who seemed to have maintained her bedside vigil, told me that it was evening, I sat up and shook off my blankets. My mother rushed up to the bed and clutched my wrist, and peered into my eyes.

'Zoltán, how are you?'

I had a stinking headache. I wondered whether I was still all there. But when I could still feel some sense of myself lingering in my head like a brimming cup of milk, I told her that I was all right, despite having a horrible pain in my head. Her relief was visible: the colour returned to her English cheeks and she patted her thick blond hair, now laced with grey. She shouted out: 'Oh Louis! Come here, I think he might be all right.'

After some shuffling of feet outside the nursery, my father finally walked in. He stood erect underneath the chandelier; the painted cherubs on the ceiling looked like they were revolving around the bald sphere of his head. I thought that one day, when I was fully grown, I would have a magnificent nose like his, although I wasn't so sure I wanted to be bald. Nobody could disagree with such a noble nose.

'Yes, he does seem to be better,' he said without moving any closer to me.

Wanting him to come nearer, I asked him what I thought to be an obvious question: 'So I'm not Dracula, am I?'

The looks of astonishment that greeted this question, both from my father and my mother, told me that they had no idea what I had been doing this afternoon. My mother grabbed her diamond engagement ring and swivelled it around on her finger, while the Count inched towards me like a naturalist stalking a wild animal.

'What on earth makes you say that?' my mother asked. 'You did just go for a walk in the City Park today, didn't you?'

I think if my father hadn't been there, I would have maintained this lie, but his presence unsettled me. Like Dracula, he was infallible and could read people's minds. It was useless lying in front of the Count.

'I saw a talkie, Mama,' I said, slowly breaking into sobs. 'But I don't think I've turned into Béla Lugosi quite yet.'

My addled brain equated Béla Lugosi with the vampirical Count because I hadn't quite worked out that there was a qualitative difference between the actor and the character he portrays.

'Béla Lugosi?' my father mused, churning over everything verbally. 'You went to see the film *Dracula* in which the main character was played by a man called Béla Lugosi?'

I nodded mutely as the black profile of my father creaked towards the bed. His shadow fell across my eyes as he continued his questioning: 'And you imagined that you had actually become this character and the actor who plays him by a process of hypnotism?'

Again I nodded, expecting the Count to bend down and give me a medical examination to see if I had, in fact, been transformed. Instead, I was surprised when the Count laughed thickly: 'Well, isn't that the damnedest thing? The poor child was persuaded of all that superstitious hokum by Béla Lugosi! Béla Lugosi. What a total incompetent he was! He managed to mess up everything in Kun's regime and he certainly could never act! Well, I never.'

My father's mirth perplexed me. I had no idea that he was referring to Lugosi's lamentable role as Minister for Culture in the disastrously short-lived Hungarian Communist regime in 1919 or that Lugosi had acted in Budapest before the war.

The depth of my mother's anger mirrored my confusion.

'I don't know how you can laugh about something like this. That wretched tutor not only lied to us but he took my children to see the most unsuitable film imaginable. I've been warning you about those yids, Pongrácz, and you've never listened!'

My father's nostrils dilated in disgruntlement. His bald head fell into shadow. He murmured: 'Now, now, let's not talk like Germans in front of the child, dear.'

My mother stopped twirling her ring and pulled at the gold bracelet that hung around the cuff of her white blouse. She curled her lip but remained silent. She followed my father out of the nursery, leaving me to ponder what yids were and why my tutors were of this species.

Interlude I

From: KarolinaTarr99@outlook.com
To: BelaPongracz9@gmail.com

Hi Béla,

How are you?

I am sorry it's taken me so long to reply.

Anyway, I wanted you to know I read your email and then what your great-uncle wrote.

The story is of great interest to me.

My grandparents lived through the war in Budapest.

I don't remember them very well because they died when I was young, but I can recall them talking about the shortages, and how much they hated the Russians. They weren't rich; they served people like your Count.

Your great-uncle makes me laugh. I really feel like I can see him: his fussiness, his worries about his health, his strange parents, and of course, Anna. I see her, I feel her. You can feel his love for her in his words. It makes me want to know what happened to them. I really like Miss Virág and Imre too. But I worry. They were Jewish of course. Do send me more of the story.

I don't feel I want to meet you just yet. I think it's better to write to each other.

I'm obviously assuming you're OK. I am sorry I didn't come and get you from the café. I hope they let you go free and that you didn't do anything stupid.

I'm sorry, Béla, but I've got to protect myself. It's been very difficult for me but getting this job with the film production company is a big deal. I want to hold onto it, even if it's just being a secretary - - at the moment. They like me. They are saying that I might have a chance to go to the States. But it's 24/7 job. No time for anyone or anything else.

And the thing is the person I fell in love with was not real. I feel a fool for not seeing through you from the start...

But you were convincing! You knew all this stuff about CGI, special effects, and you had money, and you wore nice clothes. You speak well.

But I think I could feel your neediness. It wasn't attractive. And it doesn't surprise me that you're not a CGI computer expert, I think I began to sense that. You never seemed to need to do any work, and you were always hanging around my flat. I was finding it very difficult. That's why I changed the locks. I really hope you don't come back. I am asking you nicely.

But do write to me. That feels safe. Tell me what happened after you read your great-uncle's will and how and why you came to Budapest. I am interested to know -- and send me the rest of the manuscript. I have a feeling it might make a great film.

Then, maybe, we can meet for coffee or a drink, when we know where we stand. I never led you to believe that I was committed to you forever. It was never anything like that for me. I like you Béla, but I want us to be friends – nothing more.

Yours,

Karolina.
From: BelaPongracz9@gmail.com
To: KarolinaTarr99@outlook.com

Dear Karolina,

Thank you for writing back to me finally. You're right, I am still alive. Eventually, the café owner let me go after he gave me a free lunch! But he said I had to come back, and so here I am the next day, watching the snow fall on the Danube, writing to you.

Yes, I feel a bit better knowing that at least I am in communication with you. I wish I did not love you so much, but I can't help it. It feels both good and bad to write that.

But I should explain. Yes, you wanted to know how what happened after I read Zoltan's will. Well, there was a bust-up between me and my mother. After I read the Count's story, I had all these questions. Did Mum have any photographs of my grandparents? I wanted to her to confirm some of the details in the Count's account. I won't tell you what my precise questions were because I want you to read what happened. It really is very shocking.

I couldn't take it all in straightaway. I was sort of in a daze. I even stopped gaming for a bit, and went for long walks, around Vicky Park near where I live, and imagined I was in the Budapest City Park. I visited the Hammersmith Bridge, which was built by the same guy who did the Chain Bridge. I did some research about Hungary, watching documentaries on YouTube, reading stuff on Wikipedia, going to the library and reading books. For the first time in a very long time, I was interested in something.

I felt very sad too. I wanted to talk to the Count. I realised that he would never have wanted to speak about what happened. When you read what he wrote, you'll understand why. I sort of get that. But I wanted to say to him, 'Hey, I didn't know that. I had no fucking idea. I just thought you were odd, eccentric, a bit irritating at times, I never actually really knew you.'

I partly blamed Mum. I realised that she knew and never told me. And this led to me to having one of the most productive conversations I'd had with my mother in a very long time.

She'd come back from work and was smoking in the kitchen, playing Bingo on her iPad.

She didn't look up when I said whether she might lend me some money.

'What do you want it for?'

'I am hoping to fly to Budapest and stay there for a bit.'

She put the cover her iPad and stubbed out her ciggy.

'Why do you want to go to that shit heap?'

'I'd like to do some research.'

She snorted mockingly. 'Research? What are you now? An academic? Don't make me laugh. The only research you'll do is into the cheap liquor there.' Then she winced: 'You're wasting your time you know. You won't find anything there except prejudice and poverty. You're Jewish, Béla, the Hungarians still hate the Jews. And it's getting worse with this fascist clown Orbán!'

'I'll take my chances. The Count's story has made me want to go there.'

'He hated the place.'

'You haven't read what he wrote.'

At that, she left the room, and didn't speak to me all night.

But in the morning, just as she was about to leave for work, she said: 'OK, Béla, if I give you some money, do you promise when you get back you'll make a serious effort to look for a job, or do a course or something? Do you promise? Give up the computer games and get back on track?'

And so that's what led to me flying over this January. I wanted to go in the winter because, as you see, it's an important time of year in the Count's story. I wanted partly to feel what he felt a little: the cold, the bleakness, I was kind of into that idea. And besides everything was cheaper: the flight, the Airbnb. I felt good. I had a lovely flat in central Budapest to stay in for a month, enough money to live on. I felt free and confident.

And that's when you met me, when I was touring around the Korda studios. I was full of hope that maybe I could get a job in some place like that, and that's where the lies started, and that led to me posting shit on Facebook about being a CGI guy in Shoreditch. You were so beautiful and composed behind that reception desk, so articulate, so gorgeous, and I felt somehow buoyed up by what I knew about my great-uncle. I can't explain it. Reading the manuscript gave me an inner confidence about who I am that I'd never had before.

Why didn't I tell you about his story then? Why now? I don't know really…Maybe it is because I wanted the story to be mine and mine only at that point. I enjoyed hugging it close.

And besides it was so easy to lie to you on that first night, in that bar by the Danube, getting drunk together on *pálinka*, laughing at the stupidity of the film industry, talking about films we liked. You liked all my favourites: *North by North West*, *The Apartment*, Tarkovsky's *Solaris*, *Mirror*, *Stalker*… I'd never met anyone who liked my weird old-time films, and you even liked playing GTA.

You were so beautiful, Karolina, your dark eyes shimmering by the lights of Buda, your tongue touching mine as the river slid by, your laughter, your mockery of Hungarian prejudices. I even thought I might tell you I was Jewish, I knew it would be OK.

And your life, growing up with all those brothers and sisters and having to work so hard at school. And the times we had, they were fleeting, but the best times I've ever had. I've had a shit, banal life. I went to a shit school and then went to a shit university to do a shit degree in Business Studies. I only did that because that's what everyone else was doing.

I hated it, and ended up just sitting in my room playing online games and being irritable with the Count. I didn't eat properly. When I really get into gaming I can just go at it for hours and hours; the only breaks you take are for the toilet or to eat the pizza you've got delivered. I felt safe playing League of Legends, a summoner fighting on the Fields of Justice, casting my spells, acquiring items like Athene's Unholy Grail, Bramble Vests, Corrupting Potion, Zhonya's Paradox, which makes you invulnerable for 2.5 seconds. I loved that feeling of invulnerability. Never to be hurt. Never to feel.

You see, I did have a girlfriend at school. She was called Precious, but it went very badly wrong. She was involved in some heavy shit. And I got hurt. Badly hurt. There were girls after that, but it was never the same. Just very temporary stuff, until you.

It was the way we talked. I know I only told you lies, but it makes me think how much better it would be if we told the truth.

I am glad that you like my great-uncle's story. I am going to show you *a bit* more, but I'm not going to give you the important section... Not the nightmare that happened during the second world war.

Not until you agree to meet with me. I need to trust you before I show you it.

I love you Karolina. I am feeling better now, but it would make such a difference if I could see you again.

Yours,

Béla

11: SCHOOL

I was soon to learn about the multiplicity of appellations given to Jews because our private lessons ceased immediately after the *Dracula* incident and we were both sent to school. I attended a Catholic gymnasium in Budapest while Anna was banished to my mother's school in England, Cheltenham Ladies' College.

What can I say about my school years, except that they were both banal and ghastly? My delicate constitution was not suited to being near large groups of sweaty, thuggish boys, nor were the hollows of my ears used to being pierced by the screeches and exhortations of exasperated teachers.

I don't know who was worse; the boys or the teachers. Certainly, the boys would mercilessly mock the lonely Jewish boy, Józef, who had found himself in our class; but the teachers' constant condemnation of this boy's work seemed to have much more to do with the author's racial origins than its intellectual merits. 'Of course, how could you possibly understand Hungarian history?' our fat-bottomed master would frequently comment.

I suppose I should have been grateful that such anti-Semitism was so rife because, for some mysterious reason, I seemed to be the next recipient in the pecking order of the teachers and the pupils' taunts. Unfortunately, some urchin with dreadful spots pimpling his chin discovered that I spent most of recess sipping my medicine and sticking fresh buds of cotton wool in my ears. Thus, I acquired the nickname of 'beetroot boy'. The nasty tykes would bring in beetroots and, depending on how good-humoured they were collectively feeling, would either hurl the vegetables at me in the playground or leave mouldy ones on my desk.

I don't think I would have survived if I had been a boarder like Józef. They used to beat him up in the dormitory after the lights were switched out. Often, the poor chap would surface late for registration, get yelled by a teacher for his tardiness and interrupting the Lord's Prayer, and then spend the remainder of the morning picking at some fresh wound on his legs or arms. The bullies never touched his face for fear of making their persecution too obvious.

Yet I plunged myself into my musical studies with a passion that had been wholly lacking when the Virágs had taught me. This was chiefly because I quickly worked out that the more music lessons I attended the more academic lessons I could skip. Thus, I not only continued with my violin and piano lessons, but took up the viola, the flute and the trumpet. The impossibility of one person single-handedly carrying this collection of instruments also meant that János had to drive me to and from school in the Mercedes every day. I was spared the claustrophobia of the metro.

I tried my best to fill the painful cavity created by Anna's absence by practising my instruments with fiendish diligence during the evenings. For the first and last time in my life, I had a routine based upon the concept of work. After nibbling at some sauerkraut once I had returned home from school, I would begin by completing a set of scales and arpeggios on each instrument. Once freshened up in this fashion, I would practise my pieces, usually starting with the oldest composer first and working through the centuries as I jumped from instrument to instrument.

The total control I had over my own music schedule somehow compensated for the utter lack of control I seemed to have over the events in my own life.

Respite from my strict music program only arrived in the summer when Anna would join my parents and me on holiday. These were rather grand affairs which, on the most memorable occasion in the early 1930s, involved János motoring us up to Vienna, through the Austrian Alps and up to Paris, and finally, via the Channel ferry, to London. Along the way we sojourned in the mansions, town houses and mountain retreats of the European aristocracy -- one of my parents always seemed to be distantly related to whatever family we stayed with. Often, these dignitaries weren't present to greet us but their servants always were and they always treated us with the obsequiousness that they must have shown their masters.

However, as the 1930s progressed, our holidays became less and less ambitious. England was the first country to get knocked out of the equation: British high society saw my eccentric 'foreign' father as a poor match for my aristocratic mother. I can't remember much about our stay on her parents' Northamptonshire estate except that her father and the Count went shooting grouse one morning and returned without a bird and in silence. The following summer we got as far as France but didn't make it to Paris. However I much preferred Nice's kind climate and beaches to Paris's raucous streets.

In 1935, we didn't even make it over the Alps; the highlight of the trip was a disappointing production of *The Marriage of Figaro* in Salzburg. In 1936, János didn't bother getting out the Mercedes: we took a boat up the Danube to a German-infested Vienna. By 1937, these European sorties ceased entirely and we spent the summer sweating in Budapest and driving down to a baronet's hunting lodge at the weekends.

At the time I thought that Anna's extreme sulkiness was to blame. She barely spoke a word to any of us during these trips. Instead she contented herself with reading volumes of revolutionary Hungarian poetry, Sándor Petőfi, Vörösmarty, Endre Ady and, her personal favourite, Attila József, a particularly dour and harsh poet who wrote about urban deprivation in Budapest. I remembered that Imre had espoused his cause quite passionately during one of our secretive lessons. Sometimes Anna would quote lines from him at inopportune moments -- just as we were passing underneath the gold-leafed threshold of some great mansion or sitting down to eat underneath a fantastic glittering chandelier.

> 'O night of the poor, be my fuel,
> smolder here in my heart,
> smelt from me the iron,
> the unbreakable anvil,
> the clanging, flashing hammer,
> and the sharp blade of victory,
> O night.'

Anna was never crass enough to condemn the extravagance of our lifestyle outright but her declamations did unsettle me, vex my father and severely irritate my mother who would grip her engagement ring between her forefinger and thumb and pull it up and down her finger.

'Anna, dear, I'm not sure such poetry is appropriate here,' she would agitate, and then in a lower voice, which was out of earshot of the servants: 'We might not get invited back.'

Before Anna could embark on reciting more lines, which I could see she was just about to do, my mother would continue: 'Of course, you'd probably like that, wouldn't you? You probably like it if we had nowhere but your miserable Budapest slums to stay in, wouldn't you? It's not enough that we won't be going to France or England this summer, you'd probably like it if we didn't even stay in the Baron's house in Vienna, wouldn't you?'

This would bring my father into the conversation as he tried to mollify my mother's increasing annoyance at our decreasing social and geographical horizons. 'I'm sure that Anna isn't thinking like that at all,' he would whisper, placing his hand on Mama's knee.

But judging from the sullen smirk on Anna's face I think she probably did take a measure of delight in our vanishing social world. I was to learn from Anna's moody asides to me on our dutiful tours around the various European monuments, that she hated Cheltenham Ladies' College. 'England is ripe for the worker's revolution,' she would say to me. 'Karl Marx said so himself and I can see it in that school. Bloodsuckers, the lot of them!'

Perhaps I should have guessed that these weren't her words. Perhaps I should have heard Imre's voice echoing behind everything she said and everything she read, but it never occurred to me then. I was too much in awe of Anna. She had such a magnificent presence, with her mane of black hair, her dark eyes, her high cheekbones, her striking figure that made even the modest attire seem glamorous. She was as monumental as one of the lions on the Chain Bridge, as regal as Buda Castle Palace and as fantastical as Pest's Parliament building. I never questioned the authority or novelty of her opinions. If I had been perceptive and a little worldlier, I would have realised that her thoughts were as hackneyed and unoriginal as Budapest's architectural highlights.

But by the time I was old enough to figure out that Anna must have been in correspondence with Imre, I was too pre-occupied with the happy events in my own life to give much consideration to anyone else's. My diligence at practising all those musical instruments reaped rich rewards. At the tender age of 16, I gained a scholarship to attend the Liszt Academy of Music, to specialise in the violin and piano as well as taking classes in composition.

Although my father doubted that this would be the right training for a Count – he felt I was getting to an age when I could go shooting and fishing with him at the baronet's hunting lodge – my mother was overjoyed.

'Some of these musicians get paid very well. Maybe he'll make back some of the money you've frittered away on your stupid bridges and your nights on the Corso,' she said as we were standing out on the balcony of the Opera House during the interval of a production of Béla Bartók's *Bluebeard's Castle*. My father displayed the patience of Job here because he was already considerably vexed at having to listen to Bartók's dreaded music; nevertheless, he knew it was his duty to attend a production by a fellow Hungarian. But he was far too much of a gentleman to respond to Mama's barbed comment and simply bowed at her, excused himself and bought a fresh glass of brandy at the concession stand, where I joined him during the interval. It was here that he told me about how his ancestor rescued János's ancestor from the clutches of Gilles de Rais in Brittany. 'Who, of course, is judged by many to be the real Bluebeard!' he said, sipping his brandy. 'I'm not sure what is more horrific: the thought of that awful Breton and all those child murders, or that music! Nevertheless, you know Zoltán, I am pleased you appreciate it; it tells me that you are a more open-minded person than I will ever be. We Pongráczes can be very set in our ways, and somehow I think you may have broken the mould!'

It was the nicest thing that my father ever said to me; I feel I have the transcendentally brilliant Bartók to thank for that.

12: LISZT AND LASZLO

My first year at the Liszt Academy was blissful. I spent a great deal of time just savouring the delicious Art Nouveau atmosphere of the building. After the bare, scrubby walls, bleak corridors and austere classrooms of the gymnasium, I marvelled at the gold-leafed columns, the emerald walls, the brass fixtures, the brown and red velvet curtains, the cosy practice rooms, the astonishing concert hall and the gorgeous murals of naked maidens worshipping before the fountain of art. The smell of freshly ground coffee and violin resin drifted through the glimmering corridors and twirling stairwells. The Academy seemed as exotic and gaudy as unfurled peacocks' tails.

What transfixed me the most was the notion that an institution as venerable and established as this world-famous music academy could be so decadent and louche in its demeanour. I felt it gave me the licence to experience all sorts of emotions that I had hitherto safely stowed away in the cupboard of my unconscious. However, while the Liszt Academy may have given me the key – a musical and psychic key – with which to unlock the cupboard, it took László to open the door.

When I met him, László was slim and shy, he didn't have his big, glossy chestnut moustache or his big belly and he wasn't bald. Instead he had a fine head of curly brown hair, soft lips and an endearing country accent. He had grown up in a remote Transylvanian village not far from my father's confiscated Castle. This had been what had drawn us together initially because he had heard my surname and, after an orchestral rehearsal, he had hesitantly asked me whether I was a noble Pongrácz.

When I had finished explaining the true aristocracy of my lineage, we fell into discussing the sheer size of our old family Castle. László had been around it. It was sadly abandoned now and was only used for the occasional concert or meeting.

'Yes, it's amazing place. Huge and beautiful. When the sun rises in the morning, it shines on all the turrets and towers and the Castle looks like it's floating in the air,' László enthused. 'There are lots of birds in the rafters now. They make their nests in the window alcoves.'

I asked him about my father's bridge.

László's face fell. He told me that it had been destroyed in a bad storm: it was no longer safe to cross. When he saw my dismal expression as he described the bridge's ruinous condition, he squeezed my arm heartily, saying with a bluff joviality that would become his main social bearing in later years: 'Don't you worry, your Excellency! The Führer will soon return your Castle and land to you. Don't you worry at all!'

I was surprised at this comment on several counts. Firstly, no one at the Academy called me by my rightful title – Excellency – and secondly, being a liberal place, no one spoke in positive terms about Germany's leader except when some minister from the government attended a concert and they were forced to preface the Hungarian national anthem with some paean to Hitler. I found László's faith in Hitler rather endearing. His country yokel's accent always dropped a few semi-tones when he talked about him, making it sound as though he was speaking about some distant but revered relative.

László and I strolled out of the green gloom of the academy and wandered along the Elizabeth körút towards the Café New York. When I saw that László was peering into the swirling golden interior of the Café with a profound look of wonder and curiosity, I offered to treat him to a cup of coffee and he accepted eagerly. The décor of the New York was much more agreeable to his simple rustic tastes than the more perverse furnishings of the Academy. Unlike the college, all the private parts of its painted cherubs and maidens were covered with swaddling cloths and the furniture was much more traditional than the Academy's dreamlike fixtures. The café's conservative style reassured him.

'Now this is what I always imagined Budapest would be like,' he said, gazing at the satyrs that frolicked on the gilded arches and ceiling fretted with shining seashells, eagles and angels. As he leaned back, his knee touched mine. Perhaps because I was enjoying the sensation of his strong, country leg pressing against my thigh too much, I moved it. But László immediately slid further down in his chair and his knee quickly resumed its former position against my leg. Suddenly, I was aware that he liked me a little more than a friend normally did: he wanted to touch me. And the strange thing was, I wanted to touch him, to fondle him, to kiss him. To my horror, I understood that my desires were not entirely natural. Once he had finished scrutinising the rococo flourishes of the café, he told sat bolt upright in his chair and smiled at me. He told me proudly about how he had been chosen to study at the Academy by one of Kodály's most trusted friends who had listened to every child in the village sing and play an instrument. He was the only person Kodály's friend picked from a ten-mile radius. Maybe I would have been less inclined to forgive this bragging if László hadn't informed me of this with such energetic naiveté and if he hadn't clutched my hand suddenly and said: 'But I'm only 15. I don't know anyone here at all. No one, your Excellency.'

My response was immediate and magnanimous. 'But you know me, don't you? The Pongrácz family will not let you down.'

13: WALKING ON THE CORSO

Although my father was pleased to hear that I had made a friend who lived near our former estate in Transylvania, he was extremely reluctant to let László accompany us on the increasing number of parties to which he was taking me. Initially I thought this was because László was, in essence, a peasant. I'm sure this played a part in his adamant refusal to let László take even the shortest stroll with us along the Corso, but I don't think it was the principal one. My father was a liberal man – he had, after all, employed two Jews to educate us – and he was always interested in meeting new people.

No. I'm certain that it was my detailed account of László's idolisation of Hitler that put my father off. Until I joined the Academy, the Count always kept his views on the Germans to himself, chiefly because my mother was a bit of a Führer fan as well. But once it became clear that a war with England might be a real possibility my mother toned down her praise of Germany, and the Count began to take me for long drives in the Mercedes to introduce me to many of the dignitaries at his club, the National Casino, and generally to induct me into the high life of Budapest.

When we were alone together, perhaps in the velvety alcove of the Ritz or the Carlton, or watching silver-spangled dancers perform somersaults on the dance floor of the Arizona from a secluded high balcony, he would often sip his brandy schnapps and say ruefully: 'It's a terrible thing, young Zoltán, a terrible contradiction. The Germans may give us back the lands that we want. We may even get our estates back, but what will they ask for in return? What will they want?' He was nearly always a little drunk when he spoke in this manner, and I could tell that he didn't enjoy dwelling upon his distrust of the Germans. But for the most part, he was jolly good company.

Now I finally learned what my father had been up to during all those empty evenings in my childhood when we weren't having manly chats: chasing women. No wonder our dear mother had languished in the Red Room reading Jane Austen with a permanent frown souring her English features. I suppose the Count assumed that now I was old enough, I would be following in his footsteps. At garden parties, he was forever introducing me to the pretty daughters of wealthy bankers and baronets.

For all his carousing, the Count's life was highly structured, albeit in a haphazard fashion. He spent most of the morning in his workshop tinkering around with one of his model bridges. At around eleven, János would drive him to one of the numerous cafés in Budapest; the Café Japan near the Liszt Academy was his favourite because all of his artistic friends – architects, artists, museum curators and poets – loafed around there. They were his most reliable informants about which ladies were on the prowl. Furnished with this knowledge, he would then adjourn to the National Casino for lunch. This was usually a lengthy affair and involved a few select acquaintances from the Hungarian aristocracy. In the afternoons he might return to the apartment if he was tired and had drunk rather too much wine. In this case he would sleep until the early evening. However, he might sit in the Upper House in Parliament if the fancy took him and fall asleep listening to some grandee's speech.

He would always bathe in the early evening and János would shave him with a cut-throat razor. At six, he would take high tea with his wife and dutifully try to assuage her complaints about the boredom of Budapest life. He would then invite her out for a stroll on the Corso. 'It will do you a world of good just to get out. Why only the other day Baron Serenyi's wife was asking after you,' he would say brightly. My mother nearly always refused, much to the Count's relief. Although she had a much stronger constitution than I ever had, she had the same propensity to feel ill. By then, she suffered terribly from neurasthenia.

In the springs and summers of the late 1930s, I always joined my father on the Corso at around eight o'clock. Usually he would be escorting some pretty specimen along the promenade and would glance up at me with a look of surprise on his face, as if he hadn't been expecting to bump into me. He would then introduce me to his fragrant companion if I didn't know her – after the first year I got to know most of them – and then we would take a turn along the banks of the river. He would spend a great deal of the walk expounding at length about the history of Budapest's bridges, usually returning with monotonous regularity to the marvellous reliability of the rivets in the Chain Bridge.

'Not even dynamite could separate those chains!' he would say, pointing victoriously at the incandescent suspension cables of the Széchenyi Bridge which shone like lights on a Christmas tree over the dark Danube. 'Those are the finest rivets in the world. English rivets, naturally.'

The lights from the fine hotels – the Carlton, the Bristol, the Hungaria and the Ritz – would spill onto the Corso, illuminating the gentlemen's soft, smart hats, which were the fashionable Italian hats of the period, and making the sabres, which officers were required to wear at all times, shine in the green air. These gallant servicemen with their shakos and their glittering swords would escort their belles along the riverside and then would sit down on the terrace of some elegant café, their sabres clanking on the ground as they ordered their Viennese coffees. Below us, the river would flow noiselessly, shimmering as if shivering with delight at the smell of violets drifting down from Gellert Hill and the sheer sophistication of the people strolling along its banks.

The crisp, see-saw rhythms and melodies of *csárdás* would plume out of the cafés and hotels like fire from a circus entertainer's mouth, making the marble tops of the tables tremble. The flirtatious chatter of gentlemen and ladies would reverberate through the trees and make the water ripple in the fountain in front of the Vigadó. Every now and then a leaf – or in spring, a shower of blossom – would flutter down onto a fine coiffure or a glossy hat, transforming a well-bred voice into a child-like peal of laughter. In the background, the lights of the Chain Bridge threw lion-shaped silhouettes, purling gothic shadows and huge silver raindrops onto the river. High above us, planted on Buda hill, the baroque dome and fortifications of the Castle Palace, and the bespangled spire of Matthias church, glimmered like quartz in black rock.

After this pleasant walk, which was never too long to tire me out, we would retire to some restaurant or drinking establishment that the Count had heard was serving a particularly good dish or fine wine that night. During dinner, I would watch the Count's libido rise with the glasses of wine he imbibed. Quite often, after dinner, he would pack me back into the Mercedes for János to drive me back while he 'escorted his companion home'.

Who exactly were all these women and what exactly did the Count do with them? For the most part, if the truth be told, these women were from the lower orders. Yes, on the odd occasion the Count might entertain a respectable married woman, but he certainly wouldn't have 'escorted her home'. This is why the Corso was so popular with both the lower and higher classes in the early part of this century. You could always find a certain kind of woman there -- the French call them *les grandes horizontales* – who were as delicate and as cultured as genuine 'ladies'. They had to be because they spent most of their time entertaining the aristocracy and the upper middle classes.

Of course, my father desperately wanted me to be inaugurated into this pastime. But once I had been, and had shown no particular desire to partake again, the Count stopped plying me with women and sent me home, like Cinderella, at midnight.

Although I was aware that my father's trysts were a dreadful betrayal of my mother, I was incapable of judging him because my own predilections seemed far, far worse than Papa's promiscuity -- which was, when one considered it, merely his aristocratic right. My growing desire for László didn't feel aristocratic in the slightest. I sensed that even Counts were not entitled to run their fingers up some young man's firm thighs. There was no protocol that enabled me to grasp László's muscular back and cover the stem of his neck with kisses. I decided to reserve my moral outrage at my father's rampant behaviour for a time when I had my own wayward desires under control.

The only time when my mother joined us on this promenade was on Sunday mornings when, after attending a 'scented' Mass at the Matthias church -- where incense was wafted in front of us to a nauseating degree -- we would descend to the Corso for morning coffee. Of course, it was very different place in the bright Sunday morning light from the sinful, louche locale that it became at night. The Hungarian verb *korzózni* was specially invented to describe the strutting walk that the citizens of Budapest performed along the Corso on such mornings: it means to walk at a leisurely pace, possibly showing off one's Sunday-best finery. Which is exactly what my parents did. For those brief hours on Sunday morning they were the perfect couple: all those lonely hours that my mother endured at night and my father's infidelities were forgotten and they strolled along the burnished promenade arm in arm, smiling beneficently to all their acquaintances of high and low birth. They would lean over the railings and chat amiably to each other as the river glistered in their eyes. They would nibble on Gerbeaud's chocolate in the Buchwald chairs that were dotted all along the Corso and talk about the country of her birth. As the 1930s progressed, my mother talked more and more of us all returning to England. Normally my father would have none of it but on Sunday mornings he allowed her to indulge herself and even joined in with the fantasy of buying a manor house in Surrey and living the life of an English country squire.

14: ANNA'S RETURN

Anna's return to Budapest put a stop to my father's nocturnal assignations on the Corso – well, for a while. She finished in her studies at the Cheltenham Ladies' College in June of 1937. My father was understandably reluctant to let her accompany us on our strolls but she was much more forceful than my mother had ever been and wasn't going to fill her evenings with re-reading *Pride and Prejudice*. He seemed exceptionally glum as János drove us down to the Corso on one fine twilit evening at the beginning of that month. Anna couldn't have been happier; she was clearly delighted to have escaped from the horrors of her English education. She linked arms with me in the back of the car and sang 'A Foggy Day in London Town' as the sea-shell balconies and rococo flourishes of Budapest sailed past us.

My father snapped at her and told her to stop singing. He tapped on the glass partition in the car with his silver-topped cane and asked János to set him down at the foot of the Chain Bridge and to take us onto the Corso. This was entirely unexpected. I knew that he had several young ladies waiting to meet him by the waterfront and he was bound to disappoint them if he sauntered lonely as a cloud across the Chain Bridge into Buda.

Anna ignored his irritable admonition and continued singing, barely waving goodbye to him when we left him on the bridge. Instead she cosied up to me, burying her silky black hair against my neck.

'Oh Zoltán, it's so good to be with you again,' she said, kissing me lightly on the earlobe.

I found it difficult to restrain a few tears of gratitude. For the first time in over 18 months, the smell of László's rustic hide and the imagined texture of his brown skin was not uppermost in my mind. My affection for Anna seemed to override my abject lust for the Transylvanian boy.

Unfortunately, fate was grimacing at me that night in the nasty, ironic way which it reserves for Hungarians of upstanding character. No sooner had my sister and I stepped out of the Mercedes and settled down at an excellent table at the Ritz – at a good distance from my father's hussies -- when who should appear but László. Apparently, he had been playing the piano at the Carlton and had just knocked off. Of course, this would have been the cue for most upper class Hungarian women to wave their fans in front of their faces and scarcely give the poor boy a glance, but Anna was not like that. She was a democrat of the Marxist variety and she immediately invited László to join us.

God, how different that evening seems to me now than it did at the time. When Anna and my colleague at the Liszt Academy clinked glasses and discussed how much they liked stupid songs like 'I'm an Old Cowhand from the Rio Grande' and the 'Whiffenpoof song', I was exhilarated. Here at last was a way for me to resolve the contradictory nature of my soul. I was convinced that if my sister and my best friend married then I would be magically released of my craving for both of them.

By the end of the evening, László was clearly besotted. Anna's smile, which was as enticing and dangerous as the emerald waters of the Danube at night, seemed to have lured him like a forlorn and hungry fisherman into the river. After a few glasses of wine I could see that he was already floating on that smile and beginning to sink under the surface when it disappeared.

The next morning, I was dithering around in front of the Fountain of Art that was painted on the wall in the Lizst Academy when László suddenly popped up from behind a gold-leafed pillar. There was a Transylvanian furtiveness about his movements. He must have been trained to avoid vampires in all those moonlit woods and acquired the art of concealment in the process.

His chestnut hair was tousled and his eyes were bloodshot: he clearly hadn't slept a wink all night. He grabbed me by the arm and pulled me behind a velvet curtain away from the students who were flowing past us and up the stairs. His breath made my skin tingle. We were completely hidden away, being in the curtained alcove that separated the main auditorium from the entrance hall.

'That was your sister?' he asked excitably. 'What did she think of me?'

I shrugged my shoulders but it was too dark for him to see anything. His strong fingers fixed themselves upon my shoulders and squeezed.

'What did she say?' he said.

Realising that if I told the truth – that Anna hadn't mentioned him at all – I would be inflicting a severe bout of depression upon him, I decided to lie. 'She said you were very handsome,' I said, thinking that I could smell his body odour rising above the tang of ground coffee that always suffused the entrance hall.

This was obviously the right thing to say because his soft, wet lips kissed me on the cheek and he pirouetted out of the dark alcove, becoming entwined with the velvet curtain in the process. He laughed as he disentangled himself and rested his quivering frame upon the brass balustrade that separated the naked nymphs that danced over the Fountain of Art from the student riff-raff.

15: WOMEN AND BRIDGES

I know that I shouldn't have encouraged him – after all, he was a mere peasant and she was a Countess-in-Waiting – but I found that by being their chaperone I was close to both. Anna was amused by the elaborate, quaint letters that he wrote her; they spoke a great deal about his life in Transylvania and the strange cuisine and customs of the peasants. Apparently, Bram Stoker's *Dracula* was quite accurate. They did eat paprika and a maize-flour porridge called *mamliga* for breakfast and they drank *slivovitz*, a plum brandy. They also hung up garlic to keep away the evil spirits and would often cross themselves and point two fingers to ward off the evil eye.

Largely because Anna hadn't made up her mind about what she was going to do with herself, she agreed to accompany László on many of the trips he suggested. My parents quickly got wind of what was happening and, to my joy, insisted I be Anna's chaperone.

'Women of upstanding character are like beautiful bridges, Zoltán. Your sister is one of those women. She is quite possibly to femininity what the Chain Bridge is to river crossings. That Chain Bridge needs constant maintenance. The rivets need to be tightened regularly and suchlike. Also, someone should be watching that no unsuitable traffic travels across it. Yet no one does. They just don't know what damage they're doing to the structure by allowing those great big trucks to rumble over it!' he would say, sighing as we watched hulking army vehicles sail through the arch of the bridge and boom along its delicate roadway.

László was far too much in awe of my sister ever to touch her. I would look at him gazing at her as we walked through the City Park and see a man who was entranced by a woman whom he believed wasn't entirely human. If you had never touched Anna you could well have thought that she was more an embodiment of the Magyar landscape and not merely another citizen of Budapest. Her lustrous hair seemed as fluid and thick as a mountain stream, her white skin was as effulgent as moonglow and her black eyes were as impenetrable and alluring as some dawn-lit, Carpathian forest.

Perhaps it was her Transylvanian features that really misled László. He thought that he knew her. He thought that behind the veneer of urban sophistication that she exuded, with all her talk about music, books and bridges, was a country girl; and that she wanted nothing more than to return to the area of her ancestors, hole up in some wooden-slatted cottage and have his babies. He would often talk obliquely about this with me. He had a definite plan. Because collecting traditional folk songs was still all the rage at the Academy, he thought he could return to his native area and continue Bartók's and Kodály's ground-breaking work.

'The difference is that I'm not a dilettante like Bartók and Kodály,' he would say. 'I'm going to find myself a good wife and actually live there. No one knows that area better than me. And I write wholesome music as well.'

The meetings between László and my sister continued throughout the summer. Amazingly, these encounters maintained their inaugural innocence: they rarely talked of anything else but popular songs and would sing them together as they walked ahead of me around the City Park. I can still hear my friend's rich baritone and my sister's gentle soprano singing such absurd numbers as 'Who's Afraid of the Big Bad Wolf?' 'Smoke Gets in Your Eyes' and 'I Got Plenty o' Nuthin''.

They never, ever talked about the Germans. I had almost immediately told Anna about how László admired Hitler and, although she clearly loathed the Nazis, she kept quiet. It wasn't safe to say anything critical about Germany, even in front of the servants. I suspected that Teresa, our maid, was not trustworthy at all.

I couldn't tell what Anna thought of László. After spending the summer of 1937 footling in the apartment and prancing around the park with the pair of us, she was far too busy to explain the innermost secrets of her heart to her brother. She enrolled at the Veterinary College in that month, much to my father's amusement and my mother's horror.

'But Anna, you'll be dealing with animals…' my mother tailed off, and set down *Sense and Sensibility* on the table as she tried to think of the right word. Finally, she found a suitable one after she had rubbed her tired eyes. 'You'll be dealing with animal muck! That just isn't the kind of thing that a lady does. Perhaps nursing might just be a forgivable vocation for woman in your position, but this hare-brained idea is quite out of the question.'

My father laughed off my mother's complaints. I think he was furtively pleased Anna's studying would probably mean that she wouldn't be accompanying us along the Corso. He was aware that her studies would be far more taxing than the intermittent music lessons and orchestra practice that I had at the Academy. He said, almost triumphantly: 'I'm sure she'll make the best vet in Budapest. She is a Countess, after all!'

Anna's studies seemed intolerably burdensome to me. I rarely saw her and when I did, she was often too fatigued to speak or too smelly to be approached by someone with delicate nasal passageways. She was too occupied even to see László for the odd afternoon at weekends. She seemed to be at college all the time.

László was distraught. He pestered me continually to arrange some meeting during the week and plied me with sealed envelopes to give to her. When she consistently rejected his offers, he started improving his suggestions. He would take her out for a meal at Gundels, for a drink at the Carlton, or afternoon tea at Gerbeaud's. These overtures were not lightly made: they were more expensive than the money he would make playing the piano every night at the Ritz for a month.

But Anna consistently refused. On a few occasions, she would implore me to go skating with her – a recreation I detested. When I suggested that she went with László, she sniggered but said nothing. Mind you, I was grateful that I saw her skate that winter. She seemed to have boundless energy, weaving in and out of the crowds and floating over the frozen boating lake like a ballerina. I can still see her now, her arms pumping as she sails towards me through the glittering mist, framed by the fairy-tale turrets of the Vajdahunyad Castle.

Eventually, though, she was beaten into submission by László and agreed to go to the Arizona night club with him one wintry Friday night -- as long as I was their chaperone. It was to prove quite a night. László had dug out an old suit from some fusty cupboard and appeared at our apartment door reeking of mothballs. The smell was so overpowering that I had to insist that I wound down the window of the Mercedes and let the cold November air flood in, together with a few snowflakes. Anna couldn't stop giggling. She seemed in an excitable mood, which was odd because she had made it perfectly obvious to everyone that she wasn't the slightest bit interested in my friend, much to my parents' relief. My father had an elderly widowed Baron lined up for her whom she had met on a few occasions at various garden parties at the Buda Palace Castle. The Baron only had one eye, several chins, often wore a ridiculously inappropriate Panama hat and smelt of Vaseline, but he was fantastically wealthy. Sometimes he joined my father on the prowl on the Corso and he always lavished presents on his women.

I knew that Anna would never marry such a creature: he was far too rich, far too fat, far too old and he smelt of grease.

Looking at her giggling in the back of the Mercedes with László, I almost thought that she might be seriously interested in this rough, brown-haired boy. She was wearing a red velvet basque, matching pleated dress, long white gloves and twinkly, pointed black shoes – not clothes that a dispassionate girl would wear. László was so unnerved by the plump cleavage that rose above her basque he banged his head on the door of the car as he was disembarking.

This only increased Anna's mirth, and László gained the first inkling that she was actually laughing at him rather than with him. We all hurried across the snowy pavement and hastened underneath the revolving neon sign that consisted of two couples dancing by the fantastic name, 'The Arizona'.

Inside we were greeted by what for me was a familiar sight because I had been to the club on many occasions with my father, but it was clear that both Anna and László were overwhelmed by the festive venue. In particular, neither of them could take their eyes off the star-spangled acrobats who were performing double and triple somersaults the middle of the revolving stage. That rollicking platform was a phantasmagorical whirl of powered hands and fairy feet, silver thighs and glittering calves, sequinned bosoms and golden loin-cloths, muscular arms and arching necks, dazzling smiles and impossibly immaculate hairdos.

I could tell by the way that László sat down in his seat at our candle-lit table that all sorts of forbidden thoughts were passing through his mind. I saw that he had to fold his arms across his lap when the Arizona revue girls were lowered onto the stage from a crystal chandelier. His arms remained folded throughout their ethereal, gravity-defying performance.

Although Anna was clearly bewitched by these girls' tumbling, air-borne manoeuvres, she was primarily interested in watching Miss Arizona herself. When she spotted her, she leaned over to László with her cocktail glass still in her hand and said to him: 'That's Mrs Rozsnyai herself. Isn't she incredible?'

László gazed with an opened mouth at the beautiful woman in the fiery costume who was leading the troupe and nodded in agreement with my sister.

'She's married to the chap who composes all the music,' Anna continued, now gesturing at the dance orchestra who were playing instruments that glowed like phosphorescence in the darkness behind the dancers. 'It's good music, don't you think?'

Again, László agreed.

He's Jewish, the composer,' Anna added nonchalantly, although I think she was aware of the effect that this statement would have. She knew that the country boy was, along with most of the rural Hungarian population, virulently anti-Semitic and that he would resent being lured into confessing that he liked a Jew's music.

But such was László's love for my sister that he cast this consideration aside and tried to appear curious rather than appalled by this piece of news.

'Oh, is he?' he said, gulping slightly, and leaning towards Anna's cleavage. At that moment, just at the juncture when it seemed as if László was going to plant a clumsy kiss on my sister's neck, a tall figure joined us at our table.

'Zoltán, you're looking a little healthier these days,' said a deep, cultured voice. At first I didn't know who was addressing me in such a familiar fashion because his face was immersed in the silvery, glitter-ball shadows of the Arizona but I soon recognized the distinctive scent of his Turkish cigarettes. I knew without seeing his pointed, symmetrical features that my former tutor was sitting beside me.

Anna's powers of perception were even quicker. She leapt to her feet, and sprang at Imre Virág like a tigress pouncing on her prey; she wrapped her arms around his neck and buried her face into his neck, kissing him repeatedly on the cheek. Poor old László was left craning his neck at an empty seat, his mind still swimming with thoughts of finally kissing his heart's desire, and his eyes full of the horrific vision of Anna embracing a swarthy, handsome stranger.

Once my sister had finished slavering over Imre, who didn't seem the slightest bit shocked by such an outrageous display of public affection, she turned to both of us while remaining on her former tutor's knee, and fixed her radiant eyes first on me and then László, and said, 'Zoltán, László, I want you to meet my husband!'

I was so unprepared for this statement that I refused to believe it.

'Your what?' I asked, taking a very large swig of Manhattan cocktail and wishing that I had my beetroot medicine with me.

If my first reaction was incredulity, László's response was a sudden but mighty outburst of indignation. He had spent every last *pengő* of his wages on paying for this evening, had wasted countless nights thinking about Anna and written much awful poetry about her -- only to find out that she was already married. He had been tricked.

He jerked up from his seat, knocking his cocktail glass over and obscuring a spangly wheel of limbs that was rotating behind him. Little bullets of spit flew out of his mouth like machine-gun fire as he mustered the nastiest words he could think of in the circumstances: 'He looks like a dirty Jew!'

Imre was equal to this challenge. Pushing Anna a little awkwardly to one side, he too rose out of his seat, and smiling victoriously at László, he said: 'That's because I am a Jew. And so is Mr Rozsnyai and so was Mendelssohn and Karl Marx and Mercadente and Spinoza. And the Saviour was a Jew and his father was a Jew. Your God.'

Imre's conquest seemed absolute as László slunk out of the Arizona. My friend's departure posed a tricky dilemma for me because I didn't know whether to follow him out of the club and try and patch things up as best I could, or to remain with my sister and her husband. Staying with them would unequivocally indicate that I was on their side and of a liberal temperament.

My enfeebled frame made the decision for me. My astonishment at the news had drained my body of all its physical resources and I found myself virtually paralysed in my seat with barely the strength to raise my glass to my lips. I lifted my arm in László's direction but that was the nearest I got towards pursuing him. My stationary position was no real indication my allegiance; if it had been my friend who had remained and the couple who had left, I probably would have stayed where I was.

Imre returned home with us. A snow storm had risen during the hours we had frittered away in the Arizona. The muscles and breasts of stone sculptures that adorned the Andrássy apartment buildings poked through the swirling whiteness without a single goose pimple showing on their smooth skins. In sharp contrast, a furious bout of shivering racked my body as I listened to Anna explain animatedly, as she hugged her spouse, how she had never lost touch with Imre even when he was sent to prison.

'Prison?' I exclaimed.

Imre smoothed the centre crease of his wide-flannel trousers. 'You really know very little, don't you, Zoltán? I was sent to prison shortly after I stopped being your tutor. Horthy and his henchmen don't like communists, especially Jewish communists.'

'But why didn't you tell me?' I asked Anna sorrowfully.

'How could I? I wasn't supposed to know. I knew that you would tell Papa the moment I told you. You and he are such good friends now. And then all my letters would have been checked. I would have never been able to write to him again,' she said with extraordinary equanimity, considering that she was, in fact, admitting that she didn't trust me.

János had stopped the Mercedes outside the apartment before I could remonstrate with her. Showing her customary impetuosity, Anna rushed up the stairs, flew into the apartment, and insisted upon waking our mother with the news. After donning her floral night-gown, Mama eventually materialised, her hair still dishevelled, in the Mirror Room where Anna was sitting beside her beloved and I was swigging my beetroot medicine. I still hadn't ceased shivering.

'Anna, Anna, what on earth is going on?' she said, peering at Imre's jacket with obvious distaste and incomprehension. 'It's two in the morning. Where is your father?'

As if on cue, my father stumbled into the apartment at that very moment. We listened to the slippery trajectory of his leather shoes sliding across the parquet floor in the hallway. There he was standing in the threshold of the opened double doors of the Mirror Room, his silk scarf slightly awry, his heavy coat flecked with snowflakes. His piercing eyes stared at the four of us above those high Pongrácz cheekbones.

'Imre Virág, what the bloody hell are you doing here?'

Virág stood up and approached my father with steady steps.

'I've come to tell both of you that I've married your daughter,' he said, stubbing out his cigarette in a sea-shell ashtray that he was holding in his hands. My mother peered disdainfully down at the smouldering cigarette.

'You got married?' she repeated, touching her greying hair with trembling hands. 'But you're not…'

I don't know what she was going to say next because Imre interrupted and said emphatically: 'Yes.'

Now that my mother had absorbed the truth, her reaction was predictable: she fainted. While I rang the bell for one of the servants to attend to her, I watched my father's face absorb the full force of this statement. Everyone remained frozen, immobilised by the late hour and the scandalous news.

As I heard Margaret's thundering shuffle emerge from the parlour, I watched my father begin to laugh in a high-pitched, agitated fashion.

'But Virág, old chap, this won't do at all. Our daughter is of a completely different rank and, dare I say it, race from you. It's just not protocol,' he said, hiccupping.

'It's already done. I have a copy of the marriage certificate here to prove it,' Imre said, pulling out an envelope from his inside pocket.

The Count curtailed his laughter and spent some time examining the document. When he lifted his head, there were tears in his eyes. Margaret dabbed my mother's forehead as his Excellency turned to my sister and whispered sorrowfully, 'You should have waited. You should have listened to your father.'

Glancing at her mother, who was rousing from her stupor, Anna broke away from her prostrate form and linked arms with Imre. She pointed a furious finger at the Count, who by now had tears trickling down his cheeks. 'Why should I listen to you? You made damn sure that Imre got sent to prison, you sent me to the worst school in the world...'

'But, Anna, Cheltenham Ladies College is one of the best schools in England,' my mother said, raising her head off the parquet floor.

'Your mother is right, it's a fine school, and I had such a good man lined up for you. A Baron, no less,' the Count said, opening his arms and moving towards his daughter.

Anna tightened her grip on Imre's arm.

'Papa, don't talk to me about marriage. The whole of Budapest knows what you get up to on the Corso,' she said venomously.

The Count tugged his silk scarf off his neck, rolled it into a small ball and squeezed it between his hands, which seemed to have turned blue. My mother brushed aside Margaret's skirt and eyed him suspiciously from her humiliating position on the floor. Before they could say any more, Anna swept Imre out of the room.

16: THE AFFAIR

Because we had the final rehearsals for a concert the next day, I felt compelled to drag myself into the Academy. Much to my relief and the conductor's annoyance, László wasn't there. I was just congratulating myself on this small mercy when the conductor peered at me over his glasses and said: 'You know where László lives, don't you? Will you go and fetch him for me?'

'But he lives in the Ferenc district. I've never been there,' I protested. His flat was a considerable distance from the Academy and in a poor neighbourhood.

There was some supercilious laughter from the wind section who must have felt that my complaint was not adequate. The conductor growled at me: 'Just go will you? Your playing is not good enough to cover for László's. We need him here now.'

Smarting from this insult, I plodded wearily out through the auditorium and out into the ankle-deep snow that now was streaked with dirt and grit. Snow eddied around my winter coat as I boarded the tram. What a miserable day it was! All the magical promise that the snow had provided the night before had curdled into gloom.

The sight of so many ragged people on the tram depressed me even further. Many of them weren't wearing proper shoes and had threadbare socks for gloves. Their pinched, shivering faces seemed to ooze a discontented malevolence as they stared enviously at my fur hat, my sheepskin gloves and winter coat.

I felt as though I might be stripped of my luxurious clothes at any moment as I left the tram and walked into the squalid Ferenc district. Slum tenement buildings crowded all around me. Everywhere wizened old ladies and snot-streaked boys huddled around the meagre warmth of lighted braziers on the street corners; the nauseating smell of boiled cabbage and the acrid smoke of burning wood wafted along the narrow alleyways

Eventually I reached my destination. I entered a crumbling hallway and plodded up some creaking stairs that seemed to be riddled with woodworm. The stench of rancid fat did not further endear me to the place. I knocked on László's door. It was open. Timidly, I sneaked into the room only to find that I was practically treading on my friend's mattress.

It was wretchedly small room. There was a washbasin but obviously no running water because there was a water jug on the table next to it. The mattress occupied most of the floor space and there were no other pieces of furniture. A violin was leaning in a cobwebbed corner and the snowy light filtered onto this bleak scene from a high small window with a rotting ledge and no panes of glass. A wicked winter wind gusted through the hovel. How could anyone live in a place like this? And yet people did. Families, too.

Something groaned from behind a large mound of blankets. After a few minutes of rummaging, László poked his head out of them.

'Anna? Anna?' he said.

'No, it's me, Zoltán. You've got to come now for the rehearsals.'

'Oh, yes,' he murmured sleepily. 'I will, but I need to be warmed up. I'm so cold. Will you just come here and warm me up?'

I felt momentarily paralysed with fear and desire. For months, I had yearned for this moment, much to my shame. However, now it was before me, I didn't know how to conduct myself. What was the correct etiquette? I took a deep breath and dug under those blankets and joined him in the womb-like warmth and darkness he had created for himself there. I was shaking with trepidation and excitement. But before I

knew where I was, he was hugging and kissing me. He smelt terrible -
- of cheap pálinka and sour milk – but I didn't care. Somehow I was
able to articulate my grief at Anna's betrayal by responding to his
desperate embrace.

'Oh Anna, Anna,' he said urgently. 'I need you.'

The gratification of my desires outweighed my torment at being my
sister's substitute.

* * *

This was the beginning of my affair with László. It was to last for well
over a year, until the time both of us graduated from the Academy. We
never spoke of it and he never called me by my real name when we
made love. I was always Anna to him. I felt so forlorn in wanting him
at all that I was quite content to play whatever role he required me to
enact. But now, after so many years have passed, and I have come to
know many men quite intimately, I can see that there was a tenderness
about László's lovemaking that showed his feelings were genuine. I
suppose the affair made me realise that I would never love a woman. I
knew that I was doomed to this guilt-ridden pleasure for the rest of my
life.

17: THE DANUBE FLOWS ON

A terrible silence descended upon the apartment on Andrássy Avenue after Anna's disappearance. My mother buried herself with renewed vigour into her Jane Austen novels, and my father channelled his frustrations into making his bridge-building even more complicated and vexatious: he spent most of his days and nights in his workshop trying to perfect a matchstick version of London's Tower Bridge in London. It was a monumental task and required over a hundred thousand matchsticks and phenomenal powers of concentration: the slightest misplaced match would mean that the drawbridge mechanism wouldn't operate properly. Much to the disappointment of many ladies of the night, he did not return to the Corso.

Anna had deprived him of his illusions. He had always considered himself to be a powerful man, who rarely used that power to his own ends because he had a beneficent heart; he liked to imagine that he was above the fray. Anna's marriage to Imre showed that he didn't have any control over his daughter, let alone his friends, members of state or the common people.

He had always thought that his assignations on the Corso were perfectly acceptable if his wife never learnt of them. But he felt that he should be punished for his moral turpitude if she discovered the truth; her knowledge of his wrongdoing somehow brought it into existence. His dalliances, although paraded in front of the cream of Budapest society, had been entirely invisible to his conscience before his wife was aware of them.

It would be nearly half a year before the recriminations began. It was not Anna but Hitler who was the ostensible cause of the strife. As soon as my mother had heard from a crackling BBC broadcast that Hitler had marched into Austria, she formulated the idea that she would be far better off back in England where she could assist with helping the Hungarians deal with the German threat. Although my mother was very impressed by the Germans, she had the good sense to be suspicious of them.

This deeply puzzled my father. I remember that he blew on his asparagus soup when my mother announced her plan of action one Sunday luncheon. He tasted the steaming liquid briefly and then set down his soup spoon. Glancing up at the white gloves of his butler, he gently asked János to leave the dining room.

'What on earth are you talking about, my dear?' he said in a low tone, and then dropping his voice even further he continued: 'You're not going to be any use to the Hungarians in Britain. The British aren't the slightest bit interested in helping us; they're too busy appeasing Hitler.'

But as the months of that year progressed and war loomed, my mother's resolve hardened. Her arguments with the Count became ever more furious and technical, culminating in an explosive row that they had after Chamberlain signed the Munich Agreement.

'The only people who have any influence over the Germans are the British. They are the only ones who will stop Germany invading Hungary,' she screamed at my father. 'We're sitting ducks here! They're going to overrun us.'

'I haven't heard a bigger load of nonsense since Béla Kun and his idiots tried to run this country,' my father retorted, his face reddening with ire. 'Germany has given us back southern Slovakia. Heaven knows, soon we might even get our old castle back. The Treaty of Trianon may well be outdated.'

He swiftly curtailed his bluster because he was aware that he was supporting the very expansionist policy of the Germans – a policy he abhorred -- in order to win this argument with his wife.

'You don't trust the Germans any more than I do. They'll be asking a high price for all those returned lands and you know it,' she said, planting her hands on her hips, sensing that she had caught the Count in a trap of his own making. 'The only reason why you want to stay here is because you're too fond of taking your nightly jaunts down to the Corso.'

'Oh please, Ellen,' my father begged, using her name for the first time in years. 'You know that just isn't true.'

Eventually, just after the Germans occupied the Sudetenland in early October of 1938, my mother packed her bags and sailed back to England on a rainy, windswept afternoon, promising that she would do all she could for the Magyars in London. She did invite me to join her but I still had a year to complete at the Academy and I didn't want to abandon my sister, whom my mother had signally not invited with her because of Anna's unsuitable marriage.

I had kept in touch with Anna without my parents' knowledge. At first I visited her at the Veterinary College where she continued to study. I would chat to her as lame dogs, cancerous cats and wounded horses lolled past us in that institution's ivy-entwined courtyard. However, when it became clear that I hadn't come to condemn her for her elopement and that I wasn't our parents' emissary, she relaxed and agreed to meet me on an almost daily basis at the New York Café in the late afternoon when both of us had finished our studies for the day.

Her conversation was a trifle tedious because, as if compensating for all the years when she had never spoken of Imre, she now discussed only the wonderful projects upon which her husband was embarking. Apparently, he had now become a Renaissance man. He had just been appointed a theatre director for a new Jewish theatre company at the Goldmark Hall, and was writing a polemical novel based on the poet

Attila József's sad life. The poor chap had just thrown himself under the wheels of freight train in November that year, apparently unable to endure the hounding he had received at the hands of the police for being a communist agitator.

The following year, Anna took me more into her confidence after I began to tell her about the awful rows that our parents were having. In a distant corner of the New York Café, with only two pearly-bottomed cherubs listening to our conversation, she explained proudly that Imre was in constant dialogue with the notable communists Rákosi and Rajk, currently exiled in Moscow.

'Imre thinks that the revolution is only a matter of time,' she whispered.

I didn't like the sound of this revolution at all. Apparently, we would be deprived of all our property and titles and everyone would be given an equal share of the country's wealth. Visions of László's desperate little flat invaded my mind. I was savvy enough now to know that most Hungarians lived in quarters that approximated that kind of squalor. And I also knew that living like that would be utterly unendurable for me.

Of course, I kept my own counsel on this matter because Anna wouldn't tolerate the slightest criticism of the accursed ideology. Even the mildest reproof of the doctrine, such as mentioning that it all sounded very impractical, would cause her to waggle her finger at me and say: 'Your life of privilege has blinded you to the truth, Zoltán! Blinded you!'

* * *

Although the Count had quite clearly found his wife an extremely difficult woman to get along with, he lamented her departure in the most unexpected fashion. He did not resume his promenades on the Corso, return to the café society that he had enjoyed only a couple of years before or even don his ceremonial robes and put in the odd appearance at the Upper House. His construction of the match stick Tower Bridge now consumed all of his energies. But he was unable to get the drawbridge mechanism working satisfactorily and this meant he had to demolish a good part of his painstaking work and start all over again.

Meanwhile, outside the confines of his bridge-building workshop, world events were moving on apace. Yet when János knocked on his workshop door on one bright summer morning in 1939 and provided him with the news that Germany had restored Northern Transylvania to Hungary, the Count dismissed the butler with a wave of his hand.

'Give it a few years and we won't have anything left,' he mumbled and returned to fortifying the matchstick girders that supported his precious drawbridge.

Most of the Hungarian population, overjoyed that at last the evils of the Trianon Treaty were being corrected, did not share my father's pessimism. Running concurrently with this rising sense of nationalism was an ever-growing wave of anti-Semitism. Laws banning Jews from working as journalists, actors, lawyers, doctors and engineers were passed through Parliament and in February one of the followers of the Hungarist Movement, led by Ferenc Szálasi, threw a grenade at people leaving a service at the Dohány Street synagogue. Twenty-two people were injured, and many of them died. The outcry that followed this affront led to the movement being banned – but only temporarily. Two weeks later, Prime Minister Count Pál Teleki allowed Szálasi to establish the Arrow Cross Party, the Hungarian version of Germany's National Socialist Party.

László didn't even wait to finish his studies at the Academy, such was his eagerness to join this new movement. He was offered the post of official musical director and felt that there were far more opportunities in attaching himself to a political party that was in the ascendancy rather than mouldering in an institution which didn't appreciate his nationalist melodies and strident instrumental playing.

The Party provided him with new living quarters and the possibility of real power: it was widely rumoured that the Führer himself took a keen interest in the Arrow Cross's affairs.

'I'll be coming back to this place in a few years and firing the lot of you stinking liberals,' László shouted at his tutors on his final day at the school.

Like László, I failed at the Academy. I enjoyed a few years of respite from my usual ill health but now it was beginning to deteriorate again and I found it impossible to attend orchestral rehearsals or many of my classes. I was asked to leave because of my poor attendance. Unlike László's, my departure was not a dramatic affair; I simply slunk out of the place one freezing winter afternoon and never returned.

* * *

I'm sure that it was the Count's total inability to perfect that drawbridge mechanism on Tower Bridge that finally persuaded him he had to terminate his affairs on this earthly sphere. He now spent most of his meal times pawing over big architectural books, examining the various attributes of drawbridges; most of his conversation was consumed by trying to resolve the perhaps insoluble problem of getting matchsticks to behave like metal.

'The secret may well be to cut the match sticks even more finely so that the load in the middle is not too heavy,' he would say, turning over a page of drawbridge diagrams as he slurped his soup.

Now that his wife and daughter had vanished, the apartment was deprived of the two people who talked politics, albeit in their opposite fashions. And so only passing comment was made about the declaration of war and Hitler's invasion of Poland. The two of us led an almost monastic life of isolation during the early part of the war. Mine was largely slothful and punctuated by illness, and the Count's was permeated by his growing irritation with his Tower Bridge.

However, it was the news of the Count Pál Teleki's death in April of 1941 which forced my father to concede defeat over the bridge. Prime Minister Teleki had shot himself because he realised that Hungary had become a mere plaything of the evil German regime; the Magyar people were entirely at the mercy of an irrational tyrant. My father slapped down the paper at breakfast and asked János to lay out his tweeds, bought from Gieves and Hawkes in London.

Once he was suitably attired in those stout English clothes, he set off on that fine spring morning with his walking stick in hand. I often imagine him striding manfully down Andrássy Avenue, through the Deák Ferenc and Vörösmarty Squares, and onto the glittering Corso. I can see him now doffing his hat politely at the passers-by, some of whom will be acquaintances and close friends, some of whom might be past lovers. But on this morning, he doesn't stop to pass the time of day. He leaves behind the shimmering sabres of the officers, the Panama hats of the gentry and plump bosoms of the *belle dames*. I imagine them all sipping their coffee and eating their Viennese pastries as he mounts the steps of the Chain Bridge, hurries past its tongueless lions and advances underneath the magnificent Pest arch. He lingers a little a while in the middle of the bridge, glances briefly at the Corso - - now shining in the morning sun -- and then turns to face the twisting spires and Ottoman domes of the Parliament building. Then he jumps, and the Danube sweeps his body away downstream.

Interlude II

From: KarolinaTarr99@outlook.com
To: BelaPongracz9@gmail.com

Dear Béla,

It was good to see you yesterday and walk along the promenade and talk about your great-uncle.

I didn't agree to meet up with you just because I want to read the rest of the Count's story.

Here's some guidance for you:

Advice 1: you don't need to lie about having a great job and life to get a girl. After a while, anyone with any intelligence is going to guess that you're lying. I did. That's why I got turned off, and that's why you got desperate, I think.

Advice 2: listen more. When I saw you, it was like you were just telling me things and never heard what I had to say. It was like suddenly I had become your therapist listening to how mean your mum is; how shit your life is; how much of a failure you are; how you feel bad so much.

It's not attractive. That's why I find it better writing to you.

Advice 3: don't go back to London immediately. Stay here for a while. If you smarten yourself up and write a decent CV, I might be able to get you a job as a runner at Korda. They like fluent English language speakers here.

I'll do you that favour for you because I like you. It would cost me, though, if you mess it up. You can't let me down.

Whatever you do, I don't think you should go back and live with your mum. You hate her! You seem to have this totally weird thing going with her, it's like you're dependent upon her, but you kind of despise each other.

It makes me think of your great-uncle and the strange co-dependent relationships he got into with people; with his sister, with Janos, with Laszlo. Always relying upon people, but somehow the relationships were not healthy. He was never free. It's strange but it's like your mother is your Janos, your Anna and your Laszlo.

I'm sorry but the Freudian in me thinks it's so strange how you call her every night, even on the night before you were going to kill yourself, and yet, what did you talk about? Whether you were wearing clean underpants, and getting into a row about that!

Yes, it was funny to hear that story, but weird weird weird weird, too.

It was sad about how your great-great grandfather killed himself, but it was very Hungarian somehow. I don't know but I felt that he did the only honourable thing he could do. However, he was also abandoning his children. It was cowardly.

And Zoltan -- he's both irritating and sympathetic with his endless worries about his health and his neediness. That's like you, too. It's like he had to have Anna to feel whole. I think he was jealous of Imre, more than he could say.

And then the worry for Anna and Imre. What happened to them? I must know.

You're clever there, not giving me the next bit. But you can trust me now. I will help you, Béla. I do want to be your friend. Having that chilly walk on the promenade and that big hot chocolate at the Café Gerbeaud was good for us. It reassured me that you're in a better place, that you're not going to do anything stupid, that you need to stop talking about your mother.

Go on, send me the rest of the story, and then we can meet and talk about the future.

Love

Karolina.

From: BelaPongracz9@gmail.com
To: KarolinaTarr99@outlook.com

Dear Karolina,

Thank you for writing to me. You say I'm obsessed by my mother but it's not true!

I can't stand her! You can't be obsessed with someone you despise!

And as for calling her every night, that's just because I've got no one else to talk to, and she wants to know what I'm up to. She is, after all, paying for me to be here.

OK, OK, maybe you've got a bit of a point. She shouldn't be asking me about washing my underwear. But you've got to admit, it's a bit funny, isn't it? It made you laugh, didn't it? When I told you that over our hot chocolates at Gerbeaud's, your whole face lit up and you laughed. It's the first time I've seen you laugh in ages.

And you, Karolina, you've got to admit you send me mixed signals.

You held my hand on the promenade.

I know you said it was because your hands were cold, but it was more than that, wasn't it?

It felt good to hold your hand on the Corso where my great-uncle and my great-great grandfather once walked years ago. Somehow, it felt like I had made progress.

You're right, it was cowardly of the Count to kill himself like that, wasn't it?

If you could help me get a job at Korda that would be amazing.

I know I am probably quite old to make coffee and all that, but I will give it a go. And maybe you could teach me some Hungarian?

I agree with you. I don't think I should go back and live with my mum again, but what else, realistically, is there for me to do? I don't have a degree, I have no money, the rents there are so high. I'm trapped really, unless I get something here.

I was thinking that when you've read the rest of the Count's tale, maybe we could work together and turn it into a film script or something? I think when you finish it, you'll see it makes a great story.

Strange to think that it really happened to that old man who slept in my room for all those years.

Now that I've read it so many times, I have begun to see the things he did in a different light. Sometimes in the night, he would scream out their names, Anna, László and Imre. It was very annoying and baffling at the time, but now I realise why, and I feel like I wish I could travel back in time and comfort him. But I never did. That really hurts.

Here's the rest of the story. When you've read it, can we meet again? Walk along the promenade again and have a hot chocolate at Gerbeaud's -- or maybe something stronger?

Love

Béla

Part Two: The War -- Budapest 1944-45

18: MY BED

I spent a great deal of the war in bed or languishing in a medicinal bath. While the German divisions rolled down the avenues of Budapest, I tucked up the cover of my *dunyha*, my puffy down quilt, a little closer to my neck. While Kübelwagens, half-tracks and trucks careered around corners spluttering exhaust, I stuffed nipped buds of cotton wool in my ears and sank my wasted shanks into the sulphurous waters of the Széchenyi Medicinal Baths. While the tanks thundered over the cobblestones, I ingested as many sleeping pills as I could. While the air-raid sirens howled every night, I wrapped bandages around my head in a vain attempt to block out the insufferable noise. Occasionally, I would listen to the crackle of the five o'clock broadcasts from London and hear that Germany was losing the war, but I was never a news addict. I wanted a quiet life.

One afternoon, in March of 1944, the tops of the blossoming trees in Andrássy shook in time to the sound of parading feet. Some of the branches of the horse-chestnuts had remained scandalously uncut and their long tendrils scratched my window. A spray of leaves pressed itself against the pane like a gaggle of refugees looking for a home.

Feeling my nerves atrophying at the thumping of the parade, I closed my eyes and recalled the opening march of Mahler's Sixth. I hummed it quietly to myself, trying to replace the brutal tread of those feet with Mahler's more complex rhythms.

Waltzes and gypsy tunes shimmer in and out of the march, reminding me of nights on the twilit Corso, sipping apricot schnapps with my father and watching the folds of Anna's pure white summer frock ruffle in the gentle breeze blowing in from the Danube. The lights of the Chain Bridge sparkle on the surface of the pearly river and the smell of sweet cherry sauce and roast duck wafts through the air. The melody of *csárdás* flirt in my ears. All is well. The Count is alive and still building bridges, Anna is smiling at me and spurning her suitors and Mama is recounting some anecdote about one of her eccentric uncles in England. Of course, it's a memory that never quite happened but I cling onto it nevertheless.

I pulled the covers right over my eyes and found that it was difficult to breathe. I was having one of my turns again. Still immersed in the darkness of my quilt, I stuck one arm out of my bed and rummaged through the detritus of my bedside table. A couple of empty medicine bottles clattered to the floor, and I felt the rough texture of a tatty music score and the matted dampness of two soggy handkerchiefs. Eventually I found my quarry underneath an old photograph of the Prince of Wales, now the Duke of Windsor. I could tell without looking that it was the lamentable English prince because it was the only photo I kept by my bed. For some reason, I took a perverse delight in looking at it: he had buggered things up worse than I had.

I picked up the sea-shell bell and rang it. Its chimes reverberated through the nursery, seeping underneath the heavy oak door and into the kitchen. I heard the peevish scuttle of Margaret's feet, the creak of the door opening -- János needed to oil all the door hinges in the apartment – and Margaret's breathy voice. Although I hadn't looked at her properly in the last few months – most of my dealings with the servants had been conducted from under the bedclothes – I could tell from the stuffed intonation of her words that she had put on a lot of weight.

Margaret was probably the only servant in Budapest who gained weight during the last year of the War -- at my expense. I had sacked Teresa immediately after the Count's death. I suppose I couldn't entirely rid myself of that memory of her *prakker* beating that Persian rug, which she imagined to be my posterior. Besides, Teresa had to go once the Count, my mother and Anna all vanished from Andrássy; there was no need for her. This left Margaret to eat her colleague's portion of the food. I suppose my laziness and János's indifference meant that no one had got round to cutting down the size of the food deliveries to the apartment.

Therefore, Margaret would make me fruit soups, jellied pork, egg barley, creamy potatoes, Csekonics salad, huge Transylvanian stews, sirloin steaks in the Esterházy style, veal paprika, gypsy pork slices, brain and kidney, cabbage squares, Hungarian fried bread, cottage cheese dumplings, Gundel pancake, chocolate torte and sponge cake – all acquired on the black market, of course. I would eat none of it -- leaving János and the portly servant to devour it all. I learned after the war that János saved most of his food and gave it to his starving relatives. Most of Budapest was suffering from food shortages.

But Margaret was greedy and that was why her footsteps thumped against the parquet floor. I lifted the bedcovers a little and saw her fat ankles slopping over her beribboned black maid's shoes.

'I need more medicine, Margaret! The beetroot kind! I'm choking here,' I moaned.

'Yes, of course, Your Excellency,' Margaret said perfunctorily. And then she cleared her throat, adding hesitantly: 'There is something else.'

'Please, just keep your voice down. I have an absolutely throbbing headache. And Margaret, can you please walk a little more quietly; you have no idea how much your clumping around disturbs me,' I said. I wanted to curse the bloody Germans for creating such a racket with all their stupid marching, their noisy trucks and farting tanks. But I kept quiet. I knew that, unlike János, Margaret wasn't very trustworthy. She'd betray me to them if I wasn't careful and I'd end up stretched out in the dank basement of 60 Andrássy Avenue – where the Nazi Arrow Cross Party had their HQ. I'd get fed into their bone-crushing machines by some tone-deaf yob. So I stuck to my perennial moan: 'And those air-raid sirens. How is a musical person supposed to endure such a noise as that? I haven't slept in over a year.'

'Perhaps if your Excellency would come down with us to the shelter you wouldn't hear it so much,' Margaret said, a little more boldly. She knew that I liked hearing her say this. It indicated that someone was considering my welfare. I pulled down the bedcover a little and saw that the late afternoon sunlight was filtering past the opened shutters. Dappled green leaf shadows darted across the rose-entwined wallpaper. A great Count Pongrácz painted in his ceremonial robes smiled slightly at me.

I pulled the covers back and I saw Margaret's double-chins wobbling over me. Her cheeks were bright red. Had she been drinking?

'No one's going to bomb Andrássy,' I said. 'We've got the finest Opera House in the world right next door to us. Not even the Americans would bomb that. I don't know why you're all so frightened.'

Margaret smiled. I believe she found my words comforting, if not entirely convincing. She then reached behind her back and pulled a letter out of the white-linen belt of her apron.

'This came for you today, Your Excellency,' she said hurriedly and dropped the letter onto the bed, adding pointedly: 'There was no stamp on it.'

'Just get the medicine,' I said to her, sitting bolt upright in the bed when I saw the handwriting. No matter how much she tried to disguise it, I could always recognize Anna's handwriting.

Margaret wanted to linger but I shooed her away before I opened the letter. As soon as she had shut the door behind her, I swung my legs out of bed and padded over to the writing bureau where I used my raven-headed letter opener to slit the edge of Anna's missive.

A couple of years ago, I asked János to move my father's *escritoire* into the nursery so that I could enjoy the memory of my all-too-brief childhood and yet conduct adult business as well. I don't think I would have ever have bothered to keep the family estates going if the writing bureau had remained in the Count's study. I was still frightened to enter that hallowed domain. Secretly, I thought my father's ghost still lived there. Some nights, I fancied I heard him tinkering at one of his model bridges.

Once the *escritoire* was established near enough to my bed for the journey to it not to exhaust me, I was able to conduct all my business by letter from the nursery. My correspondence with the estate manager meant that the vineyards continued to run smoothly throughout the war. My dressing-gown transactions provided me with a better income than it ever did for the Count, who was always incurring extra costs with his high living. Apart from my predilection for expensive and largely ineffectual doctors and medicines, my need for money was minimal. I hardly ever went out, I bought no clothes, I had sacked one servant, cut back on János and Margaret's wages and neither my sister nor my mother asked me for money. Food was the only expense.

This money was what I suspected Anna would be demanding in the letter. Although my wretched illness prevented me from reading the newspaper or attending any functions, I knew from listening to the rambling conversation of my anti-Semitic masseur at the Széchenyi baths that the Jews were not enjoying their old privileges. The fat old Hungarian was a peasant from the Eger region.

'At last, the Magyars are getting back all the gold these dirty Jews have been stealing from us all these years,' he would say with a throaty chuckle, dousing my buttocks and back with oil. 'Back home, we're really getting our own back.'

Although I found his coarse prejudices distasteful, whenever the word Jew was mentioned the image of Anna being married to that back-stabbing tutor of mine always popped up, and I couldn't bring myself to contradict anything he said.

Various laws had been passed which restricted the rights of Jews to own property or to hold jobs. The arrival of the Germans couldn't mean that their lot was about to improve.

Anna's note was too brief to suggest what she was thinking. It wasn't written on her husband's customary headed notepaper or even on good quality paper. My fingers felt quite grubby after reading it. It simply said -- or demanded: 'Make sure there are no servants around tonight. I will arrive at nine. Leave the front door open. Do not greet me. We will talk in the music room. A.'

I wouldn't have minded giving Anna money but this note suggested she wanted more than that. Did she know how ill I was? How could I dismiss János and Margaret tonight when I might suffer another attack? Her prejudice against them was unreasonable and selfish.

As it was, I took no immediate decision about the dismissal of the servants. Instead I rang the bell and asked János to itemise the clothes in my closet. I soon realised that I was in a terrible dilemma: I had nothing suitable to wear for my sister's visit. 'What the hell am I going to wear?' I complained in between swallowing more medicine.

János shut the emblazoned doors of the cupboard and turned away from its flamboyant corners, dusting the front of his black tail-coated jacket. Margaret really needed to give all the closets a thorough cleaning and dusting; what did that woman do all day except eat? I was about to articulate my concern about her slovenly habits when János spoke: 'If Your Excellency would kindly tell me who you are seeing, then perhaps I could make a suggestion?'

I mumbled something and then decided that Anna's paranoia about the servants – and János in particular – was absurd.

'It's my sister. If you must know,' I said grudgingly.

János's dull eyes lit up momentarily and then simmered in the gloom. He put both his hands together as if in prayer.

'May I suggest a light blue evening suit, Your Excellency? I know that the Countess has always admired that colour and I do know that I could obtain one tomorrow morning from the tailor's on Váci street,' he said obligingly.

'That's no bloody good. I'm seeing her tonight.'

'Your Excellency, I will see what can be done,' János said quietly.

What an wonderful chap János was! Do you know he actually went and dragged the tailor to the apartment that very evening? The sniffy little tailor was able to furnish me with a stylish light blue suit. Although the cut wasn't perfect – I was horribly thin -- the tailor was able to tuck and sew the hems and cuffs so that, at least, I looked presentable.

* * *

I asked János to leave the door open and keep himself out of the way, but I really felt beholden to allow him and Margaret to stay in the apartment for Anna's arrival. What if there was an air raid? I had heard them affirm on a few occasions that the basement cellar was the best shelter in Pest in terms of comfort and safety.

I stood by the marble fireplace and waited. And waited. The material of the blue suit began to make my delicate skin itch. I think I was allergic to it; I began to develop hives. I sat down at the piano and started playing some Chopin in an attempt to forestall my growing impatience.

Unfortunately, the blasted air raid siren started wailing before I could enjoy the full benefit of Chopin's melancholic cadences. János plodded dutifully into the room and urged me, with his customary servility, to join him down in the basement while he opened the windows and pulled down the regulation black-out blinds.

'Don't be ridiculous. No-one would bomb Andrássy. They haven't touched the Champs-Élysées, have they?' I shouted above the siren, retreating from the piano and sitting down on a high-backed chair beside a marble griffin.

János switched off the lights and absented himself with a courtly bow. He disappeared with Margaret into the basement. I leaned back and in the dim light scrutinised the all-too familiar outlines of Beethoven, Mozart, Haydn and Bach, whose heads were moulded in stucco on the ceiling. In that caterwauling darkness, I felt irrationally jealous of the quiet that these composers must have enjoyed during their lives. Beethoven may have had a few of Napoleon's cannon balls whizzing around his ears but he didn't have to endure the noise of air raid sirens. This hideous hullabaloo probably would have made him deaf at an even younger age.

A strong but delicate hand gripped my mouth before I could tell myself that it wasn't fair. I started up from my seat and found the whites of two eyes glinting in the darkness. I could smell an acrid stench of city dust, cleaning fluid, and possibly urine. I nearly gagged from the pressure of the tough hand against my mouth and the appalling stink.

The air raid sirens had stopped whirring but I could hear the distant, ominous rumble of aeroplanes. I inhaled through my nose for more air and realised that lurking underneath these horrid smells was Anna's unmistakable apricot scent; the odour of her youth. I tapped on the gagging hand and Anna, now convinced that I wouldn't speak loudly, let it drop from my face.

'Anna,' I whispered as softly as I could. 'You're late.'

Anna pressed her head against my ear. Her breath made the side of my neck goose-pimple. She hissed: 'You didn't get rid of the servants.'

'I don't know why you're getting so worked up about them. János is totally trustworthy and Margaret's too stupid to say anything,' I retorted irritably, wishing that she wasn't kneeling quite so close to me. Her physical proximity ruined my train of thought. It made the blood rush through parts of my body that I had thought my illness had killed off.

She yanked me up and out of my seat, making one of my brittle leg-joints crack. This was unendurable. Did she know how ill I was? But before I could elaborate upon my ailments, Anna had clenched me by the throat and was waving a badge, a five-pointed star made from canary-yellow felt, in front of me.

'In a couple of days' time, we all have to wear this!' she said, slapping the star into my hand. Even in the comparative blackness of the room, it seemed to emit a nauseating glow. Before I could inquire what the object was – I had a pretty good idea – Anna continued her rant. She pressed her body urgently against mine. The fabric of her summer dress seemed thin and worn. She chanted in my ear: 'I need money, Zoltán, I need letters of recommendation from you for me, my husband and Miss Virág, and I need a new passport.'

I gulped. Her words made me feel quite dizzy. The stuccoed composers spun about my head. Passports? Letters of recommendation? Why wasn't Anna using any of the time-honoured civilities that a Countess should employ when addressing her brother? It was so presumptuous.

'Anna…' I said, grabbing onto the only word that I could think of saying.

'Bring them around to this apartment as soon as you've got them,' she said, pressing a folded piece of paper into my hand. 'I must go now. Have you got any cash on you?'

She picked the star out of my hand and squeezed my arm. I raised my other one in alarm to grab her face by way of some kind of response. Yet, instead of feeling her plump skin, I felt her skull. The years had given her cliff-top cheek-bones.

'Anna, don't be so ridiculous,' I said in a normal voice, finally breaking away from her. 'I don't know why you're being so melodramatic. This is Budapest, not Berlin.'

'Keep your voice down, Zoltán,' she whispered.

There was a moment of silence as we both caught our breath in that darkened room. In the distance, I could hear a flurry of explosions. A fire or a flare must have sprayed over the rooftops because a jag of orange light, making Anna's cat's eyes shine, momentarily illuminated the octagonal mirror. I saw her fragile hand brush a lock of hair back behind her ear.

'I don't know why you have to be quite so rude,' I said finally.

Another glow of fire in the octagonal mirror made me see that Anna was gritting her teeth. 'Just get the money, you pip-squeak!' she growled.

Having a sister is such a mysterious thing. There has rarely been a moment when I loathed her more than that evening. Even after her ghastly wedding we managed to maintain civilities. As more time passed, it became apparent to me just how much she had betrayed me by marrying Imre. She knew that I loathed my former teacher's strident self-righteousness and the inevitable danger it would bring to everyone and she had pursued her selfish and reckless union. Did she not care at all for what I thought?

All pretence of friendship had been dropped now. But oddly I hadn't felt quite so close to her in years. I hated her then, but I discovered that at the bottom of my hatred there was an unfathomable love too.

I trailed out of the Music Room and groped my way down the hallway. The ebony clock ticked quietly, providing me with some idea of where I was. I opened the door to the nursery and the bloody thing creaked on its hinges – tomorrow I would command János to do something about that.

Once in the nursery, I heard Anna gasp. I was conscious that it reeked of my sweaty fevers, my beetroot medicine, my blackcurrant pálinka, and dirty linen.

'You moved back to the nursery,' Anna said. Her voice was soft with astonishment and what I thought might be pity.

I had to light the oil lamp in order to find my way around the papers heaped on the bureau. The silvery light flickered our shadows against the wallpaper as it had done when we were children. Except that the shadows were much taller and gaunter now. I caught a glimpse of Anna's face in the light.

Although she had lost a lot of weight, she was more beautiful than ever in that shabby summer dress. She looked more like an adolescent boy than a woman in her late twenties: her hair was shorter, her breasts seemed smaller and the slant of her cheekbones made her face angular and angry. Despite the creases around her mouth, I could see that her full, red lips were still the same.

As I rummaged through my papers, I wanted to tell her how I had managed to run the estates so successfully from my little desk. By writing to Mama's banker in London, I had managed to invest the Pongrácz money wisely in the United States and in Swiss bank accounts. But Anna's fidgeting manner informed me that she was too preoccupied with other things to be interested in my life.

As soon as I gave her a wodge of *pengő* that I kept in the bottom drawer, she fled. All those years of marriage to Imre and living in Leopold Town seemed to have erased her manners. She was an ingrate, like her husband.

Astonishingly I managed to sleep well that night. The next morning I was sufficiently refreshed to don my blue suit again and venture beyond the confines of the apartment. Barring the odd intrusive nozzle of a tank lurking behind a few street corners and a few trucks and Kübelwagens racing up and down the avenue, you really wouldn't have known there was a war on if you strolled down Andrássy that morning. The lemony sunshine seemed as if it would waken the slumbering sphinxes outside the Opera House; the nostalgic scent of violets and honeysuckle drifted through the open courtyards. I was reminded of that brilliant morning when Anna and I set off for the City Park -- and our childhood adventures really began.

Just past the Opera, my fragile health finally truncated my sprightly promenade. Luckily, I could park my wheezing lungs at the Művész café and sit down underneath a rather second-rate crystal chandelier. For the first time in over a year, I took breakfast. As I sipped my coffee and nibbled at a slightly stale slice of brioche, I ruminated upon my sister's visit the night before. I held an imaginary conversation with Papa about her and this helped me to get things in perspective. The Count agreed that she had been jolly rude in not adhering to the usual formalities, but pointed out that this might indicate she was in some kind of distress. We both thought that as a Countess there was little chance that she, personally, was in any danger in Budapest -- but her husband was probably doing his damnedest to get her implicated in some perilous intrigue.

'I need to go round there and tell them that if they keep their heads down then no one is going to hurt them,' I said silently to the Count.

Yet as I was leaving the café, he urged me to do more. He always did have a soft spot for her. I could hear him saying: 'Anna, look to Anna.'

That morning I busied myself in the nursery. I got János to oil the door hinges in the apartment and Margaret to dust all my clothes cupboards thoroughly. I took the bold step of entering the Count's study and working at his governmental desk; the place where he conducted all his business with the Upper House. I took out a few sheets of notepaper embossed with the address of the Upper House, the family crest and the family name and wrote a letter to the Minister of the Interior, requesting that my sister's family and I were all issued with new Hungarian passports. And then, following the instructions that Anna had given me in her scruffy missive, I wrote letters of transit and exemption for Miss Virág, Imre and Anna.

By lunchtime my work was finished. I sent János to deliver the letter to the Minister by hand at the Parliament and I hung up my blue suit. I flung on my silk pyjamas and collapsed onto my bed, exhausted by my exertions. I hadn't worked this hard since those miserable days at the Liszt Academy of Music.

Now all I had to do was to wait until the passports arrived.

I was dismayed the next day to receive another curt and grubby letter from Anna asking me where the passports were. I don't quite know what else she expected me to do; I couldn't very well send my butler to wait in a dirty queue at the Ministry. She would just have to be patient. I wrote her a quick note informing her of this and spent most of the day nursing a howling headache in bed.

My nerves were not improved by shenanigans in the sky that night. Some blasted British plane – I was reliably informed by János – dropped the most almighty stinker of a bomb in the inner city. This was the first time that any incendiary device had been dropped on civilians in Budapest. Until now the Allies had only bombed the obvious targets -- railways, factories and public buildings. The noise of the blast was unbelievable – I felt it strike me in the chest – and the whole of the apartment shook. The octagonal mirror dropped from the wall in the Music Room, the portrait of the Count in his ceremonial robes was sent askew, some crockery smashed in the kitchen and the peachy bottoms of the cherubs on the nursery ceiling seemed to shiver.

I was so winded that I wasn't able to stand up, let alone struggle down to the basement. Oddly enough, the shock of that reverberating detonation had the effect of sending me into a profound slumber; I hadn't slept better since the last air raid. It says something, I am sure, about my character that I can't sleep properly unless my life is in mortal danger.

When I woke in the morning I rang the bell and János emerged from the butler's pantry in his dressing gown with his hair uncombed. Streaks of grey were visible because he hadn't had the chance to brush them back. If the sight of my butler in his bedclothes wasn't surprising enough, the spectacle of his grey hair was positively alarming. János, immortal János, was getting old.

'Can I help you, your Excellency?' he croaked. His voice seemed suddenly tinged with irritation and tiredness.

'Can you sponge down my blue suit immediately? I think I shall go out for breakfast. I quite fancy a slice of brioche at the café Művész,' I said, startled by my own chipper demeanour.

János brushed his ruffled hair back with the palm of his hand. He really did look rough; there were oily bags underneath his eyes. Had he been drinking during the air raid?

'I think you might find, your Excellency, that the café is shut,' he said. 'A fire bomb hit the Inner City last night, sir.'

'Just fetch my blue suit, will you János?' I retorted. Sometimes his Magyar pessimism just took the biscuit.

On Andrássy, I had to pick my way over bits of charred wood, screes of rubble and glass. The sky was overcast and clay grey. The smell of burning hung on the chilly breeze. In my current state of health I shouldn't have been venturing out on such an inhospitable morning, but my spirits were such that I ignored the warnings of my body and continued towards my destination.

Contrary to János's predictions, the café was packed, if a little dishevelled – one of its chandeliers lay on the red carpet like a fallen star. The bombing seemed to have animated the rhythms of Pest's conversation. I heard snippets of talk about Béla Lugosi, Pablo Picasso, the astronomical price of chocolate and the nasty taste of wartime carrots. Everyone was talking but they didn't say much about the bomb.

After a thoroughly stale slice of brioche and some extremely weak coffee, I braved the cold breeze and wandered back. A piece of paper fluttered up out of the gutter when I passed the Sphinxes and plastered itself on the breast pocket of my suit. I peeled it off and read the bold, crude letters inscribed upon it. It was some kind of Arrow Cross nonsense -- printed in the night, I supposed -- about how the bombing was the responsibility of Judeo-terrorists. 'A thousand Jews should be executed for every dead Christian,' it said.

By the time I reached the apartment I had formed the opinion that I should pay my sister an immediate visit, even though I didn't have all the documents she had requested and I didn't have the physical resources for such trip.

I told János to fetch the Mercedes from the garage and I plucked Margaret from the kitchen where she was surreptitiously nibbling at a plum dumpling. She followed me to the nursery while I rifled through the racks of my father's suits. Eventually I settled upon the charcoal grey with its silver silk lining. I handed Margaret the suit, ordering her to have it sponged and pressed in less than half-an-hour.

While she was thus employed, I hastened through the Red Room, flung open the French windows and wandered along the balcony that overlooks the inner courtyard. Margaret seemed to have been remiss in watering the pot plants and flower trays; I had a devil of a time trying to find a fitting boutonnière. The rhododendrons and the carnations seemed to be on their last legs; their petals were turning dry and brown. Eventually I managed to locate a reasonably presentable rose and settled on that.

However, by the time I stepped into the back of the Mercedes I felt armed for the battle ahead. Checking myself in János's driving mirror, I decided that the rose complemented the grey suit. My brother-in-law could hurl all the insults he liked at me but I would be unswerving: they must accept the charity I was carrying in my briefcase.

The drive was a short one. We had barely motored past the Western railway station and turned off the Szent István körút when János brought the car to a halt. There was a great crater in the middle of the road; the tarmac around its edges seemed to be sweating and letting off steam.

A young boy in a green shirt and wearing an Arrow Cross armband told János to halt and instead of apologising for the blockage, demanded to know why we were travelling down this road. He seemed unimpressed by János's mumbling and I was forced to explain that I was visiting my sister, a Countess.

The boy's face was covered in pimples. His sneaky eyes peered into the back of the Mercedes. I wanted to protest that he seemed to be snooping around like a policeman and that, as far as I was aware, the Arrow Cross carried out no civic – or remotely useful -- duties. But I kept my mouth shut; he had a rifle slung over his shoulder.

'You'll have to leave the car here, I'm afraid, mate. I'll look after it for you if you like,' he said with an insouciant grin. He knew full well that calling me 'mate' and not 'your Excellency' was the height of bad manners. But my desire to see my sister was such that I ignored him and continued my journey on foot; my destination was only a block away. I told János to park at the side of the road and wait for my return.

To my mortification there seemed to be no porter at the entrance to my sister's apartment building and the door-bell system had been smashed in. There was graffiti on the wrought iron door: *dirty Jewish pigs*. I knocked with my bare fists, feeling a rising sense of panic as I called out for someone to let me in.

No one answered. But I found that after my repeated poundings the catch gave way and the door swung open with a screech. I stepped into the hallway and the overpowering smell of human excrement assaulted my nostrils. I gagged and reached for my rose, pressing it against my nose as I ascended the stairs, hoping that its scent would eradicate the foul stench. The place was not how I remembered it; there had been two portraits of Kossuth and Széchenyi hanging in the stairwell and mosaics lining the walls back in 1940. Now the tiles had been hacked away and the portraits had disappeared, leaving two ghostly rectangles. Why didn't Anna tell me about this? Did she seriously think that I would have allowed this to happen to her apartment building?

I knocked on her door which, thankfully, seemed to be intact; a carved dove still spread its wings over the knocker. I rapped hard but received no reply. Soon, I heard the distant scratching of feet.

I shouted: 'This is Count Pongrácz. I've come to see my sister, the Countess.'

This had little effect. No one answered. I knocked on the door again and said: 'I know someone is in there. I'm not going until someone answers. As I've said before, I am the Count Pongrácz.'

In truth, I didn't know how much longer I could wait. The fetor from the hallway was beginning to aggravate my sinuses to such an extent that I thought I was going to be sick. The door opened before I was about to flee. A little old man, his neck stooped with age, stood on the threshold and glanced at me quickly. He was wearing a threadbare magenta jumper with holes in the elbow. A dirty white apron was tied around his midriff.

'Where is the Countess?' I asked immediately.

'She told me to give you this,' he said, reaching into the pocket of his apron and passing me an envelope.

He had shut the door before I could ask him any more. I tore open the envelope and read: 'You were too slow. We have gone away to the country. We can't say where. Please give any money you have on you to Ervin, the man who now lives in our flat with his wife and family. Love, A.'

I snapped open my briefcase and stuffed the cash I had through the letter box and left the building in haste. There was something dreadfully final and infuriatingly vague about Anna's note. 'We have gone to the country.' Whatever did she mean? The words of my masseur seemed to have a chilling significance now: 'Back home, we're really getting our own back.' What the hell did he mean by that? Did Anna know what people like him were saying about Jews who lived in the country? Would she be considered a Jew if she was only married to one? She was first and foremost a Countess. She was about as Jewish as Winston Churchill.

I stumbled onto the street feeling bewildered. I had expected to find Anna, her husband and Miss Virág still living in a comfortable, if slightly gauche, apartment. I had expected to be able to give them their money and their papers with due decorum and depart, knowing I had taken care of them. I hadn't expected that nasty pimply Arrow Cross boy spying on the road with his blobby eyes or that putrid hallway or that pathetic old man and his threadbare jumper.

Also, she couldn't have been too angry with me if she had written 'love' at the end of the letter.

Relief spread through me like a soothing melody.

I began to look at the other people in the street to see if there was any sign of her or an acquaintance of hers. There was hardly anyone around. I saw the back of a coat hurry into a splintered doorway near the crater and a middle-aged woman who seemed to be enduring a bad attack of hay fever – she couldn't stop sniffing – passed by me with one of those nasty bright yellow stars sewn onto her coat. Surely Anna wouldn't have to wear one of those?

I discussed the situation with János as we drove back onto Andrássy. Being a simple man, he had very few remedies to suggest and I was forced to think for myself. I considered going to the police but Anna's furtiveness seemed to indicate that she didn't want the authorities involved. Knowing her husband's political convictions, I didn't put it past him to be inveigling her into some Bolshevik plot that might make her fall foul of the law.

I asked János to drive me down to the Parliament building. Maybe if I wandered into the Upper House, I would find one of my father's friends – some decent Baron or Duke -- who would be able to assist me. The car was diverted by a road block before we reached Kossuth square.

Two SS officers in their tan raincoats and their brims of the caps winking in the cloudy light were spinning shiny handguns on the ends of their fingers in front of a wall of sandbags. They seemed to be holding some kind of competition over who could spin the guns round the fastest. Well, what could you expect from an elite army?

In the far distance, I could see two tanks plastered with swastikas trundling past the Parliament building. The whole atmosphere of Pest had been transformed overnight by the German occupation. The inmates had taken over the asylum; rushing around with their armoury and toting their guns.

I tapped János on the shoulder and asked him to re-route towards the Corso. I needed a stiff drink.

* * *

Once my limbs were resting on a leather chair in the Carlton and I was sipping a fine brandy, I began to collect my thoughts. Outside, I could see the familiar crowds milling around on the promenade, the immense lions protecting the entrance to the Chain Bridge and the Danube water flowing underneath it. Here, at least, some sort of civilisation still prevailed.

The alcohol blunted my fear. Anna was going to be fine. There was no way that the Hungarians were going to harm a Countess, her husband or her sister-in-law. I asked the barman to bring the brandy bottle over and drank to their good health. Anna would contact me in time.

Since there wasn't anyone around at such an early hour in the morning, I offered the barman a drink and he accepted eagerly. Apparently he had a bad scare in the night. A bomb had dropped near to his flat. When he didn't automatically blame the Jews for the whole thing, I was prompted to ask him if he knew what was happening to them.

He shrugged his shoulders and said that he had no idea.

On the way back, I asked János to buy me every newspaper he could from the stand at the beginning of Andrássy. I was too exhausted to read them immediately but, after a long nap, I read the newspapers from cover to cover, searching for any morsels of information. There wasn't much, apart from what I had already seen with my own eyes; the Allies seemed intent upon pounding Budapest to the ground and the wearing of the yellow star was compulsory for Jews. What I read next caused me concern. Mass deportations of Jews to labour camps were occurring in the country and no Jew was allowed to leave Budapest.

I didn't know how to react to this. I felt my left eyelid twitch with anxiety. I tried to convince myself that Anna couldn't have gone to the country. But even if she hadn't, did this mean that all Jews in Budapest were safe? Or just the opposite?

I decided that it was time to pay a visit to my old friend, László Bródy, who I had heard was now a high-ranking official in the Arrow Cross. He might not have known where Anna was and I certainly had no intention of sharing my present worries with him, but he, of all people, would be able to set my mind at rest. He would know what the Germans' plans really were. I wrote him a note saying that I had been suffering from a prolonged illness but now I had recovered sufficiently to resume my social engagements. I would be delighted to meet up with him again. I sent János to deliver the letter by hand to the headquarters of the Arrow Cross Party at 60 Andrássy Avenue.

While I waited for László's reply, I contemplated visiting Imre Virág's last place of employment. I knew that he had assisted with the musical evenings at the Goldmark Hall during the early part of the war. Indeed, I had attended one before my health worsened. It was a very jolly affair. The poet Ernő Szép was the compere, Zoltán Kodály and his wife were in the audience and Imre had acquitted himself as best he could reading some of Attila József's poetry.

Since János had taken the Mercedes in order to deliver the letter, I entrusted my faltering pins to make the journey from the apartment to 7 Wesselényi utca where the Goldmark Hall was. It was – and still is – barely a half hour's walk for a healthy person but I found that it was far too much for me. As it was, I couldn't have completed my journey anyway because a group of Arrow Cross oiks were busy erecting some sort of barbed-wire barricade in the middle of the street. I decided to turn back.

I would phone up instead, I thought. But when I tried I found the line had been disconnected.

János brought back an immediate reply from László: he would be delighted to see me in the Café Lukács tomorrow at noon. My day's exertions, which amounted to more physical exercise than I had performed in the past year, rendered me incapable of doing anything else. I fell into a profound slumber in the Count's great red leather chair in the library, my hand still clutching the telephone receiver.

I awoke in the night to find myself in my silk pyjamas, safely tucked up beneath my *dunyha*. The ceiling spat slivers of light and the whole room seemed to be shaking. It felt as if some devil had released a trapdoor in the floor and dropped my bed from the innocent, childish sanctuary of the nursery into the outer regions of hell. The droning of the aircraft overhead, the crack of exploding bombs, the spurt of flares and the sound of the air raid siren made me reach frantically for my beetroot medicine and swig half the bottle down in one gulp. I then complemented the medicine with a shot of Scotch whisky from a bottle that my mother had sent me for my birthday.

This didn't have the desired effect of drowning out the insufferable noise. Instead it sent me running to the bathroom where I was ill for the rest of the night. But at least the noise of my retching succeeded in partially blotting out the infuriating wail of the siren. In truth, there is some aesthetic pleasure to be derived from the sound of dropping bombs once one has grown accustomed to it; a deep, resonating rumble follows the detonation and then, if one is close enough, the satisfying crackle of fire follows. Add the shimmering drone of aeroplane engines and the whoosh of flares to this assortment of noises and one has to concede that there is something almost symphonic about an attack. However, the air raid sirens ruin the effect. They have no redeeming aspects; they sound like a thousand chickens being plucked, a million dogs howling. Not even these bloody car alarms that go off so frequently nowadays can match the aural torture of an air raid siren.

* * *

The early part of the morning was consumed by deciding what to wear for my meeting with László. My first thought was to sport something casual but elegant such as my father's tweed jacket and trousers. Gazing at myself in the mirror, which had inconveniently acquired a lengthy hairline crack in the night, I decided that tweeds were far too

English. The blue suit was too feminine and the charcoal grey suit would not have set him as his ease.

In the end, János came to the rescue again by suggesting that I asked the tailor from Váci street to visit me with a selection of his clothes. I really don't know how I would have survived without János during the war. I smiled at him gratefully after he had phoned the tailor and informed me that he would be coming over right away.

'Was it you who put me to bed last night?' I asked my butler.

'Yes, your Excellency,' he said perfunctorily.

A mixture of embarrassment and gratitude caused my cheeks to smart. János had undressed me, slipped my pyjamas on me, folded my trousers and hung up my jacket. János knew the most intimate secrets of my nakedness – and had known them since I was a very small. I imagined his meaty hands buttoning up the front of my pyjamas. What a grand Magyar he was! They were very few left like him.

'Thank you János. You know, I never will forget this,' I said, wondering if I should pat him on the back. I resisted.

The tailor rested a row of suits on the long, varnished table in the Red Room and peered up at me from behind his glasses. I opted for a light grey double-breasted jacket, a shirt with red bow tie and flannel trousers with neat centre creases. The suit's simple and unstuffy cut and subdued colours would counter-balance the gaudy bow tie perfectly. I would look every inch the stylish Count-about-town and yet not appear too flashy.

As the tailor was leaving I asked him as casually as I could if he knew what was happening to the Jews in the country. Although he didn't shrug his shoulders like the barman at the Carlton, the way he pushed his glasses back onto the bridge of his nose had the same effect. 'I don't know,' he said evasively. 'They're going away, I think.'

'Where?' I pressed him.

'I don't know,' he said, and hurried from the apartment with my banker's cheque in his top pocket and his suits safely folded up inside his big brown leather case.

Since it was such a lovely morning I decided to walk up Andrássy Avenue, even though my muscles ached from all my rushing around the previous day. But I knew that striding along the promenade would allow me to plan out my strategy with László. I swore to myself that I would not let on what my true purposes were; I would just question him gently about the Jewish question. His anti-Semitism was such that I probably wouldn't have to probe very hard; if any measures were being taken against the Jews he would no doubt brag about it.

I was pleased to see that the war had left the Opera House untouched thus far; the sphinxes still winked at me in the sunlight. I hurried past Liszt Ferenc Square, trying not to think about my ignominious student days. At the Octagon, the Arizona night club seemed shut up: its big neon sign had been switched off and the posters and photographs in the window for the cabaret had been removed. But the cafés were still in full swing behind blacked-out windows; the chatter of cultured voices and the smell of roasted coffee drifted out of their doors. Budapest wasn't finished yet.

I quickened my step past number 60, the so-called House of Fidelity where the Arrow Cross had their main headquarters. Rumours had abounded about this place since the late 1930s; my masseur claimed that there was a torture machine in the basement into which they pushed Jews like linen through a mangle. The masseur didn't seem too distressed by this image but I felt my limbs contracting at the thought of it as I passed the bland, phoney exterior. Anna couldn't have got herself taken into there, could she?

László would know, he would know, I kept repeating this to myself I walked with jittery hands into the Café Lukács. The high cane-backed chairs didn't help me recover my equilibrium; the cane reminded me of the *prakker* that Teresa used to beat the Persian rugs with. Nor did the sight of the marble tables, hand-wrought lamps, stately chandeliers, gilded mirrors and ornate mantelpieces help me feel at home, for the smell of rancid goulash reminded me of some advice that my masseur had given me; never eat beef or pork in the Café Lukács.

'I've heard that the reason why they have the best supply of meat in Budapest is because they get their joints from the basement at number 60,' he said once, slapping my buttocks with enormous hands.

A reedy country accent was hailing me before I could dwell upon this any longer. 'Count Zoltán Pongrácz! Your Excellency! There is a place waiting for you here.'

I recognised the Carpathian inflections of László's voice immediately and was immediately set at my ease -- he had both addressed me correctly by my title and his tone seemed deferential but friendly, as befitted his social station.

He was wearing his Arrow Cross uniform: a freshly pressed green shirt and an Arrow Cross armband, heavy duty grey trousers and knee-high leather boots. The war and his rank had smartened him up; he radiated a bluff, confident, affable air. He had lost the haunted, country boy look he had carried around with him at the Liszt Academy and had filled out; his bony nose seemed longer, an extra layer of fat now disguised his weak chin and he had grown a moustache that gave him a manly dignity.

The moustache was a fortunate addition because when he took off his cap and shook my hand, he revealed a balding head. 'Count, what a pleasure it is to see you again,' he said, quite disarming me with his civility. He had been such a coarse boy at the Liszt Academy. But I could tell this was a man now used to dealing with the great and the good. He shook my hand warmly and we sat down at a pleasantly secluded table in the corner of the room. László called over the waiter.

'Now let me see, I think the Count will have a brandy schnapps, if I'm not mistaken, Excellency?' he said, bowing slightly at me as he addressed the waiter.

I congratulated him on his good memory and proceeded to inquire after his family. They had moved from Transylvania to a small hamlet in the country near Kislang. He smiled: 'Oh, they're doing very well. My father has just taken over the local baker's shop. After years of slaving away by the ovens, he's finally got what he deserves.'

'How did he manage that?' I asked brightly.

László glanced away from me and rubbed the underside of his chin 'He requisitioned it from some dirty Jew,' he said.

I wanted to ask him what had happened to the previous owner but I knew that this would be a mistake. László was examining my jacket and bow tie admiringly.

'You're looking very dashing today, Zoltán,' he said, stroking his glossy moustache.

'And you are too. In your uniform,' I replied, pulling my chair further under the table so that he wouldn't see my shrunken waist-line. His eyes seemed to be reconnoitring my body very thoroughly.

Our drinks arrived. Being a tee-totaller, László had asked for a cup of camomile tea and so we couldn't clink glasses in the normal fashion. We raised our drinking receptacles and he said: 'Long live Szálasi!' I felt reluctant to toast the crazed leader of the Arrow Cross Party but I mumbled something to stop László from becoming suspicious.

I was surprised but relieved that László did not ask after my family and stuck to moaning about the Judeo-terrorists who were trying to blow up the whole of Budapest. His words and thoughts were uncannily like the leaflet I had picked up yesterday morning near the Café Művész. I wondered if he had written it. He spoke more loudly than he had before and seemed keen that the German officers and Arrow Cross men, who were sitting at two neighbouring tables, should hear what he had to say.

'These fucking yids need to be taught a lesson,' he exclaimed, adding with a grin: 'And they will be soon, I can assure you.'

'What's going to happen to them?' I asked quietly. I glanced anxiously over my shoulder at the German officers at the next table and then regretted having done so. Fortunately, László didn't seem to have noticed.

'The ones in the country are already helping Germany with the war effort. Herr Eichmann is in Budapest at this very moment making all the necessary arrangements. It's a testament to his brilliant skills and the Magyar spirit that he's got so far already,' he said dryly, sipping at his tea. He put the cup down in its saucer and smiled. There are smiles and smiles in the world but I had never seen one quite like this one. Often anti-Semites smiled when they spoke of getting their revenge on the Jews but lurking behind their creased lips and crinkled eyes was always a knotty, vindictive anger, a fury at their impotence. They wished the Jewish race doom and disaster but they weren't sure that it would ever happen. None of this petty-minded viciousness hovered behind my companion's smile; this was the placid smile of certainty.

I was sufficiently disconcerted to let my brandy glass slip slightly in my hand. I blinked. There was a real possibility that Anna was dead. This was a proposition that I had never considered until this moment. The full force of her absence hit me. I remembered the smell of her hair as she carried me on her back around the nursery. I remembered her rushing around the zoo, her mouth sticky with candyfloss.

I set my drink down on the table and buckled forward, touching László's knee in the process. A stinging pain ran through my face.

'But Anna, Anna,' I mumbled, pulling my hand off his knee and planting it on the table for support.

László took a moment to react, mystified by my sudden collapse. But once he realised I was talking about my sister he helped me to my feet and stated loudly for the German officer's benefit: 'You're still wounded, aren't you Count? I'll have to take you home.'

Once we were back on Andrássy, he bundled me into the passenger seat of a dusty Kübelwagen parked on the verge by a cherry tree sapling and a few sandbags. It wasn't until he had started up the engine and we were speeding along the Avenue that he spoke, shouting above the motor's roar: 'We'll get you sorted out. I know just the place. Just remember we can never talk properly in Pest. Never speak to me in Pest. We're going to a place where we can talk properly.'

His driving was the precise opposite of the sedate progress János made in the Mercedes; it was reckless to the point of suicidal. We overtook two bread carts and a creeping tank and swerved past a police car at which László tooted his horn loudly. The gendarmes waved back cheerfully, clearly familiar with the vehicle.

'This is the Arrow Cross's city now,' László said proudly. We passed Elizabeth Square, rattled over the Széchenyi Chain Bridge and raced up Castle Hill where two SS guards at a fortified checkpoint motioned us through without stopping us. László pointed at the Buda Castle Palace where the Regent Horthy lived with his two sons and laughed. 'They say old Horthy cries all day. He knows it's only a matter of time before Szálasi takes over. The old buffer is kaput!'

The Kübelwagen skidded to a halt on the Hunyadi János road, not far from the Renaissance spire of the Matthias Church. László pushed me through a black door and I found myself following him down an endless set of spiralling, metal stairs down into the caves that burrow underneath the Castle Hill. Our steps echoed against the chill, dripping walls. Once we reached the bottom our breath plumed with mist. I shivered. I had not come properly clothed for such a voyage; my jacket felt very insubstantial.

But I wanted to hear what he had to say. We walked on an inadequate wooden plank along an oppressive rocky tunnel, dimly lit by electric storm lamps. We passed a few small grottoes, roughly hewn out of the rock which looked like they were serving as air raid shelters because mattresses, blankets, suitcases, water vats and small stoves, partially covered in tarpaulin, were neatly arranged against the limestone walls.

There wasn't anyone around; I didn't suppose anyone would want to hang around here unless they really had to. We passed under a glittering fringe of gypsum looking like sculptured snow and found ourselves secluded.

'I will help you,' László said. 'But first you must do this.'

'What?' I asked, turning round to look for him. I couldn't see a thing. I could only smell the moist reek of slimy rock and hear the crunch and rasp of his boots shifting in the gravel. There was a pause.

My heart beat faster and I reached out, hoping to touch something solid. I grasped only blackness.

'Where are you?' I asked desperately.

'Don't worry, I'm here. Now you must take off your clothes, your Excellency.'

This time his voice was laced with sarcasm and contempt. I swallowed hard, and the blackness boiled in front of my eyes.

'But it's cold. I've just recovered from a serious illness. I'll catch pneumonia,' I complained weakly.

'Just fucking take off your fucking clothes you fucking queer!' László shouted. The echo of his voice rang against the stone.

'But where shall I put my jacket and trousers? I only bought them this morning,' I said plaintively.

László grumbled irritably and then struck a match. The light flared, illuminating his moustache and his beady, peasant eyes. He reached out a hand, snatching my jacket impatiently and then my trousers.

I don't know exactly what he did with them but they were still clean when I put them on again some time later. Once I had taken off my clothes and I could feel the iron claws of the cold grasping me, László told me to bend over. I heard him light a match again as he moved closer to me. I could feel its meagre warmth tickling my back as he entered me.

Everything about him seemed to have grown; my poor passageway could barely cope with the size of his member. I groaned in agony and he seemed to like that because my cry of distress triggered off a volley of obscenities and a furious bout of rutting.

The strange thing was that I didn't actually find the whole incident traumatic while it was happening. I reflected that I probably deserved this for my neglect of Anna and that as punishments went, it wasn't the worst I could think of.

Nevertheless, my equilibrium didn't last much longer than the rape itself. When I got back to the apartment, I consumed the remainder of my mother's bottle of whiskey and threw myself onto my bed.

* * *

I spent the next month in bed suffering from the worst bout of fever I had endured since the war began. Margaret sat for many hours beside me with a damp cloth, washing the sweat off my head, chest and arms – I wouldn't let her go any further – and glugging my medicine down my throat. I doubt whether I would have survived without her ministrations.

All the doctors that examined me were useless. They claimed that they could find nothing wrong with me and prescribed plenty of fresh air and exercise -- a bit rich as the air raid sirens were blaring every other moment. Even the most able-bodied person would have had difficulty in going for long walks in Budapest in 1944.

János consoled me by reading bits and pieces from the newspaper. In particular, he informed me that those Jews whose spouse was non-Jewish were exempted from wearing a yellow star -- and thus from deportation. They were Aryan couples, and shouldn't be touched by the authorities. This news, in combination with the five o'clock broadcasts on the radio from London, speaking confidently about the relentless Russian advance and English and American successes, made me feel, somewhat irrationally, that Anna must be safe.

I was assailed by guilty dreams. I was back on the merry-go-round in the Városliget fair and riding on the horse behind Anna. I waved to her and tried to attract her attention but when she turned round I discovered, to my horror, that László's moustache lurked underneath her dark curls. The merry-go-round spun faster and faster and the scenery around me changed: I was back in the Buda caves and Imre was scrunching up the score to Béla Bartók's *Bluebeard's Castle* into little balls and shoving it down my throat.

I would always wake choking. Bartók's opera was quite indigestible.

19: THE RESCUE

Unaccustomed noises awoke me one morning in June. High-pitched yelps; when I struggled to the window, I saw bedraggled men and women in ragged overcoats emblazoned with yellow stars pulling wooden carts heaped with battered leather bags, books, suitcases, pots, pans, cutlery, oil lamps, lampshades, framed photographs and tins of food. The Jews were being herded into the ghetto that was just behind Andrássy.

I know I should have found it a heart-rending sight but the squeak of the carts' wheels was so painful to my ears – I was suffering from a terrific migraine at the time – that I slammed down the window in a rage against those poor people and tried my best to get some sleep. I kept my head buried in my pillow for the rest of the day.

Should I have braved my illness and gone out there to search for Anna? I told myself over and over that she was an Aryan. She wouldn't be so foolish to allow herself to be caught up in the whole thing. Besides, they were being moved for their own safety. Once they were altogether in the ghetto they could help each other. It would encourage comradeship.

János brought me a mysterious, anonymous note the very next day. 'Look in the school on Wesselényi utca. Go now.' I peeled back my quilt and looked at János who was standing over me, his face, from my bed-stricken vantage point, blotted out by the silver tray on which he had brought the note.

'Who brought this?' I croaked.

'It arrived with the post, the rest of which I placed on your desk, your Excellency,' János said.

Maybe my horrific afternoon in the Buda caves had reaped some dividends after all. Maybe László had found Anna. I crawled out of bed and examined myself in the cupboard mirror. I looked frightful with over a week's growth of beard and sunken cheeks.

I ordered János to follow me into the bathroom and give me a shave straight away; it was still an art I had not fully mastered. János's hands were so steady that he was able to use a cut-throat razor without giving me the slightest nick.

When my ablutions were complete, I quickly chose my suit – the one my father always wore for diplomatic functions. It was a sober jet black with a silk waistcoat and an Eton collar. Before I left, János thoughtfully suggested I should take my passport and entry papers for the Upper House.

János drove me as far as the Dohány Street Synagogue but we were prevented from going any further by a road block. Two Arrow Cross thugs lolled by it, smoking cigarettes and laughing like only the victorious can. The sharp tips of their bayonets twinkled in the morning sun.

One of these yobs blew smoke into the face of my butler and then demanded to see my papers. He was a little more respectful when he saw them and asked me, with a chuckle: 'So Excellency, why do you want to visit all that's left of *Judapest*?'

My retort was immediate and confident: 'To fetch my sister and her husband. They are an Aryan couple. They've been taken here by mistake.'

He snorted something about how they'd better have the papers to prove it and then he said that I could go into the ghetto by foot. I told János that he should wait in the Mercedes by the Astoria that was just opposite the synagogue on Múzeum körút.

I ventured into the ghetto. Most of the houses and apartment buildings had large yellow Stars of David hung from their wrought iron balconies or stuck on their front doors. There were a few people milling around the streets: I first saw two old men disappear into a dilapidated café, and a woman carrying string bundles of bread on her back. Further up, some kids were playing football with a rusted tin can.

Everyone I passed was wearing yellow stars and all of them gazed at me with curious, fearful eyes. The smell of old boiled cabbage wafted out of the opened windows and the sound of low, animated murmuring would intermittently emanate from shadowy doorways. There were many more people indoors than outdoors; it felt as if they were all watching me.

I entered the school building at 44 Wesselényi utca and was greeted in the hallway by the nightmarish screams of some poor chap who seemed to be in the last throes of life. It was not a sound I had heard before; it was more animal than human. I quickly retrieved my perfumed handkerchief from my pocket and pressed it against my nose – there was a horrible stink of bleach and vomit.

I staggered backwards – and then unmistakably long, delicate fingers placed themselves on the sleeve of my jacket.

It was Anna. Where had she come from? She had her hair tied back in a bun and was wearing a makeshift nurse's uniform; a tatty, badly sewn white apron and cap. Her apron was covered in what looked like fresh blood. She appeared to have emerged from one of the entranceway's side doors because they were still flapping.

'What on earth is going on?' I cried as I steadied myself on my feet.

'They're just playing that guy one of your compositions,' Anna said, pointing to the ceiling from whence the appalling, wordless yells seemed to be coming.

I couldn't believe that she could be so flippant at a moment like this. The man was obviously dying. I looked at her in disgust, shook off her hand and strode decisively onto the street. How could she be smiling when all this terror was raging around her? The last time I had seen her, when she had visited me at the apartment, there had be no time for jokes or smirking.

She had followed me outside but before I could reprimand her ill-judged humour, she had yanked me into the doorway of a neighbouring building, pushed me up a rickety set of stairs and elbowed me into a barren apartment.

'Where the hell have you been?' she said, peeling off her apron and flinging it in a chipped, porcelain basin.

'Well, well …I…'

I took a moment to catch my breath; I hadn't had such vigorous exercise inflicted upon me since, well, that afternoon in the Buda caves. I plonked myself onto the threadbare sofa and examined my surroundings. There didn't seem to be much to this apartment except crumbling plaster walls, bare floorboards, and a single plank nailed onto the wall that served for a bookshelf. There were a few leather-bound volumes of my father's on it, including Bram Stoker's *Dracula*.

'How did you know I was coming?' I asked.

When Anna explained that she had written the note and had been waiting for me all morning, I realised, with some sense of relief but also disappointment, that László could not know where she was. When I inquired what she was doing in the hospital, she said that she was working as a nurse there. There was an awkward silence.

The door to the bedroom creaked open. Miss Virág tiptoed out into the empty living room. But where was all the elegance and grace of movement that I remembered her by? She walked slowly, and seemed slightly bowed as if she was curling up in herself like an autumn leaf. Nevertheless she greeted me with her familiar graciousness, kissing me warmly on the cheek. It was clear she was not well. She was painfully thin; her porcelain skin seemed to be fissured with hairline cracks and her normally immaculate frilly blouse seemed much the worse for wear.

'Oh, Zoltán, it's so good to see you, my boy!' she said, touching the golden locket around her neck.

The magnitude of my actions struck me. A little lump of sentimentality lodged itself in my throat. I separated myself from Miss Virág's embrace and held her manfully by the shoulders.

'How are you?' I asked. Suddenly I was aware that I hadn't actually seen her in ten years. What had she been doing all this time? Had my parents looked after her? Somehow, I doubted it. She had been forgotten when she stopped tutoring us.

She took a moment to reply.

'We have seen better days,' she said, swallowing hard. And then, recovering herself, she stepped backwards and whispered: 'Caliban has taken over the island, Zoltán. Taken over.'

I leaned forward, not sure whether I had caught her words properly. What on earth was she talking about? Had she lost her marbles? And then I remembered how Miss Virág had taught us *The Tempest* with such enthusiasm. But it was such a long time ago that I couldn't recall the story properly.

Miss Virág's chilly, calm reply unnerved me and the ensuing silence seemed to suck all the air out of the room. I found it difficult to breathe.

'You must come with me now,' I said hoarsely: 'All of you must stay with me. We have to forget everything else and you must come home.'

Miss Virág was clearly moved by this speech; she looked at me with shining eyes and said, 'I'm glad to see that you know that it's not enough to help the feeble up, but to support them afterwards.' However Anna didn't seem so impressed and snapped at her sister-in-law that they weren't feeble. Miss Virág's reaction to this riposte was surprising. In the old days, she would have reprimanded Anna for being rude but now she just bowed her head. She did indeed look feeble. Was this because she acknowledged that Anna was her social superior or because the fight had deserted her? I couldn't tell.

Anna tugged at my sleeve again. I shook her off.

'It's not as simple as that. Your servants,' she said. 'You need to get rid of them.'

I cogitated on this.

'I don't know how you can say that,' I answered. 'János and Margaret are virtually part of the family now. Well, János definitely is. And there would be no one cook for us if Margaret went.'

Anna planted her hands on her hips and moved closer to me, saying in a low voice: 'I was followed after I visited you that night. We were raided. We nearly got caught.'

As she was speaking I heard the scrape of laggard footsteps rasping in the bedroom. It sounded like a sack of cement was being dragged across the floor. Suddenly the bedroom door sprang open and a stooped, long-haired figure lurched into the room, supporting itself with a thin, varnished walking stick.

When a puff of wind blew the tousled fringe away from this waxen person's eyes, I was astounded to recognize Imre Virág. His brilliant eyes seemed to be the only trace left of the old, proud Imre. His chiselled jaw and his straight nose seemed to have shrivelled away. The fine carriage of his body had been dismantled, leaving only a burnt-out shell.

Most distressing of all, I could see he was deprived of his left arm. The sleeve of his lank shirt hung limply around the stump of his shoulder like the Hungarian flag hanging on top of Buda Palace on a windless day.

'They're spies, I tell you that. They're spies,' Imre said, raising his walking stick and pointing it at me as if it were a bayonet.

I was completely unprepared for Imre's appearance. His disintegration made me clasp my hands tightly together.

'Look, I'll see what I can do,' I said, retreating from my broken brother-in-law, adding: 'But are you coming now?'

Imre shuffled towards me, still pointing his stick.

'Don't you see, you buffoon? We can't leave with you now. No one must see us. Otherwise they'll know where we are, won't they?' he said, deliberately slowly. He was speaking to me in the same way that he used to when I was in the library.

'Yes, yes,' I said. 'So I'll prepare things then? It will all be ready when you come. You can stay in father's workshop, that's hidden away. It'll be safe.'

'Good,' Imre said, producing from the depths of misery a sickly smile. 'We will arrive tomorrow morning. Wait for us by the maid's entrance.'

I left the ghetto quickly. When I reached the Astoria and found János reading the newspaper in the front of the Mercedes, my horror at seeing Imre subsided and I began to think things through.

I couldn't get rid of János. He was one of my limbs. Losing him would be like losing my arm. I thought of Imre. I, for one, could not afford to lose an arm.

* * *

I ordered Margaret and János to take the morning off and come back in the late afternoon. I instructed Margaret to leave a pot of goulash on the kitchen stove and János to clear my room of all medicine bottles, soiled handkerchiefs and abortive musical scores.

Once the two of them had disappeared, I waited as bidden in Margaret's tiny, windowless bedroom and unlocked her door, which opened out onto the servants' stairs, with my master key. I hadn't been in Margaret's bedroom since Anna led me through it all those years ago when she showed me the two maids beating the rug with the *prakkers*. It was truly a dismal place: just a buckled camp bed and several stacks of biscuit tins spread across the bare floorboards.

The air raid sirens never seemed to stop wailing that day and I wondered if Anna would ever materialise. However, due to my lack of sleep the night before – I had spent all night fretting about my servants and my family's fate – I fell asleep in the crater of Margaret's bed. The sound of scuttling feet woke me from an evil dream. The frilly cuff of Miss Virág's blouse poked past the door and I saw the silhouette of a hand grope for a light switch. I turned on my torch and whispered; 'Miss Virág, it's me, Zoltán.'

For a split second, she stood in the glare holding two large suitcases. Her skin looked more like alabaster than porcelain. Somehow the light erased, momentarily, her wrinkles. I discerned that she must have been a very attractive woman when she was young: her strong nose, her determined eyes and her perfect skin must have made her look like Diana: a lean, bounding huntress. How strange I'd never noticed this before!

She hugged me again and I could feel the muscles in her back relax in my embrace. She knew she was safe here. We waited by the doorway for Anna and Imre to arrive. While we stood there in companionable silence, Miss Virág began to shuffle her sandals across the floor, creating an enervating rustling sound. At first, I thought this was her impatience for their arrival but it soon became apparent she had other things on her mind.

'Your Excellency,' she said with surprising formality. 'There is another family coming to stay with us. The Róths. I hope you were aware of this. I hope Anna told you.'

'No one told me,' I said, agitated.

Miss Virág blinked. All that youthful vigour, which I detected in her only a moment previously, seemed to drain out of her like a bucket of water being tipped down the sink. She opened her mouth to speak but no words came out. This distressed me because I was used to her sprightly lectures, not her silence. She merely uttered weakly: 'Listen…'

The sound of footsteps filled the void where Miss Virág's lecture should have been. Who was coming? And who were the Róths? Before I could express my trepidation, Anna clumped into the room with Imre draped over her shoulders. Husband and wife were both breathing heavily, although Anna was taking healthy gulps of air and Imre was wheezing like an ancient engine. I could smell fresh sweat on Anna and a mouldy, cheesy smell issuing forth from Imre.

Five unfamiliar silhouettes quickly followed the couple. I hesitated for a moment, unsure what to do. Could I, as master of the household, order this family back out onto the streets? Although the Róths looked pitiable in their current destitute state, I could recognise the lineaments of fine people; the father clearly was, in his prime, an impressive patriarch with bold, impressive features and a greying beard, and the mother, although very thin and pallid, was still a beautiful woman, with full lips and dark eyes. The children all clearly worshipped their parents, looking up to them with a kind of pathetic expectation that even in this dire situation, they would make sure that everything was fine. Pa Róth clapped his hands together and told his charges in a rich deep voice that they'd all do a crossword puzzle soon; he fished a piece of paper out of his pocket and waved it triumphantly at them. His children smiled and all seemed keen to embark upon this game. Gratified that the young ones seemed cheerier, his wife hooked her arm through his, leaning with ineffable poignancy against his shoulder. I thought: this was a family who loved each other. Could I ever say that was true about my own family?

János coughed politely behind me, and I ruminated upon the protocol that one should follow in situations like this and came to no firm conclusions. As yet, I hadn't seen a book about wartime etiquette for persons of the higher classes.

Anna pushed me in the back and said that I should take them to the hideaway right now. She was insistent that there was not even time for the Róths to introduce themselves to me.

The ragged troupe from the ghetto hurried after me through the hallway where the ebony clock still ticked, past the nursery door, through the library, and into my father's old study. No-one said a word as I unlocked the secret mirror door. It sailed open without the slightest creak.

We stepped into the Count's workshop and I switched on the light. It was an ideal hideout: there were no windows, and it was, if all the model bridges were removed, large enough to accommodate eight people.

However, neither Anna nor Imre were particularly happy with the sight that greeted them. Three large models of bridges dominated the room. Tools and tat were strewn everywhere: hammers, spanners, an old saw, screwdrivers, boxes of tacks and nails, a big lathe littered the workbench and the floor. An inauspicious combination of wood shavings, sawdust and grey dust covered every surface.

'I thought you said that you were going to get things prepared for us,' Imre hissed. I avoided looking into his eyes but I could see the tip of his walking stick pressing so hard into parquet floor that it seemed to be gouging a small hole in it.

Miss Virág came to my rescue. The presence of the Róths seemed to have animated her; she shrugged off the despair I had sensed earlier and mustered these upbeat words: 'We will have this sorted out in no time. All we need is some cleaning things and some bedding.'

The Róth family nodded collectively. In the light of the workshop, I could inspect them properly for the first time. They were a tiny family: old man Róth was barely over five foot and his wife was a good few inches smaller than he was. Their three children, who I was told later were three, five and six years old, didn't reach their parents' elbows.

All of the family was bundled up in their overcoats even though it was a hot day. Their belongings were tied up in bed linen. They put these rumpled sacks in the corner of the room and placed their coats neatly on them. The children's scrawny faces peered up at me expectantly, waiting for me to give them a job to do, while Papa and Mama Róth introduced themselves.

'We are very proud to meet you, your Excellency,' Mr Róth said.

Anna had fetched some cleaning implements from the kitchen and gave them to the family before they could express their gratitude properly. She put some dusters into Papa Róth's hands and gave a mop to Mama Róth.

My allergy to dust meant that I was unable to assist with the clearing out of the workshop and I returned to the nursery, wondering when I was going to get the chance to tell them about the servants' continued employment on my premises. I decided that I would catch Anna alone before lunch-time and tell her then.

Unfortunately I over-slept and when I woke I found both János and Margaret had returned. János was winding up the clock in the hall and Margaret seemed to be baking a cake, judging from the sweet buttery wafts of hot air emerging from the kitchen.

There was absolutely no sign of my new lodgers -- except that when I entered the Count's study I found his big model of Blackfriars Bridge situated on the floor. János followed me into the study and expressed his surprise at finding the bridge there.

'Oh, I was just wanting to have a look at it,' I mumbled, and then asked János to give me some privacy.

The moment János left the room, the end of Imre's chewed walking stick poked out from behind the mirror door, beckoning me to approach and enter the Bridge Room. I hesitated, wondering whether I could escape back into the nursery, swallow a few sleeping pills and leave everyone else to sort out their enmities without my mediating, and possibly extraneous, presence.

But the thought of Imre further cursing my uselessness to my sister and the respectable Róths without my being able to offer any kind of defence persuaded me to venture in. I shut the door quietly behind me and found the stump of Imre's shoulder flattening the sleeve of my dressing gown. I tightened the knot of my silk belt and tried my best not to inhale the rotten-egg stench of his breath.

'Are you trying to get us all killed?' he asked. There was a deadly calm in his voice.

His mouth was close enough for me to see his blackened teeth.

'I...I...' I muttered, glancing around the room, hoping to catch sight of Miss Virág's kind and forgiving eyes. Her arms were folded and she stood resolutely behind her brother, not looking me in the face and fiddling with her golden locket.

They had cleaned the room remarkably well. Somehow they had managed to stack the remaining bridges away in one corner and had cleared all the dust and scattered tools. They had put down their bedding by the furthest wall of the room, laid out a little library of books against the skirting board and even put a decorative bowl of fruit on the worktable. In the dim, reddish-brown light the room looked like a still life by Vermeer. I said with forced merriment: 'You've done a jolly good job with tidying up this room.'

Imre clapped his hand over my mouth. His fingers were still twined round his walking stick and its knotty wood pressed into my cheeks. Imre's palm felt like a mouldy orange peel, all dried up. My wet lips moistened its surface.

'Keep your voice down,' he said.

I nodded furiously and he let go, twirling his walking stick expertly around his knuckles in the process. Seeing that Anna was sitting silently on her mattress with pursed lips, I walked over to the Róths, who were staring up at me from their makeshift stools. The three children shared two upturned buckets between them and the tiny couple had squashed up together on the only cane-backed chair that was in the room. Since they knew nothing about my servants I hoped that they would take a more balanced view of the situation.

'My servants are very good people,' I said, walking on tiptoes and speaking in a reassuring and quiet voice. 'There's nothing to be frightened of.'

'We'll be better off in the ghetto,' Imre said, coming up behind me. 'If we stay here, we'll have to tell them. They'll already suspect something since we put that stupid bridge out there. I told you we shouldn't have moved that thing.'

Imre seemed to have given up talking to me now and was addressing Anna. But she remained impassive on the mattress. Then she did something I hadn't seen her do since before her marriage: she reached behind her head and untied her hair. Her black locks tumbled over her shoulders. I hadn't realised that she had kept her hair so long. It seemed as inexhaustible as the Danube.

'My brother is not a Csekonics,' she said, still not looking me in the eye. She was cleverly twisting a familiar Hungarian saying that is used when someone asks for something beyond the other person's means. Gyula Csekonics lived in the middle of the 19th century and was the hopeless rascal of an ancient aristocratic family. The patriarchs of his family were prominent political figures, offered charity to the poor and all became famous horse breeders. Csekonics frittered away vast sums of money betting on the horses. By saying that I was no Csekonics Anna was effectively claiming that I was pathologically incapable of sacking my servants – it was beyond my means. It was both a compliment and an insult.

Imre revolved quickly on the balls of his heels and faced me: 'Well, can we trust them?'

'You have my word as a Count,' I uttered solemnly.

The corners of Anna's mouth curved into a smile but Imre seemed maddened by my vow.

'I don't want your word as a Count. I just want to know the truth,' he said.

I didn't deign to reply. I knew that Imre's comment was connected with his refusal to accept the hierarchical structure of Hungarian society; he couldn't concede that the higher classes had a decency and courage that most of the lower orders didn't possess.

To my displeasure, it was Anna who punctured my haughty pose by lacing her words with a heavy irony. 'You had better go and use your Count's words on János and Margaret now and make sure that they keep quiet – and bring us something nice to eat. I rather fancy a Csekonics salad.'

I interrupted Margaret scooping a palm full of raisins out of a large glass jar. A single raisin remained stuck on the top of her thumb as she turned round to face me. She stifled a gasp.

Behind her, flies buzzed around the huge kitchen sink that was piled high with dirty dishes and my empty medicine bottles. The smell of stale food and cake mixture and the horrid flies encircled me.

I restrained myself from screaming at the fat maid for the disgraceful state of the kitchen because I knew that I was going to need every droplet of goodwill I could extract from her. I smiled a sickly smile that was inevitably infected with my mortification at the state of the kitchen. Had I been eating food prepared on those filthy surfaces?

Margaret peered up at me from the table and quickly licked the raisin from her thumb, shoving the jar to one side as if she had never had had anything to do with it. She said, 'Oh, your Excellency,' with a trembling chin and seemed to be on the verge of tears. It occurred to me that Margaret might be a human being with feelings and not a rotund guzzler who was good at making food and useless at most other things.

'Margaret, I have something very important to tell you. Your mistress and her husband have returned to live with me...' I trailed off, distracted by Margaret's widening eyes. 'And another family, the Róths, too, a very fine family. It really is most moving and edifying to learn that they all do crosswords together; this is never something I did with my own parents. Perhaps, things would be different if I did. But the Róths... no one must know about this.'

I was stunned by Margaret's reaction. She tottered out of her chair and actually fell at my feet on her knees. I reared back in alarm at the noise of her great carcass hitting the floor. She clasped my hand before I could get away.

'Oh, bear I knew it, I just knew that you were a good man.' She kissed my fingers. 'My mistress is back. The Countess has come back! I shall not disappoint you, your Excellency. No one shall know and I shall cook such meals and I shall clean the kitchen and I shall cook such meals!'

She was so overwhelmed that she continued to ramble on in this fashion, tiresomely repeating herself. I had never heard her talk so much in my life. It seemed as if she was both articulating her anxiety for Anna and celebrating her safe return to the fold.

Once I managed to calm her down, I ordered her to get cracking on the Csekonics salad. Margaret seemed a little put out by this request. 'Doesn't her Ladyship want her favourite food?'

'What on earth might that be?'

'Why, Hungarian strudel stuffed with black cherries, of course!' Margaret chirped merrily, wiping away a couple of tears from her eyes with the back of her hand.

'Possibly, for pudding,' I said.

'Yes, yes. I see. Yes. I shall go out and buy a chicken and some tomatoes straightaway,' Margaret said.

This gave me some pause for thought. It would look suspicious if Margaret suddenly started buying much more food from the butchers and the grocers. I instructed her to go far afield in her search for food.

'I'll buy it from the market. No one will notice anything there,' she said. 'No one shall find out about the Countess's return from me.'

János was much more measured in his response to the news. He was dusting the leather volumes in the library when I told him. He stopped cleaning, descended the step ladder and put on his glasses. He was silent for a moment. I could see him calculating all the points he had to consider before he said: 'Will her Ladyship be requiring service in the normal fashion or shall I take a more casual approach?'

It was a very good question and I was unable to furnish him with a satisfactory answer. Eventually, I said that he would have to ask my sister herself.

I was disconcerted to find that János was not happy with me fobbing him off like this. 'As master of the household, you have absolute authority still, and it is for you to establish the protocol in exceptional circumstances,' he said.

This felt like a rebuff – although I couldn't quite put my finger on why. But I felt a little cornered when I said: 'You should deal with the Countess and her charges – her husband, Miss Virág and the Róths – with formality, I think. Yes. We mustn't let this bloody war destroy centuries of proprieties.'

'Quite so,' János said. He bowed slightly and then ascended the stepladder and resumed his dusting. His painstaking care of the volumes made me think that there was something immortal about János. Nothing -- not a German invasion, nor the Arrow Cross bully-boys, nor the Allied bombing raids, or the imminent invasion of the Russians -- would put him out of kilter.

Anna's reunion with Margaret proved to be a moving, if comic, event to behold. According to custom, János, wearing his white gloves, carried the main course – the Csekonics salad – on our best silver platter. Margaret tailed him closely, with impatient, thudding steps. I opened the secret mirror door and he and Margaret followed me into the den. Imre and the Tiny Couple – as I now thought of them -- were fast asleep on the mattresses and Miss Virág was sitting on the only chair staring into space, her eyes not focused upon her immediate environment but obviously recalling some long, lost memory. She hardly noticed that I was there. She undid the catch of her gold chain and gazed down at the picture in her locket tentatively. This made me curious to know what was inside it. I edged towards her to get a peek but as soon as she heard my shuffling feet, she clicked the locket shut and continued her staring.

Anna and the small children were crouching over one of the Count's bridges – the dreaded half-completed matchstick model of London's Tower Bridge. I thought about warning them about the dangers of attempting to finish this model. After all, it had driven my father to suicide. Or had it? I considered the notion that it hadn't: there were other reasons. I let them fiddle with the bridge, unheeded.

Anna was explaining, as she handed out matchsticks and glue to the children, about the time when she saw London Bridge in real life. It was a great disappointment because she thought London Bridge was Tower Bridge. Her black hair was still loose around her shoulders and obscured her features. When she revealed her thin, almost cadaverous, face, the silver platter quivered slightly. At first, I thought this was because János was alarmed at seeing his mistress's emaciation, but I quickly realised that János's trembling had a great deal more to do with the fact that Margaret was barging past him. The moment Margaret and Anna's eyes met, I comprehended the depth of the love that they felt for each other. Their two bodies dissolved into a tangle of hugs and kisses. Unfortunately, Margaret also managed to collide with the silver platter and the Csekonics Salad was sent flying into the air. Although János managed to catch the dish and the cover, he was splattered in an unsightly array of cooked chicken breast, king prawns, lettuce, caraway seeds and mayonnaise during the process of retrieval.

'Oh, your Ladyship, I have made such a good salad for you,' Margaret said, still locked in an embrace with my sister but starting to weep as she saw most of the salad residing on the dour butler's head and shoulders.

There was silence as we all surveyed the damage. But then Anna burst into a peal of laughter that rang out like a cleanly-struck bell. Soon, all of us were tittering at the sight of János's usually immaculate butler's uniform plastered in prawns and lettuce leaves. Even Imre, who had been woken up by the commotion, laughed.

The only person who failed to see the funny side to Margaret's clumsiness was the butler himself.

20: DRESSING UP

Anna brought a colour and light to the apartment on Andrássy Avenue that it had never seen before or since. Liberated from the influence of our parents and knowing that she could push me around in any way she wanted, she filled those mahogany rooms with laughter and games.

While we were careful not to make too much noise, we knew that the walls and ceilings of our residence were thick enough not to let any sound filter through to the rooms above or next to us. We had most fun in the Music Room that the Count had had sound-proofed.

Anna found the old gramophone and her records packed away in a cupboard in her bedroom. With Mr Róth's help – it turned out, fortuitously, that he was a trained engineer – she rigged the thing up and played all her favourite *csárdás* whenever she got the chance. At first, having failed to recruit any adult partners – I was too unfit, Imre too busy reading communist literature and Miss Virág too depressed - - she taught the children to dance with her. This looked extremely odd because her height and slender figure was such a contrast to those fledgling gnomes. She looked like a swan teaching her cygnets to swim.

Exasperated by the inadequate physiques – it was, after all, meant to be a courting dance -- and poor rhythmic sense of her dancing partners, I reluctantly volunteered my services. My sister had never got beyond teaching the children the slow section of the *csárdás*, the *lassú*, but Anna and I quickly managed this almost immediately, snapping our feet inward and outward in time to the music. Soon, we were whirling round as the music went faster, the *friss*, and, with a week's practice, we could improvise to the compelling, syncopated rhythms of the more complicated *csárdás*.

I had never felt so exhilarated in my life as when I was dancing the *csárdás* with my sister that summer. My physical ailments melted away when I was close to the warmth of Anna's body. Her breath stroked my cheeks, her long hair brushed my neck and her hands clamped my hips. Her feet matched perfectly the steps of my own. Sometimes she would press herself tightly against my ribs and I would feel her heart beat against my chest as we whirled around and around.

But by late July, Imre had worked out that something was going on. He'd caught me on a few occasions with my shiny dancing shoes on, tiptoeing down the corridor in my turned-up trousers and creamy white shirt with the billowing sleeves.

He soon made it his business to do his reading in the Music Room. At least when Anna and I danced in front of him, he made no comment, but, after that, he always insisted on dancing with his wife whenever it looked like she and I were going to take a turn. Anna battled bravely in order to dance successfully -- and even romantically – with her husband but it's hard to swing with a one-armed man. The man always leads when a *csárdás* is exultantly performed; the woman is swept along in his wake. After a few weeks' of cavorting, I led the exhibition with passion and confidence. Imre could never lead; he had no passion or belief in the music; his handicap was the least of it.

After this realisation dawned upon him, he became bitter and claimed that we should never dance to the gramophone because it was far too noisy. Someone in one of the other apartments or out on the streets was bound to hear.

If he had been able-bodied I don't think Anna would have listened to him but it became increasingly clear that she pitied her husband desperately. She knew that his only feeling of power was derived from ordering her to obey him. As a consequence, she would, more often than not, accede to his wishes. 'You're going to dance with me now, aren't you?' he would say. Instead of Anna asking him to repeat his request in a polite fashion, which she surely would have done with anyone else, she would smile and, with love in her eyes, would say softly: 'I'd like nothing better, my darling.'

Thankfully, Raoul Wallenberg's arrival in Budapest enabled our *csárdás* to continue. The great Swede arrived in early July, just after Regent Horthy pulled his decrepit bones together and decreed that there should be a halt to the Jewish deportations. News that a diplomat was issuing passports and papers to the Jews from the Swedish embassy in Buda quickly spread through the city. As soon as Imre heard about it, he hobbled out into the streets -- despite his sister's and his wife's protestations that it was dangerous for him to do so -- in search of papers for himself, his family and his friends. Mercifully, he ordered his wife to stay at home, although she longed to come with him. 'But no one's going to hurt me,' she would plead, only to be rebuffed Imre's sharp retort: 'There is no way you're going out there and that's final.'

I noticed that Imre no longer called anyone comrade now. At first, I had assumed this was because he was in a foul temper for most of the time and he no longer harboured such feelings. But now I realised there was a different reason. Imre wanted to battle against the Germans and his disability alone. We were no longer his comrades. His suffering had isolated him from his wife, his sister, and his friends.

As a result of Imre's prolonged absences, our games and dancing continued unabated throughout that glorious summer, only interrupted by the air raid sirens, meal-times, and Imre's return at dusk.

But Anna's merriment was a kind of desperation. She needed constant distractions to stop herself fretting about Imre. As a result, she invented an unending stream of activities to keep the Róth children occupied. Since some deep-rooted insecurity within me meant that I felt healthy only when I was bathing in the sapphire glow of Anna's presence, I mucked in with all the rather undignified and childish games.

However, once I had shed my inhibitions, I felt as if I was enjoying a second childhood. The satisfaction I felt when we completed the matchstick model of Tower Bridge was the equivalent to the enjoyment I gained from making the dolls' house zoo with Anna when I was so young. I also believed, in some obscure way, that we had partially righted the wrong of our father's death. Anna's enthusiasm was infectious and soon the Tiny Couple had cast aside their books and started playing hide and seek.

However, the Róths didn't participate in the most enjoyable lark of the lot: dressing up. This riotous activity commenced when Anna unlocked all of our parents' wardrobes and unearthed the true extent of our dear mama's hats and complicated dresses, her racks of shoes, her drawers full of jewellery and make-up.

Anna had no inhibitions about stripping down to her petticoats in front of me and the children. I suppose I should have put my foot down and insisted that she conducted herself with due decorum in my home, but I was enjoying myself far too much for that. Anna brought such a feeling of joy and laughter into my wizened old heart when she played those risqué games that I found myself totally disarmed.

I have a vivid memory of Anna at that time. She is standing in front of mama's colossal wardrobe mirror in a hat with a wide brim and large crown swathed with silk chiffon, and a full gathered skirt trimmed with bands of ribbon. Now she takes her hands off her hips, and reaches for a small metal object she keeps in the pocket of her skirt. She blows quietly on it; it's a mouth organ. I recognise it as one I have kept hidden away in the drawers of the nursery. She's been rummaging around my room, I think with a pattering heart. She talks to the children while she picks various dresses out of the wardrobe. Each time she finds a dress she likes she blows in triumph on the mouth organ.

'Now *gyerekek*, how do you think I would look in this? Do you think I would look a real lady? Hey, Helen, I've found a string of pearls for you!'

The children giggle as Anna bends down and loops the pearls around Helen's neck. Once all of us had donned the clothes that Anna was happy with, she would give us all new names.

'Now Sándor,' Anna says as she addresses the blushing Róth boy. 'I am going to call you Petőfi after our great revolutionary poet because I know that you are going to be a great hero. I think I shall make Helen Cleopatra, Queen of the Nile, and Susan shall be Queen Elizabeth I of England. Zoltán here can be our slave; we'll call him Boris and he can do exactly as we say.'

Anna leads us to the dining room and explains that we are now in the Queen of England's palace and we expect Boris to bring us a luncheon of the highest quality. I rush feverishly to the kitchen where I find that Margaret is making pancakes. When I re-enter the dining room carrying the silver platter and wearing white gloves, and pulling a expression which is uncannily similar to János's impassive glare, Anna says: 'Bravo, Boris, bravo!'

Invariably, the dressing up game would always end up with me playing the role of some unfortunate: a beggar, a barman, a fool, a servant, a clown or a slave. Anna, and then the children encouraged by her boldness, would order me to fetch them food and drink, or perform some daft task such as doing a handstand (which I could never manage) or crawling on my hands and knees on the floor. The hilarity engendered by asking a great Count to do these demeaning labours was huge and even had the Róths and Margaret in stitches.

I don't think I would have participated with such good grace if Imre had been there: he would have delighted in seeing me humiliated, whereas the laughter of the others was charged with affection and, in Anna's case, genuine love. I could feel her returning to me with every silly role I adopted. She was becoming mine again.

The only people who didn't laugh were János and Miss Virág. János carried out his duties with the same elegant polish and refinement as always but I sensed he wasn't happy with such frivolities.

Miss Virág's lack of mirth had different origins however. I don't think that she was distressed, as János clearly was, because we were breaking so radically from aristocratic protocol. She was a democrat of the Kossuth variety and didn't care a fig for upper-class codes. No. Her dourness was an altogether different phenomenon. During the first weeks that my new guests were staying in the apartment, I endeavoured to cheer up my miserable governess by bringing her some of the books that she had used to teach us. I fetched Vörösmarty's *The Flight of Zalán* from the library and inscribed the book to her, giving her it as a present. She smiled weakly up at me from her position on the bed, where she spent most of the days and nights sitting and staring.

'I thought you might like this,' I said gently.

She put on her spectacles and examined the book.

'Now why would I want this book?' she asked me with such quiet resignation in her voice that I didn't find the question a rebuff at all. I reminded her that she used to teach it to us.

'Do you remember what it is about?' she said.

I said I did and then proceeded to recount with rather too much pride all the incidents that I could recall from this epic which describes the conquest of Hungary by Árpád nearly a thousand years ago. I quoted some of the most patriotic lines about the triumph of the Magyar spirit that Miss Virág had insisted that we learnt off by heart.

'You see, you taught me so well that I can remember it still after all these years,' I said.

To my surprise, Miss Virág had buried her head in her hands and told me that she didn't feel very well. 'I'd like it if you could just go away now,' she said from underneath the knuckly cage of fingers that encased her face. I retreated reluctantly and deeply puzzled. She didn't seem proud at all of her superb teaching.

Later that day, I asked Anna what was troubling her sister-in-law and mentioned our conversation about *The Flight of Zalán*. Inexplicably, Anna was furious with me for disturbing Miss Virág with such a piece of literature.

'Are you completely insensitive?' she said, with her hands on her hips.

'But she used to love that poem,' I persisted, wilting under my sister's severe glare.

Anna took me by the arm and led me into the library, well out of earshot from anyone. She sat me down in the red armchair where I had used to sit when participating in one of my father's manly chats. She then explained that Miss Virág had suffered a great deal after our parents sacked her following the *Dracula* incident: her brother was thrown in prison and she hadn't been able to find any more work because she was Jewish. She had nearly starved to death during those years. When Imre was released her situation improved but at the beginning of the war, her flat was sacked by some Arrow Cross thugs. When she complained to the police, they had laughed in her face.

'Neither of us knows quite what happened to her then but she has never been the same since,' Anna said. 'Apparently, the police didn't even regard her as Hungarian even though she knows more patriotic poems off by heart than the whole station put together.'

Despite my dreadful, unwitting faux-pas, I persisted in trying to find a book that might cheer up my governess. Anna's explanation spurred me on. Although I wasn't willing to admit it to myself at the time, I felt, deep down, that my family had let her down. My next two choices of books met with the same silent head-buried-in-the-hands response as before. On reflection they weren't very suitable options – *The Tragedy of Man* and *The Death of King Buda* -- but they seemed to be at the time because I thought that they might be a good reflection of Miss Virág's gloomy mood.

The moment that I abandoned trying to find a Hungarian book that might interest her, I began to be more successful. She did not cover her face when I raided my mother's library and started reading *Pride and Prejudice* to her. However, she derived most pleasure in having Anna and I read Shakespeare's comedies to her.

Repeated exhortations for her to act a part in *Twelfth Night* managed to rouse her from her bed. I was forced to play Malvolio, while Anna took Maria's role, and Miss Virág, cast against type, opted for Sir Toby Belch. We all dressed up and produced a hectic performance of a few scenes for the mystified Róths – who didn't speak English.

But it was one of the few times that I saw Miss Virág laugh during the war. After the performance, her spirits recovered enough for her to read on her own, although her melancholia did seem to return in part. I think her constant re-reading of *Twelfth Night* didn't help; she started quoting lines at us and taken out of context they did seem rather sour. Sometimes, I would see her scrutinising her locket and hear her muttering to herself in bed; 'Dost thou think, because thou art virtuous, there'll be no more cakes and ale?' and 'Is there no respect of place, persons, nor time, in you?'

Once as Anna and I were sitting at the table in the Bridge Room and trying our best to pretend that our former tutor wasn't talking to herself, I leant over to my sister and asked her, in a whisper, just what was in the locket. Anna shook her head.

'You don't want to know, believe me, Zoltán, you don't want to know,' she said very quietly.

Of course, this just aroused my curiosity even further and I continued asking her. But she would never give me a straight answer and I didn't manage to peek inside the locket because Miss Virág would always click it shut at any time someone approached.

Often Anna would distract me from asking questions about it by entertaining me in some way. When she was not playing games, she agonised about whether she should be with Imre or working as a nurse in the ghetto hospital. This was what she had been doing before I rescued her. Although she didn't talk much about it, I could tell that it hadn't been a pleasant experience. Yet she felt it was her duty. Imre, however, forbade it.

It was the one thing that they argued about. 'Why won't you let me help? I can help. I can go back there during the day, I'll back here at night like you are.'

Imre would shake his head decisively; I almost admired him for it. 'You're not going back there. I want you alive when this war is over. That hospital is vulnerable. The deportations may have stopped now but you never know when they might start again.'

Anna didn't speak much about what had happened to them in the time we'd been separated, except to say that Imre had lost his arm in a forced labour camp in the Ukraine. Apparently, he was shot in the arm while trying to escape from the camp. The wound festered and his arm became gangrenous: it had to be amputated. 'It's meant that he hasn't been called up again; you're not much use with just one arm, even in a Hungarian work camp,' she said ruefully. I winced as Anna told me this story and clutched my arm as she finished her explanation, checking to see it was still there.

Anna gave me a pained look. 'Maybe Imre is right, maybe all your illnesses are imaginary,' she said abruptly. 'You just don't know what real suffering is like, do you?'

'Do you?' I retorted immediately.

'I've seen some things. In the hospital I saw some things,' she said enigmatically, refusing to elaborate. But I believed her. One rarely wants to talk about the truly ghastly things one has endured.

Imre generally returned home in the early evening in time for the five o'clock broadcast from London which all of us listened to in the Bridge Room. The large varnished wireless had been carried into this room at Imre's insistence; he claimed that he needed it to know what was happening both in Budapest and in Russia. I wanted to know more about what he was up to, but whenever I asked him what he did during the day, he would snap back at me with an evil chuckle, 'Mind your own bloody business! Believe me, a coward like you wouldn't want to know!' That made me shiver. Imre's charm had been replaced by a brutal sarcasm which I found deeply disturbing. I could scarcely bare to look at him and indeed didn't need to; whenever he was in the room I could feel his presence bristling malevolently and could sense his changeable moods – moving from triumphantly self-righteous to darkly savage – just by the sounds of his workmen's boots tramping across the varnished floors and lush carpets. For a few days, I resisted Anna's pleas for the great hulking wireless to be taken out of the nursery and then eventually relented after she threatened to stop dancing with me and exclude me from all her games.

János, Mr Róth and Imre's arm all assisted with carrying the radio into the secret room and placing it next to my brother-in-law's mattress. It was a victory for Imre and he liked to remind me of it by sitting up on his bed and smiling proprietarily as he turned on the radio and twiddled the knobs.

As the summer progressed a silly competition developed between Imre and myself when it became clear we were reacting somewhat differently to the news of the Allied victories. Whenever we were informed in those clipped, correct BBC tones that the British and the Americans had taken a town or won a battle, I would nod sagely at Imre and say: 'We're getting there. We are.'

But Imre was much more enthusiastic about the Russian victories and he would always turn up the volume when one was being reported. Afterwards he would brag: 'We're getting there faster!'

In late August it became increasingly clear that Imre was going to win our unspoken wager. I was trying my best to celebrate the surrender of Paris while Imre could scarcely conceal his joy at the news that the Romanians had switched sides and were now in alliance with the Russians.

The war had hardened Imre into a fanatical Marxist-Leninist. He read nothing but *Das Kapital*, and often left the book lying around on my sofas and chairs even though he knew I could have been arrested for having such inflammatory literature in my home. When I upbraided him about this, he would laugh and say: 'I'm just getting you prepared for the Revolution. It's coming whether you like or not.'

I looked to Anna when he spoke like this, but she always seemed enraptured by her husband's words; I could see visions of an egalitarian utopia swimming in her eyes. Politically, she was very naive. In an attempt to knock her out of a communist reverie, I once asked Imre: 'What's going to happen to me in this paradise of yours?'

Imre twirled his walking stick around his knuckles, like Charlie Chaplin. 'Rákosi is a reasonable chap,' he said with a grin, referring to the most notable Hungarian communist in exile in Moscow and who was, coincidentally, Jewish. 'But I expect you'll have to share this grand apartment of yours with a few of the proletariat.'

To my frustration, Anna simply nodded in agreement as if this seemed a perfectly rational idea.

21: RUSSIANS

When the Russians invaded Hungary at the very beginning of October 1944, Imre's victory was so categorical that he began to make friendly overtures towards me. There had been an air of unreality about his triumphant crowing about the Revolution back in August, but now it seemed extremely likely that some kind of socialist state would be established in Hungary under what Imre presumed would be the benevolent guardianship of Uncle Joe.

Yet perhaps Imre was a little scared of this prospect -- or maybe he took pity on me. After all, as a Count and supporter of what increasingly looked like Horthy's doomed regime, I would be first in the firing line. Perhaps he was beginning to wonder, along with the rest of us, whether this would be a metaphorical or a literal firing line.

One evening in October, he tapped me on the shoulder while I was playing the piano and asked me whether we might take a stroll down the hallway. I agreed with some trepidation because I imagined that he was going to complain about the way I was behaving with his wife or embark on a tirade about how the Hungarian upper classes had always oppressed the working man.

'I will make sure that you are protected, you know,' he said to me as we walked slowly past the ticking ebony clock. 'I won't forget what you have done for us when the time comes.'

His head remained bowed as he said this but I caught a good glimpse of his face. He was evidently having difficulty articulating his words. Whether this was because he didn't want to praise his brother-in-law or because he was choked by emotion, I couldn't be sure. But I did notice that the gnarled anger that had knotted his features when I had encountered him in the ghetto had been vanquished by three months of Pongrácz hospitality. He had put on weight, his sallow cheeks had fattened up, his eyes had acquired the intellectual sheen of old and Margaret had shorn him of his bedraggled, greasy locks. Anna had found that some of the Count's clothes fitted him.

In a smart white shirt and trousers, Imre looked respectable and distinguished. The civilised environs of the Pongrácz household had tamed his handsome but wild virility. Instead of looking like some half-crazed cross between a gypsy and an unkempt Franz Liszt he seemed more like a cultured intellectual.

He patted me on the back, adding with an acerbic chuckle: 'You may be a coward and a hypochondriac, but you stuck around. You stuck around.'

I was sufficiently moved by his speech to mention it to Anna the very next day as we were waltzing to Strauss. I pressed my cheek against hers and said: 'Your husband thanked me yesterday, in his own strange way. I can almost understand why you married him now. Almost.'

I didn't get a chance to see her reaction to my comment because there was a loud knocking on the door. People called occasionally and everyone knew the drill: Anna and the Róths ran to the Bridge Room while Margaret and János cleared away any evidence of them in the flat. Usually, Miss Virág didn't have to run anywhere because she was in bed reading a Shakespeare play. In the meantime, I was to stall the callers by answering them as casually as I could.

It was László. He was not hiding behind his Arrow Cross uniform but had put on his lederhosen instead: voluminous leather shorts, braces, a short-sleeved shirt, knee high socks and brown sandals. Although little of his legs were exposed, their hairiness was embarrassing: tufts of black hair even covered his kneecaps. He coughed nervously, frowned and said that he needed to speak to me.

Mercifully he didn't ask to come in and he explained that he had come alone. 'There are things that I have to tell you,' he said: 'We could take a walk.'

I did my best to suppress a smile at his ridiculous get-up, but asked, 'You're looking very Germanic today, László!'

'Yes, I do believe we Hungarians have a great deal to learn from the Germans,' he said quietly. His tone seemed somewhat abashed.

'What in particular?'

'Maybe it's that they are so practical and efficient. This lederhosen, for example, it's so marvellous to move in; I feel very free in it. Yes, in most areas, the Magyars could learn from their allies...'

Even with this explanation, I didn't understand his newfound humility or his outfit: why was he aping the Germans with his lederhosen? Was this all a trap so that he could lure me back to the Buda caves? Or had the realisation that the Germans were losing the war finally dawned upon him? Perhaps he now knew that he would need my support if he was going to survive its end. Reluctantly I agreed, thinking that he could very well turn nasty if I refused his request; I knew László. I fetched my cape and plucked my father's silver-topped cane out of the rack.

The Kübelwagen was waiting underneath the bare, autumn branches of a horse-chestnut tree on Andrássy. I stood in front of it, tapped the mud-spattered bonnet with the tip of my cane and shook my head: 'Oh no, I'm not getting in that!'

But again, László adopted his humble approach, touching his moustache in an agitated fashion while he implored me in whispering tones to get into the Kübelwagen. 'Nothing will happen to you. We can only talk in there!'

His mouth was puckered and small. He looked like he was telling the truth. For all he had done to me, I trusted him, in an inexplicable fashion. I climbed into the passenger seat. He sprang in beside me, yanked on the gear stick and we revved up Andrássy. It had been a while since I had been out, having been pre-occupied with making bridges and playing games with Anna and the Róth children. Although the villas and apartment blocks on Andrássy still seemed relatively untouched by the bombing raids, I could see strands of smoke tapering away into the evening sky, and smashed-up buildings peppering the side streets.

The sun melted behind the fairground in the City Park; the tracks of the rollercoaster were blistered with gold sores. We swerved past the archangel Gabriel standing aloft on his great column in Heroes Square; his face and wings radiated a greenish glow in the clear, autumnal air. Once we had passed Gundels and the Zoo, and the Vajdahunyad, László turned down a small road and drew the Kübelwagen to a halt under a canopy of trees.

'We can talk here,' László said, lighting a cigarette and offering me one. I declined as he gripped me by the shoulder and drew me into a latticework of shadow created by the branches of the tree we were standing under. 'They know, Zoltán. They know you're hiding that Commie Jew and they're going to come and get him.'

I took a moment to absorb this information and then I asked for one of his cigarettes. I wasn't a smoker and so I felt even more nauseated when I inhaled. I flung the wretched thing to the ground in a fit of coughing.

'I've kept them away until now. And perhaps I still can,' he said, drawing on his cigarette. His eyes gloated in its glow. The last rays of the sun trickled over the treetops and then dwindled into the black wood. I didn't say anything. László moved closer to me, breathing smoke over my neck. It tickled a little, reminding me of the way Anna's hair brushed me when we danced together. I recoiled from him.

'This time we can do things right,' László said quietly. 'We can be nice to each other.'

I didn't return home until well after midnight, but despite the late hour I lay in bed that night thinking about the encounter. Just how much did László know? He had only mentioned Imre and failed to allude to my sister, Miss Virág or the Róth family. And yet, if he knew that Imre was hiding in the flat, he must know that Anna and Miss Virág were with him. Perhaps he was only interested in getting Imre?

How did he know?

Should I warn them?

Or had I done enough to ensure László's silence? My whole body ached from what I had endured in the City Park. It seemed strange to me that once I had actively desired this man. He seemed so repellent to me now; his actions and demeanour were no better than Caliban's, perhaps worse.

I couldn't stand the thought of Anna leaving me again but I also realised that if I didn't say anything, her life might be in danger.

All these questions were thrust aside by the momentous events of the next day. It was Sunday, October 15th, and János's white gloves were ladling out generous servings of bean soup to the small Róth children – who now were not so tiny -- from a big tureen when Imre burst into the room, twirling his walking stick in the air. During these more liberal months, Imre normally spent most of the day outside of the flat: he had numerous passes and papers that enabled him to travel anywhere in the city and because he was married to Anna he didn't have to wear a yellow star. As a consequence, we very rarely saw him at lunch time.

Hence his sudden, gleeful appearance was a surprise. But before we could ask him what was happening he had switched on the radio and turned up the volume. The elderly, frail voice of our incompetent Regent, Admiral Horthy, crackled across the air waves. Mrs Róth dropped her spoon when she heard him say: 'It is obvious to any sober-minded person that the German Reich has lost the war.'

We all set down our spoons and listened without taking so much as a slurp at our soup. It was a testament to János's professionalism as a butler that he continued to bring two breadbaskets to the table and disappeared when he had completed his duties. However, Margaret soon waddled in and listened with us.

Horthy said some hypocritical nonsense about Hungary's heroic role in the war and then admitted: Hungary was about to conclude a military armistice with her former enemies and to cease all hostilities with them.

When the broadcast had finished, Imre leapt up from the bed and shouted at the top of his voice something I never thought he would say: 'Hurrah for the Regent! It's over Anna, it's all over. You see when I've been going out, I haven't been idle. The secret committee has been moving and shaking!'

As if to underline this point, he grabbed Anna and insisted upon doing a little *csárdás* with her. Of course, the dance lacked both music and any sense of rhythm or grace but it was a touching sight. When Imre had finished, he picked up his walking stick again and, with the authoritative air of someone who feels he is going to be holding a position of power very shortly, proclaimed: 'There's still work to be done. I'm going to take a trip down to the committee. I should be back in the early evening.'

'Maybe you should wait here until we know for certain what has happened,' Anna said, blocking the door with her outstretched arm.

'Don't think that this is the be-all and end-all,' Miss Virág added cautiously.

Imre took his sister's hand and kissed it, laughing a little.

'Darling, I know what I'm doing, I really do,' he said, dropping the old governess's hand and kissing his wife lightly on the forehead. With a twirl of his walking stick he was gone.

* * *

The German forces seized the Hungarian Radio in the late afternoon and Ferenc Szálasi, the lunatic leader of the Arrow Cross, addressed the nation, ordering the armed forces to fight on. The euphoria which we had felt at lunch-time quickly changed to abject fear. Miss Virág and Anna began to discuss whether to go and fetch Imre from the ghetto where they knew he was meeting with his committee.

Miss Virág clutched at her locket and fretted, 'I know it's not safe. It's not safe anymore.' Anna concurred and stated that someone had to get him back to the apartment.

I counselled against this. 'He'll know what's happening. There's no point in putting all of our lives in jeopardy.'

Yet there was one person who could bring him back to the safety of the flat without putting his life in danger. Anna edged closer to me, ruffling the eiderdown on Imre's mattress where the three of us were all sitting, crouched around the radio.

'You could go,' Anna said quietly to me, putting her arm around my shoulder, adding as if to reassure herself, 'they won't touch you.'

'But we don't know where he is,' I protested.

There was a pause.

'We do. They're in a house in Vörösmarty utca, no 16.'

I blinked. 'But that's right next to the Arrow Cross HQ!' I exclaimed.

Anna smiled. 'Precisely.'

'You mean...'

Suddenly I understood what Imre had been doing for these last two months; he'd been spying on the Arrow Cross. He was either a lunatic or a very brave man. László's comments now made sense: Imre was a marked man, no matter what. My intervention was useless. Or was it?

Anna collected my coat and hat and gave me all the papers and passes from the Swedish embassy that she could lay her hands on. I stepped out onto the dark street and walked once again up Andrássy Avenue. A chill wind blew into my face. Fallen chestnut leaves swirled around my legs. My brogues crunched over broken glass and bits of blasted masonry. I heard feet pattering after me and walked faster but I soon recognised those delicate steps. I turned around and saw Anna's silhouette in front of me. The black hood of our mother's winter coat shrouded her head.

'Zoltán, go back home. I want to go instead.'

'Anna, don't be a bloody fool, you know I'm by far the best person to do this,' I said.

'Just give me the papers,' she hissed, holding out her hand. She was clearly impatient with my sudden attack of courage.

A whispering, bickering argument then ensued about who was going to fetch Imre. Now I'm not quite sure what we decided upon. I can remember being strongly tempted to let her go instead of me, but I'm sure I wore her down and she returned back to the flat. But on the other hand it's just conceivable that I did let her go. I just don't know.

Everything is swamped in my memory by what happened next. We both turned round and headed in our different directions. Almost immediately after we had parted, the air raid siren started howling and a Kübelwagen without its headlights switched on screeched to a halt beside me. The tentacles of numerous radio antennae quarrelled on its roof. A burly man in a black shirt and jackboots jumped out of it. I recognised the slightly humped-backed form and the ample buttocks straightaway. It was László. The starlight caught his face at an angle and I could see that his moustache was beaded with soup or sauce. Evidently he'd interrupted dinner to find me.

'You, come here,' he said, pointing fiercely. He seized me by the arm. He threw me into the back of the Kübelwagen between two Arrow Cross thugs stinking of sweat and *pálinka*. They both stuck their handguns into my chest. As the Kübelwagen raced down the road I saw Anna's silhouette hurrying back home. At least they hadn't got her.

'Now Count, you have a choice,' László shouted from the driver's seat. 'Either you tell us where the Commie Jew is and point him out to us or we shoot you and all your family.'

The thugs snorted with laughter and prodded me in the ribs with their guns: 'Speak up, your Excellency!'

Everything seemed to slow down. I shut my eyes and saw the most peculiar vision. I felt as if I had been crushed into a tiny ball and had been shoved down my own throat; I had somehow ended up living inside my own heartbeat. My poor old heart was finding it very strenuous to keep pumping the blood around my body. There seemed to be no sound around me except the deep bass of my heart's strangulated beating. Then suddenly, I seemed to have popped out of my chest and I was in the outside world again: the muzzles of those guns burned into my stomach, the roaring engine of the Kübelwagen rang in my ears and the smell of oil, *pálinka* and sweat smashed into my nostrils. The muffled sound of bombers droned overhead.

My head fizzed from a lack of oxygen. The Kübelwagen pulled up outside the Vörösmarty utca house. Sirens whirred and huge flares flashed across the sky, bathing the street in a purple light. Flak pulsed around the city. Bombs dropped and exploded in the distance. We all gazed up, momentarily distracted and bedazzled. Huge green and orange lights whooshed among the stars. Even in my terror, I could appreciate that it was a beautiful sight.

László grabbed me by the hair and whispered that I should never call him by his first name again. The two thugs had run on ahead and seemed to have apprehended someone in the hallway of the building. A walking stick clattered to the ground and they pushed a half-naked figure before me.

Another flare fizzled. In the ethereal glow, I saw Imre. His face was bleeding and he was stripped down to his underpants. I saw the raw, red stump of his arm. As the turquoise light dyed away, I caught a glimpse of his abject eyes, blood trickling across his crow's feet, dirt smeared into the white hair of his sideburns, and the tight wrinkles around his mouth. He was shaking.

'Is this the fucking Commie Jew you have been keeping in your house?'

I don't know what I said. My body was convulsed. Perhaps that was admission enough. For a split second, Imre's eyes caught mine. I think that second is one of the most painful I have ever endured. He knew he was going to die and there was nothing I could do. And now, reflecting on that stare from a distance of more than fifty years, I can see that there was something even deeper than fear in Imre's eyes, something more frightening: there was love. Love for his wife. He was begging me in that last split second to look after her. Perhaps that is what is most agonizing. Not my failure of nerve then, but what happened next. I don't know. Thinking about it is like holding your finger in a fire: it's unendurable to dwell upon it for any length of time.

The Arrow Cross boys gripped Imre's shoulders, and then László stomped up to him, put a gun in his mouth and shot him, his brain splattering against the singed brick work of the house. My bowels emptied and I smelt a terrible smell as László strode up to me, and hit me on the temples with the butt of his revolver, leaving me semi-conscious on the pavement. Then they drove away, laughing.

Somehow, I managed to crawl home. Anna greeted me as soon as I shut the front door. I didn't look at her but tried to inhale her scent instead; the stink of those Arrow Cross thugs' body odour still lingered in my nose. Warm blood trickled down my throat and my clothes stank of shit. Anna broke away from our embrace and bit on her fingers as she asked: 'Did you find him?'

Perhaps my worst crime was not telling her the truth there and then. Images flashed in my head: the stump of his arm, his goose-pimpled skin, László's determined stomping, the gun in the mouth, the bits of his skull and brain flying through the air, the laughter as the Kübelwagen screeches away. Images that have haunted me for the rest of my life. I shook my head and quickly handed Anna my coat that was covered in tiny fragments of broken glass and dust. She didn't attempt to brush them off but hung the coat up on its hook. My pants were really beginning to bother me.

'I need to wash,' I jabbered.

We walked into the Red Room.

'They took you away,' she said.

'I really need to get clean,' I said.

'László was in the Kübelwagen. I saw,' she said. 'Did he know where Imre was? Did he mention him at all?'

Her questions threatened my sanity. I thought to myself: this is what it must be like to take leave of your senses, to feel disconnected from your body, to descend to a lower level of existence not rooted in the world of sight, touch, taste, smell and sound. I staggered into the dusty bathroom and shut the door. Luckily, János had left a bucket of water there because there was, of course, no running water. I stripped off my clothes and washed myself with a towel. All the while, I could hear Anna waiting outside, pacing up and down. Eventually, just as I beginning to feel cleaner, and now cleaning my trousers in the bucket, Anna banged on the door.

'What happened? What happened!'

I hung up my trousers on the railing and tipped the dirty water down the plughole, and then wrapping myself in a towel, I opened the door, pushed past Anna and bolted into the nursery, where I gulped down two bottles of my beetroot medicine that Margaret had placed on my bedside table during the day.

Anna followed me into the room and sat down beside me on the bed. She repeated her question. I knew the only way to stop her interrogation was to divert her onto another topic of possibly equal weight: my suffering.

'László did things to me,' I mumbled and got up off the bed and fetched the whiskey bottle from the bottom drawer of the writing bureau. I swigged at the bottle and then I fainted.

When I awoke, it was still night time and Anna was lying beside me in the bed. Her arms were wrapped around my head and she was running her fingers through my hair. She seemed to be murmuring something to me. An incantation or a song, I thought. And then I realised that she was recounting the fairy story that she told me that night when she stole into my room after she found out Wenceslas was being so beastly to me.

'Zoltika, there was a little boy and a little girl and together they lived in a snow palace and went skating on the frozen lakes...'

As I opened my eyes, she bent down to kiss me.

Was I dreaming or did it actually happen? Did we actually kiss and make love or was that my dream? I remember the physical sensation of her body so well; the softness of her breasts, the downy hair on the small of her back and the taste of her mouth as I kissed her and moved inside her.

The most peculiar aspect is that I fancied that Imre, shivering and naked, limped into the room as we were making love and hovered in the shadows by the wardrobe. The winged silhouette of the carved golden eagle that perched on top of the wardrobe shadowed his face as he watched us but I knew the top of his head was blown away.

When I looked up again, he had vanished.

22: THE CELLAR

I suffered a relapse in my health and I was confined to my bed for the next few days with barely the power to speak. My temperature rose and I was feverish. Without Margaret's constant ministrations and my beetroot medicine, I doubt whether I would have survived.

Surfacing every now and then from my delirium, I would notice the hem of Anna's black dress was spread across the coverlet. I would feel her cool fingers stroking my cheeks and smell that apricot scent. There were tears running down her face.

'If only you had seen where he went. Maybe they said something? Anything?'

She asked me over and over again, but I was ill enough to be able to feign deafness. I would sink back into my pillow and close my eyes and try and hear the running water on our old country estate and my father's miniature Chain Bridge.

Surreptitiously, when Anna was not tending to me, I could ask János to go to Vörösmarty utca and see if he saw anything there. 'Anything striking at all…' I said very feebly.

'Yes, of course, sir,' János said.

Some hours later, he returned to say that he had seen nothing that he did not expect to see.

'What does that mean?' I said, lifting my sweaty head off the pillow.

'Anything that may have disturbed her Ladyship if had encountered this area has been removed, if this is what you mean,' he said.

Pain sizzled through my body. I looked him in the eyes. We both understood each other perfectly. He knew. This was a tremendous relief somehow. I could bear holding this secret by myself.

'Thank you, János, thank you,' I said, feeling myself relapse into an even worse fever. Descending down, down, down into wracking agony. And yet, it did occur to me that it might be a happy thing if I died. Yes, that would be a solution.

After I began to recover, a few days later, I was further vexed by an odd note from János which he presented to me in the most formal fashion possible: on a small silver platter. I grabbed at it angrily and tore open the stiff, parchment envelope. The note informed me that my butler, in his new capacity of superintendent of the building, desired a brief, private conference with me in the library.

This request irritated me exceedingly. Couldn't the bloody man see that I was rolling around on my death bed? I barely had the energy to raise a bottle of beetroot medicine to my lips, let alone suffer the journey to the library. And what was he doing sending me a note when he was conversing with me every other hour?

I impressed these points upon him and, after some typical János silences, he conceded and agreed to talk as I stayed in bed.

'And what's all this nonsense about you being the superintendent of the building? I thought Iván did that job,' I said, referring to the sour old porter who resided like a weather-beaten gargoyle in the hallway of our apartment block.

'Yes, he did. But he was killed by a bomb,' János said, smoothing down the front of his jacket. Had his new position made him vain?

'Near here?' I asked, with tired indifference.

'Yes, your Excellency. Just a hundred yards down from here,' János said.

'It must have been a Russian bomb. The English wouldn't do a thing like that,' I said, considering the point for a moment.

János didn't reply to this and didn't seem unduly concerned that the bombing raid on Andrássy showed that the Russians were attacking the cornerstones of Hungarian culture. Instead, he cleared his throat and, in quite an uncharacteristic gesture, cracked his knuckles like a petty gangster might have done.

'Your Excellency, I must speak to you because of a conflict of interest arising from my new appointment. All superintendents must make people of Jewish extraction report for duty tomorrow morning at 10 am.'

'For duty?' I asked. These words were like slimy pebbles of rock in my mouth.

'Yes. All sons of Israel between the ages of 16 and 60 and every daughter of Israel between the ages of 18 and 40 are to be sent to assist with the war effort,' he said with the same, constipated formality that infused every word he spoke.

I drew breath. What was going on? I had always chalked János up as a thoroughly good egg. The Arrow Cross and the Nazis couldn't have cracked his Hungarian shell and made that great Magyar soul leak out of him. Or could they?

'The question is: do you harbour anyone of Jewish origin under your roof, your Excellency?'

I hesitated of course. János knew about the Róths, about Miss Virág and Anna; he'd seen them with own eyes, he'd served them soup. Why was he asking this question? And then, pulling myself out of the fog of my illness, I realised why János had requested such a formal interview. He wanted to ask me this question as a Count, not as his employer. My word as a Count was absolutely binding; a Count would never lie. Whatever I said would be taken as the truth. Finally, I mustered a quiet, hoarse reply: 'There are no Jews living here.'

'Very good, your Excellency. I will inform the proper authorities that this is the case,' János said. He bowed before me and then departed quickly from the room.

Between us, János and I had saved the lives of my sister, Miss Virág and the Róth family.

Obviously, my illness prevented me from seeing what had happened to my charges, but I took the appearance of my sister at my bedside the very next day to be a reliable indication that they had not been rounded up and marched off to a camp. Anna's agitation seemed to have increased tenfold.

'Zoltán, Zoltán, you've got to wake up,' she said, shaking the covers.

My nose twitched at the sight of two damp patches underneath Anna's arm. She needed a bath. I would have to instruct Margaret to run her one as soon as possible.

'They're taking them all away,' she said, wiping some clear mucus away from her nose with the back of her hand. 'Do you think that's what happened to Imre? Do you think that they took him to a camp?'

I pulled the covers over my head and curled up into a ball. She ripped the eiderdown off me and began to yell, 'They're killing anyone who goes out into the street. Just shooting them. Did you know that? Did you know that?'

Anna's words were pickaxes hacking away at the smooth, fragile surface of the protective shell I had built around myself. She began to shake me as I plugged my ears with the palms of my hands.

'Why don't you just get up out of bed and see what's going on all around you, you – you – you --!'

She was so enraged by my enfeebled response that words failed her. Often, I look back and wonder what she meant to say then. Perhaps to call me a pathetic hypochondriac or a useless little shit, or the worst Hungarian that ever lived, or the most useless brother that ever walked the face of the earth. Some such phrase, I am sure. Because she failed to say it, I'm forever filling in the blanks.

I had never been thankful for an air raid siren until that moment. As the screeching noise whirred into action, Anna stopped rattling my fevered bones and said, in a low, urgent and choked tone: 'You better come with us. It's not safe here. Margaret has found a secret cellar we can all stay in.'

Without saying anymore, Anna pulled me out of my bed and pushed me through the hallway where the ebony clock was still ticking. I stumbled into the kitchen, through Margaret's bedroom and then down the maid's stairs. We were following exactly the same route that we had taken all those years ago, when my sister showed me Margaret and Teresa beating the rug with their *prakkers*.

When we reached the bottom of the dark, narrow stairs, we turned right and continued down into the distressed bowels of Budapest. In the flickering candle light of the cellar, the frightened eyes of the Róth family and Miss Virág watched Anna as she set me down on a bare mattress.

Apparently, Margaret and János were staying in the other big cellar with all the residents of the building so that there wouldn't be a total absence of people from our apartment in the main shelter; this might have caused suspicions. My non-appearance could be easily explained because I had never, until this moment, stepped into a cellar on Andrássy.

I don't know how I would have survived that bleak winter without the restorative qualities of my beetroot medicine and the technical genius of János. I don't think I saw daylight for the next three months; the air raids were almost constant and I was too ill to make the return journey to the nursery as much as I would have liked. Instead I decided to cultivate a kind of nest in the corner of that miserable, dusty cellar.

A few days in that stinking hole forced me to send an order to János to bring down my bedside table. It's a testament to his skills as a butler that he could manage this feat without being detected by anyone and without chipping any part of my furniture. I gave it a thorough check and there wasn't the slightest spot on it.

Once I had a few months' supply of beetroot medicine, I found that I could sleep with some degree of satisfaction despite the fact that the damp walls gnawed away at my weak chest and the dust exacerbated my allergy. Luckily, Miss Virág and Anna were usually on hand to read me some Shakespeare if I found it particularly difficult to sleep. Margaret would bring us down food that sadly decreased in quality and quantity quite drastically after November. St Nicolas's night was a particularly miserable affair: we had a fake sugar supplement which we sprinkled on bread.

By late December, we had trouble getting clean water and we were forced to drink filthy rainwater. This played havoc with my insides and I spent quite a bit of time on the chamber-pot and would have stayed there even longer if it hadn't been so bloody cold. Sometimes my bottom froze to the pot and I had to use a candle to thaw myself off it. In the process of this difficult manoeuvre I invariably managed to burn my backside. My skin was so numb by then that I scarcely cared.

The amenity arrangements left a great deal to be desired because we had to do our business in chamber pots that were emptied by Mrs Róth, who kindly volunteered her services for this unpleasant duty. Anna didn't seem bothered by this filthy procedure. In fact, she seemed almost to relish it and would quite brazenly proclaim what kind of substance she was going to produce and told everyone to hold their noses, more often than not.

I suppose her years with Imre had made her forget that she was a Countess. But I jolly well hadn't forgotten my rank. I made János hang a screen of noble Transylvanian design and place my chamber pot, which was far more luxurious and ornate than the others, on a pedestal. This meant that my joints wouldn't crack in the laborious process of crouching down and it sent the right signals to the Róths and Miss Virág.

I offered Anna the opportunity to sit on my throne but she declined, and seemed surprisingly galled by my generous offer. 'My shit and your shit are the same as everyone else's,' she said and then blew a raspberry in my face.

I would have taken offence if I hadn't known that she was still thinking about Imre. She fretted about him most of the time, endlessly asking Miss Virág and I whether she should go out and look for him.

Miss Virág, who had kept her own counsel on the matter of her brother, would warn against this notion in a somewhat desperate and muddled fashion, saying over and over again: 'There shall be no more cakes and ale, no more cakes and ale. No more. Cakes. No more.'

Unfortunately, Miss Virág's health was badly affected by the frightful conditions in the cellar. Her refined white hair became infested with lice and even when Anna shaved all of it off, the wretched little mites wouldn't go away and the poor old lady had to have the patience of a Pongrácz not to spend most of her idle hours scratching her head. Inevitably, she succumbed to the temptation in between her readings of Shakespeare, and soon her head was covered in nasty, suppurating sores that were, quite frankly, rather alarming.

Miss Virág's woes were augmented by a chronic shortage of fresh vegetables and fruit; she quickly became malnourished and her teeth began to fall out and her gums to bleed. When I found her one day singing hoarsely to herself 'For the rain it raineth every day' through lips that were blistered with oozing cold sores, I offered her my bed which, thanks to János's ingenuity, was heated around the clock by a large silver and aluminium bed pan containing slow burning charcoal.

She was too ill to reply and so Anna and I lifted her into my bed without saying more. As I smoothed her brittle hair on the pillow and pulled up the sheets to her neck, I discovered the opened locket lying about her throat. At any other time in my life, I would have jumped back in fright at the sight of the picture inside it, but I had been through so much and my body was so racked with tiredness and misery that I was scarcely able to absorb the magnitude of what I saw. It was my father's portrait – painted in much younger days when he had something resembling a head of black hair.

Once snugly tucked up in the warm sanctuary of my bed and having been given a good dose of my beetroot medicine, Miss Virág's health improved a little.

Of course, the moment I swapped Miss Virág's bed for my own, I discovered that all the afflictions of the previous occupant were visited upon me. I suffered appallingly from the cold and the lice caused havoc to my hair. I also found that my gums were regularly bleeding. But in an irregular way, I felt that I deserved this suffering. I slid in and out of nightmares haunted by the spectral figure of my father. I believed that I was being punished for his sins. I could see now that his so-called 'assignations' were far worse than I had previously supposed. My governess had been one of his conquests and yet he had sacked her and left her to endure near starvation. For all his talking about doing the right thing, he had betrayed everyone: his wife with his infidelities, his daughter by cutting her out of his life, his lover by leaving her in penury, and his son by committing suicide. He had left me here to deal with the mess he had created.

By this time, I learned that János himself had fallen ill and was unable to visit me in the tiny cellar. Everyone was sick and we barely stirred from underneath the mountainous piles of our blankets. I generally preferred not to expose my face to the cold air and remained underneath my numerous eiderdowns, taking sips of my beetroot medicine and cursing my luck to be the son of such a feckless father.

Anna was the first person to tell us all that the Russians had arrived. She had been up and out for a couple of days, looking for Imre and for food in the snowy streets of Budapest. She pulled back the covers and caught me having a tipple at my medicine. She was carrying a large lump of firewood in her arms and, in the swaying candlelight, I could see she was smiling tepidly.

'It's over, Zoltán,' she said. Although there was a triumphant note to her quiet words, I couldn't help noticing that her smile quickly disappeared. She held out the lump of firewood and continued: 'We can move back to the apartment but we're going to need fuel.'

Somehow, I had the strength to follow her up the maid's stairs and back into the apartment. The place was in much better shape than I thought it would be – most of my antique furniture was intact -- except that nearly every single window had been shattered. There was glass everywhere: it meandered across the parquet floors and the Persian rug like the sloughed-off, brittle skins of snakes. Shards of glass glittered in the low winter sun.

I ordered Margaret to sweep up the detritus straightaway and asked János to sort out replacing the windows. All the telephone lines were down, the trams weren't running and the roads weren't clear enough to drive along and so János had to make the journey to the window pane supplier on foot – though it would, of course, be a fruitless journey. Yet, he didn't seem disheartened by this prospect and went with good grace. Likewise, Margaret seemed only too happy to get back to tidying the apartment and preparing my beetroot medicine in the kitchen.

Anna scarcely seemed to notice the household's return to some semblance of order. Her eyes were distant and nonchalant as they surveyed the smithereens sprayed across the nursery floor. She didn't even suggest that it needed to be cleaned up or ask whether she could have a bath – none of us had washed in months. Instead her heavy boots, which she had worn throughout her time in the cellar, crunched aimlessly over the glass and stopped before the window sill. I watched her in her dirty, thick dress, a woollen shawl wrapped around her shoulders, poke her head through the shattered window and lean out into the street below and shout: 'Imre! Imre! Imre! Imre!'

I was too stunned by her shouts to say anything. I had already heard from Margaret that it wasn't safe to draw attention to oneself because the Russian soldiers, who were now swarming over Budapest, were looting and pillaging from many of the wealthier houses. But I was unable to stop her.

Fortunately, Miss Virág was passing by the nursery and heard her sister-in-law wailing out of the window. The elderly governess tottered past my frozen body and tried to drag Anna away from the window and only partially succeeded in doing so. 'Come away, come away. Not you too,' Miss Virág cried weakly and then collapsed on the floor.

Anna was too distressed to notice that her sister-in-law had fainted and continued to shout. Outside, I heard gunfire. I tried to distract her by saying that Miss Virág didn't seem well and that we should help her to bed, but Anna ignored me. She fled from the room and said with a sheepish but slightly insane grin in the heavy oak threshold of the nursery: 'I know where he is. I think I know where he is.'

She ran out of the apartment. If she had been speaking sense, I probably would not have followed her and tended to the unconscious Miss Virág. But my sister wasn't herself at all: there was a desperate light of optimism in her eyes, the kind of optimism that quickly dwindles into suicidal depression once it has been disappointed. I felt that she was in more danger than my tutor.

I pursued her onto Andrássy where she slackened her pace, otherwise I wouldn't have been able to keep up. I called out to her to come back but she ignored me and, thus, I trailed after her through the nightmarish wreckage of Budapest all the way down Attila József utca right down to the river.

The relatively intact state of my apartment had been an exceptionally misleading indication about the general condition of our capital city. How can I begin to describe its ruinous state? The streets were strewn with overturned tanks, burnt-out trams and cars; flames still lapped at the ruins of great apartment blocks and grey smoke drifted around the tree-tops. Great swathes of the apartments on the ring road around Deak Ter had been obliterated, leaving only charred timbers, pulverized bricks, broken tiles and smashed glass, and the dead bodies of dogs and cats. The corpses of Germans, Hungarians and Russians littered the gutters. Although most of the bodies were of uniformed soldiers, I did come across one unfortunate Swabian flower vendor who was still holding out a sprig of heather and lavender in her hand as if she was just about to sell the pitiful herbs. Her throat had been slashed and the blood had dried around the deep wound like old egg yolk.

After that I determined that I wouldn't look closely at anything lying on the frozen ground unless I absolutely had to. However, despite this pledge to myself, I couldn't help discerning that much of the snow was streaked with bright red blood and many of the icy puddles were the colour of English strawberries. Her determination to reach her destination seemed to make her oblivious of the carnage around her; she hopped over bodies, skipped across gutters full of bloody pulp and twisted metal, and ducked around the abandoned trams and tanks.

As we approached the Danube, we heard feet tramping through the snow and the howling screech of a Russian officer. I swivelled round and saw that a large infantry division was marching in our wake: the sound of a drum reverberated through the eerily quiet, snow-thrilled air.

I managed to catch up with Anna on the fragmented remains of the Corso. She had come to a dead stop in front of what used to be the Carlton hotel and was staring at the Danube. The snow mocked us as it fell so peacefully onto the icy water.

'Ahhh!' Anna screamed.

I rushed up to her and took her arm by the railings of the promenade, which were now as looped and bowed as shoe laces. Then I embraced her, and she buried her face in the crook of my shoulder. As I held her, I could see what had happened to this once beautiful part of Budapest: every bridge had been blown up and all the great hotels on the Corso were simply piles of rubble with the occasional glint of a chandelier or hint of red carpet poking through the devastation.

I remember thinking it was a good thing that my father was dead: he couldn't have borne the vision of the Chain Bridge's lions with their manes blasted away and the middle of the bridge sliding into the unforgiving currents of the Danube. Nor could he have endured to see the great Buda castle's dome stripped of its green copper finery and its inner scaffolding exposed to the elements. Most of all, the smell of burnt flesh and rubber and wood, and the crackle of simmering fires eating up the great hotels of the Corso would have told the Count that everything civilised about Hungary had been lost, irretrievably cast to oblivion. And yet, I couldn't help feeling that my country deserved it. Quite frankly, I didn't care that the Chain Bridge was totally destroyed.

I should have told her about Imre then. I could have done so. I was on the verge of doing so. And I have regretted for the rest of my life that I did not. What a terrible thing to do to a person, not to tell them that their husband is dead. What a terrible thing.

But I said nothing. And may I be cursed for the rest of my days for my silence. Silence, my only retreat.

Anna broke free of my clasp and looked down into the snowy water of the Danube. I tried to hold her again but she shrugged me off. I hovered around her, noticing that she seemed to have fattened up a bit; she had acquired a bit of belly during these months of starvation. I assumed she must have been eating my food rations.

A rat scuttled over my snow-encrusted boots and rudely truncated my ruminations. I tried not to shriek: its incisors were clutching the ragged end of a human finger. I bit my lip. I didn't want to draw attention to us, it wasn't safe to be outside.

I continued to hesitate behind my sister, agonising over whether I should tell her about my last night with Imre. But as I gazed at those smashed lions on the Chain Bridge, I knew that there was no way I could ever tell her now: I should have told her immediately or not at all.

Eventually, Anna pulled herself reluctantly away from the railings and we walked in silence back to the apartment, numbed by what had happened to us and by what we were seeing. We took a different route back, past the Vigadó, the ornate 19th century concert hall and through Vörösmarty Square, where we chanced upon the unfortunate sight of an old man who seemed to have been cut in half. The crumpled top half of his body was propped up against the ruins of the patisserie-confectioners, Gerbeauds. He had the slightest suggestion of a brownish smile on his face as if he had died nibbling on a piece of chocolate tort. His legs were to be found nearly twenty-five yards away by the entrance to Franz Josef underground. He hadn't tied up his shoelaces.

We hid in a collapsed doorway at the bottom of Andrássy and dodged a few Russian soldiers who were depriving a dead Hungarian soldier of his watch and hip flask.

Once we reached the apartment, we found that János had returned and was sporting two bloody bruises on his cheeks. Margaret dabbed anxiously at his wounds as he said somewhat breathlessly: 'I fear your Excellency, that it is not safe here. The Russians are... well, I can't say it in present company.'

Anna said impatiently: 'János, I have probably seen more than all of you put together. Just tell us.'

János didn't meet Anna's eyes or even acknowledge her comment, but continued to address me. 'They say that the Russians are ransacking every building and raping all the women.'

Margaret stopped dabbing János's face and asked: 'Even old women?'

János didn't answer this but it was clear that he thought that the Russians would violate everyone and everything they laid their hands on. I took a swig of the beetroot medicine that Margaret had considerately handed to me the minute I had entered the flat. It was growing dark outside; clouds of smoke drifted past the kitchen window. The barking of a dog interrupted my thoughts. Suddenly, a shot rang out and the barking stopped.

'My God, they're even shooting the dogs,' I said.

János stood up and dusted down his butler's jacket, which he had just put back on that very day.

'Your Excellency, I have prepared for this contingency. I had initially thought that we might be able to leave the country in the Mercedes but I think this is impractical: it would draw far too much attention to ourselves and it couldn't cope with the roads. What I have managed to get hold of is a Kübelwagen, good for going over rough terrain and unobtrusive, in its way. I suggest that we depart at the earliest available opportunity.'

Lost in thought, I wandered into the wrecked library. A few of the bookshelves had toppled over. Leather bound volumes lay splayed on the floor like shot birds with their wings outspread. I kicked at a few volumes of Petőfi's poetry and found, to my surprise, Miss Virág was sitting, covered in blankets, in my father's armchair, reading *Twelfth Night* by candlelight. She put down the book and greeted me with chattering teeth.

'Zoltán, I was adored once too,' she mumbled, adding: 'Come away, come away, death and in sad cypress let me be laid.'

There was method in her madness, no question. But my brain was too full for me to deal with it at that moment. I offered her a swig of my beetroot medicine and said, 'We're going now, Miss Virág. You need to get ready.'

She said, 'I am a great eater of beef, and I believe it does harm my wit. But beef would be nice, would it not?'

I had no reply for this and left the library, trying not to think about succulent slabs of beef or Miss Virág's incoherence. I had my own survival to think of.

Now, where would I be without János? He had saved me on too many occasions to mention, but our departure from Hungary was a masterpiece of butlering skill. As well as getting his hands on a Kübelwagen, János had managed to find several cans of petrol. We spent most of the evening travelling down the maid's stairs and loading up the vehicle, which was parked by the smashed fountain in the courtyard, with my beetroot medicine and pills, my clothes, my musical scores and a few precious artefacts such as the ebony clock and my father's model of the Chain Bridge. Fortunately, there was room for a lot of my stuff because Margaret and Anna claimed that they only wanted to take a few clothes. The Róth family decided to stay in Hungary, reckoning that being of working class origin, they were less likely to suffer at the hands of the communists. No mention was made of Miss Virág and rather shockingly, I was extremely reluctant to bring the matter up. I wasn't sure whether I could endure her sitting in the Kübelwagen, muttering fragments of Shakespeare at me.

So much of the night was absorbed by preparing for our departure that I scarcely stopped to think what it meant to leave my home for all these years. I felt certain that I was saying only a temporary goodbye: when the British had instilled some semblance of order to Europe, I would be able to return. In the meantime, the Russians were to be avoided at all costs.

It was clear that Anna thought differently, for when dawn broke and we were just about to climb into the Kübelwagen, she lingered in the dark courtyard, kicking absent-mindedly at the wheels. She hadn't said a word during that frantic night.

'I have to stay here. I need to find him,' she said, lifting her head and twining a coil of her black hair around her finger.

I was already sitting in the back of the Kübelwagen with several blankets wrapped around me. Margaret stood behind her, looking solemnly down at the ground. At that moment, there was some shuffling on the balcony above us and I saw Miss Virág leaning over the balustrade. Unexpectedly, she waved at me, 'It's so nice of you to leave me the library,' she said with something approaching a smile. 'But I shall miss you, Zoltán, my dear.'

I looked in puzzlement at Anna.

'She's staying here with me. I've said that she can make her room in the library. Apparently, that's where she wants to live and heaven knows it's the least that we can do for her,' Anna said. Somehow, she knew that I had seen the locket.

'But…' I wanted to protest that the library wasn't a room for living in but I knew that this would be a pointless comment. Finally, I said, 'But you've got to come. It's not safe. The Russians –'

'Imre was a friend of the Russians, Zoltán. They won't touch me. And they'll help me try and find him, I'm sure. And besides who else is going to look after Miss Virág? She is going to need someone to watch her for most of the time – and she wants to wait for her brother to come back too,' she said. 'But you're right to go. You must go. It's not safe for you here.'

My mouth was open. I knew this was my last chance to tell her about Imre. I could never write it down. But the tragic hope in her eyes made me think I never could: it was the only thing that was keeping her alive. The thought that she might see him again.

János started up the engine and before I could say any more we were whistling out of the courtyard and up Andrássy at a speed that I didn't know my butler was capable of driving. He dodged around the disused tanks, the tumbled-down trams, and the clopping horse-drawn carts that were stacked with furniture and suitcases and were slowly making their way out of Budapest.

The Swiss Red Cross sticker on the Kübelwagen meant that we weren't stopped. It fooled me too -- alarm shivered through my body when I realised that we were escaping in László's Kübelwagen.

I shut my eyes as we drove. I didn't want to see how my beloved country had been annihilated. I didn't want to see the heaps of rubble that were once fine mansions, the smoking timbers that were once peasants' cottages, the emaciated, bleeding ghosts that were once women and children, the ragged sticks of filth that were once soldiers. But inevitably I caught glimpses.

János drove on. And on. And on. I would stare at his impassive face, his moustache flecked with grey, his strong arms on the juddering steering-wheel as he drove. His eyes were fixed on the horizon; he seemed to see nothing of the suffering that surrounded him. As we motored along the broken roads into Austria, I uncovered my eyes and saw the desolation on the faces of the soldiers, the children, the women, and the old men who were trudging home. But were they returning home? It seemed to me that they no longer had a home to return to. The notion of having one seemed to have gone up in smoke.

I saw that the whole concept of civilisation had been smashed to pieces. All of Europe's brilliant culture – its picturesque medieval streets, its Baroque palaces, its classical gardens, its nineteenth century theatres, its proud, nationalist people, even its languages – had been crushed.

It felt a bit like stumbling into a magnificent concert hall and finding that the orchestra and audience has been massacred: the mad conductor has his head blown off, blood drips onto Stradivarius violins, the lopped-off hands can be still found on the instruments but the players have disappeared, the grand piano's top has been torn off and its snapped strings are revealed underneath. In a distant corner, a dying man is humming the melody that once resonated so beautifully and loudly in the hall. But that is the only sound left. The rest is silence.

As I observed countless men and women -- who were obviously once refined -- spit at the ground, wail at the top of their voices, fall in fits of tears, kick at their children in anger and frustration, I began to fancy that János and I were perhaps the last remnants of the old order left. We were the only master and the servant who still adhered to the old protocols of decency and respect.

When we left Germany and continued through France, János was forced to steal a new vehicle in which we could continue our journey. We abandoned this at Calais and boarded a ferry that took us onto England.

As I gazed down at the swirling grey waters of the Channel, I thought of all that I had left behind: my home, my wonderful warm bed, the streets I knew so well and once loved so deeply, the Danube and all that beautiful music, and, of course, most of all Anna. Oh Anna! My lovely, gorgeous sister, how could I have left her in that condition? Even though the waters were calm, I couldn't help feeling horribly sick, and spent the journey retching over the railings, sobbing into the speckly rain that descended like a veil as we neared the white cliffs.

In London, my mother, after expressing her relief that her children were alive, did not show great pleasure in seeing me. She had re-married a Conservative Member of Parliament shortly after my father died. But to be honest I was not bothered by her lack of concern: she didn't ask me any awkward questions about Anna. Now that fear for my own welfare had vanished, I was beginning to worry about my sister: János should have pushed her into the Kübelwagen when he had the chance.

My mother gave me some money and made it quite clear in so many words that she didn't want to see me again. I had no idea what I wanted to do. London seemed grimmer than Budapest: it was just as badly bombed in places but at least its bridges were intact. I took this as a good omen. János and I stayed in a boarding house in Paddington. Unfortunately, my health suffered a relapse as soon as we found this place and I was confined to my bed for a couple of months.

When I surfaced again, I found that János had made some excellent contacts with refugee Hungarians, some of whom were even of my social class. He had also discovered that there was a serviceable Turkish bath near our lodgings. That decided it. Using the profits from the vineyards in Villány I had invested in a London bank, I bought a large house near the baths: prices were very low after the war.

A couple of János's contacts were Hungarian film makers who had been paid by the government to make propaganda films during the war, but now were setting up their own studios to make horror films. They needed a composer to churn out music for their dreadful flicks. My life in England had begun.

Part Three: English life

23: FILM MUSIC

As the communists planted mines on the Hungarian border, I lifted a bone-china cup of tea to my lips and listened to the gay babbling of a film director. As my sister cried out in the agonies of childbirth, I leant back in the womb-like darkness of a cinema and gazed at the jumping shadows on the screen. As dissidents were rounded up and sent to gulags, I took out my pen and put the final changes to a rondeau that would accompany a car chase. As Anna watched her son be indoctrinated by Stalinist propaganda, I made important decisions about whether a minuet or waltz would be suitable for the hero's theme. As the secret police raided the apartment in Andrássy Avenue and dragged her away, I added little fluting trills and embellishments to enhance the comedy of Alistair Sim's walk in a St Trinian's farce.

It was a period of leisurely success for me and yet I was aware that I shouldn't have been enjoying myself. Rákosi, the bald, loon-faced paranoiac who was the head of the Communist party in Hungary, was inflicting a reign of terror upon the country that was far worse than anything that had gone on before the war. Of course, the full truth of his atrocities didn't emerge until after 1956, but I kept in touch with the ex-pat community in London and heard enough horror stories from them to convince me that there was a lot of truth in the rumours.

As if to compensate for my frivolous occupation, I wrote to Anna incessantly. I would sit at my old wooden desk, dip my pen in the inkwell, survey the smoky roof-tops of London from my attic window and then begin to write. I wrote about how much I missed her. I didn't refer to any of the incidents in the war. I didn't mention Imre but I sent my love to Margaret. I tried to present myself as an entirely new person. I redrafted the letters endlessly and ruthlessly expunged any maudlin self-pity that crept into my prose and endeavoured to sound cheerful. I would tell her about my life as a composer in the film industry and try to justify it by saying that I was working for the proletariat. I wanted to bring some comfort and joy into the workers' lives with my cadences. I wrote with such conviction that I almost believed myself.

Just after the war many of my letters reached Anna. She even replied telling me of the amazing political developments occurring in Hungary. She was confident that a new brand of Marxist-Leninism would be established in the country and that some sort of perfect state, paradise even, would happen as a result. 'Imre's work was not in vain, you see. What he fought for is going to come true; it is going to happen,' she wrote in one letter. Unfortunately, in the very same letter she told me that Miss Virág had died. Anna wrote: 'As much as I hate to say this, I have to confess that it was for the best. She never recovered from the war. She didn't really know what was going on. She died from an awful bout of pneumonia. We buried her and wrote on her tombstone that she was the beloved sister of Imre...'

Anna never alluded to the discovery of Imre's body: I'm assuming it was never found. Terrible. What a terrible thing I did. However, it was clear that she had come to terms with his disappearance; I think that all her impassioned exhortations of the communist cause were ways in which she celebrated him. In those immediate post-war years she obviously believed that his spirit lived on in the political movements that were stirring the Magyars.

But after 1949, after the Soviet administration was established in Hungary under the stewardship of Rákosi, I never received any replies to my letters. I waited for them every day and mourned their absence every night when I returned home from Ealing Studios. The only way that I could overcome my sorrow was by writing to her yet again; my own letters always seemed to bring hope to me. I started to lie shamelessly. Instead of being an assistant composer – who didn't receive a single credit – I portrayed myself as the maestro. I was composing all the scores for all the best movies and my work was gaining such recognition that I was dictating what material went into the films. I had quite a few projects in the pipeline. I was the author of a historical epic about our ancestor's life as a Count in Renaissance Transylvania. I had used all our father's stories about ghosts, sultans and chivalry to create a teeming, gleaming epic. Movie moguls were enraptured by my large canvas, my exotic and aristocratic heritage, and were falling over themselves to make the film. There was even a remote chance that they were going to shoot the movie on location in Transylvania and Budapest and that I might be visiting Anna soon.

I did know in my heart of hearts that this was all fantasy -- but I found it increasingly easy, as the years progressed, to slip into a reverie during the day and imagine I was going back to Hungary imminently.

But, nothing was panning out as I would have wished. It was certainly true that I was working in the movies, but what cultured Hungarian was not in the immediate post-war period? When I turned up on my first day on the set of *Cherries for Stanley*, a ghastly children's caper, I was astonished to hear so many Magyar accents. It seemed as if Hungarians were everywhere: applying make-up to the chubby brats' cheeks, adjusting the massive lights, shouting through conical loud hailers, taking down notes for the director and issuing scripts.

I turned to János, who was always at my side then, and asked him what was going on. It was insane. It seemed as if there were more Hungarians here than in a coffee house in Budapest. He brushed his moustache, which was now quite white, and seemed to exude something that was perilously close to a smile as he explained: 'It is quite correct, your Excellency, there are many of our fellow countrymen here. They are all exceptionally talented and certainly have improved the quality of recent English films. I believe that the renaissance of what is termed the Ealing Comedy can be largely attributed to the sudden influx of Hungarians.'

As I drew closer, I began to make out the beaky, dark features of these Magyars. To say that the sight alarmed me is an understatement. I very nearly fainted. I had last seen the make-up artist in the Hungarian Parliament; he was a Baron who had been vociferous in his denunciation of legislation that sought to rid the streets of gas lighting. He had attained the sobriquet of what could be loosely translated into English as 'Gassy Gus'.

I waved at him and attempted to greet him, using his nick-name, in Hungarian. He looked up at me for a brief second, blenched and turned away, slapping on that flesh-tinted make-up with such force that the fat recipient cried out in pain for him to stop.

'But János, he just ignored me,' I whispered as my butler hooked his arm underneath mine and escorted me away from the suspicious crowd.

'I don't think it would be advisable to address anyone you recognise, especially in a public context,' János said as we left the huge, high-ceilinged studio and walked down a narrow, claustrophobic corridor. 'I don't think it would be advisable at all.'

I didn't say any more. I knew exactly what he was talking about and now understood very well why none of the Hungarians wanted to be acknowledged. They were probably all fascists; Horthy's henchmen in one way or another. Although I didn't put myself into this category, I was aware that I, too, had secrets that I would rather were not divulged. Someone amongst that lot would have known László and therefore would probably have some notion that I was involved in my brother-in-law's death. The Nuremberg trials were still fresh in everyone's memory: the victors were still looking for perpetrators of war crimes. If I was not careful my indiscretion could easily lead to some calamity.

And so, I decided not to mix with the other Hungarians that I encountered at Ealing Studios and they chose to avoid me. They were not so numerous as I at first supposed; they just happened to always work together. I was initially somewhat perplexed as to why they did this, because they rarely spoke to one another and when they did they always enunciated their words in the most careful English. But over the years I realised that this cabal of renegade fascists were inextricably entwined with each other. I discovered that in the privacy of some Hungarian cafe or restaurant away from the glaring lights of the studios, they drank together, they danced *csárdás* with other's wives, they played cards and recalled the glory days of the Austro-Hungarian empire.

But why did they avoid me? I think it was partly because the composer with whom I was working, Eli Goldstein, was Jewish. I could tell that they didn't like him by the way that they refused to look at him when he was on the set. He was a very elderly man -- great straggly fronds of white hair dangled from his head as he leaned forward to scrutinise his scores – and he was virtually blind and deaf. He hardly seemed to notice that the world existed, let alone that there were anti-Semites in our midst. His entire family had been killed during the war. He seemed permanently on the edge of tears but miraculously maintained a smile for most of the day.

He was also a great film composer. I would sit with him, watching the rushes of a film, and he would shut his eyes. He would never actually look at a film he composed for. This was why he so desperately needed an assistant to tell him what was happening during the film.

It was a jolly awkward job. While I was watching the film I had to also provide a running commentary for Eli. I would press my mouth against his ear and shout my commentary into it. He would nod and then try conducting with his hands. We would watch the film like this for four or five times and then would retreat into the recording studio where Eli would dictate the score to me. I don't quite know how he managed to produce such perfectly timed music for the films; he seemed to have an internal metronome in his head that enabled him to keep an exact record of when certain dramatic scenes would happen. Usually within a week, we had the complete score and the results always perfectly matched the film.

In the early days I moaned bitterly to János about having to press my mouth to this smelly old man's ears for so many days at a time. I was terrified that I might have developed mouth ulcers. My health, apart from the immediate post-war relapse, had been remarkably robust considering that I was now working five days a week – a punishing schedule that I hadn't even had to endure at the Liszt Academy of Music. But I felt that the ear germs my lips were being subjected to were unprecedented. Not even during the siege of Budapest had such bacteria so unremittingly bombarded me.

János wasn't much help, though he did buy a boxer's mouth guard for me and a few bottles of perfume. But the mouth guard proved to be a ridiculous idea; with it in, none of my words were remotely audible to Eli. The old man was very concerned for me; he thought I had been in a fight and had lost all my teeth. When I appeared the next day with my teeth all intact, he marvelled at the brilliance of my dentist. I was very reluctant to disabuse him of this notion and, thus, whenever Eli introduced me to the various luminaries that occasionally strayed into the recording studio, he would always preface his introduction with a celebration of my dentist. 'This man has the best dentist I ever known. He lost all his teeth you know. None of those teeth are his own. His dentist replaced them all within a day. It is quite remarkable,' he would marvel.

It became very embarrassing and obviously something of a joke throughout the studios. The story of my teeth even reached the most famous actors who appear in the Ealing comedies. And so now I have the claim to fame that such stars as Alec Guinness, Roger Moore and Joyce Grenfell have all inspected the inside of my mouth and remarked on its miraculous repair.

It got rather awkward when they asked for his name and address because I didn't even have a dentist. The sole custodian of my oral hygiene was János; he actually made sure that I brushed my teeth and, after giving a heavy dose of codeine, would pull out any rotten ones. My teeth were, in fact, not in the best condition; years of drinking that sticky beetroot medicine and the neglect they suffered during the last months of the war meant that although they were perfectly serviceable, they weren't pristine. This, of course, all added comedy to Eli's eulogies about my dentist. And I suspect it was the humour of the whole thing that sent so many people to the recording studio; they always did seem to be suppressing giggles.

Gradually, Eli allowed me to do more and more of the composing. By the mid-Fifties he wasn't even bothering to sit through the rushes; he would wait for me to produce the score and then check it over. Without knowing it at the time, I had learnt a great deal from him. Somehow his internal metronome had begun to tick in my own head. I had an instinctive sense of what music should go where and how long it should last; often I didn't even have to time it by my watch. I think this is because most film directors and writers do not think in terms of story and character development; they think in terms of time. Two minutes thirty seconds for a chase, four minutes for a love scene, a minute and ten seconds for an argument, seven minutes for the final climax to the film and a couple of minutes for a resolution scene. They work by numbers and so did I, laying down my timed base rhythms first, my harmonies next and the melody last of all.

It wasn't easy work but by the autumn of 1956 I found that I loved it. I can see now that I had always lived entirely in my imagination – I was a fantasist forever constructing stories for my sister and I to live in – and the film composing was an extension of this fantasy world. Where once I had imagined my sister and I living in the belvedere of our dolls' house, I now replayed jolly English murders, comic misunderstandings and sugary romances in my head and put music to them.

I hardly noticed my physical surroundings. Such was my happiness I had entirely lost my phobia against travelling on the underground. As

I took the train from Paddington to Ealing every morning I didn't register the broken, grey city of London, I didn't see the pinched, angry faces of its inhabitants, I didn't feel the depths of English misery felt by most of the population during those rain-soaked years. Nor did I really consider the plight of the Hungarians. I was too busy writing the music for my films or mapping out the story for my great historical epic about the Count Pongrácis during the reign of Corvinus.

24: UPRISING

The Hungarian uprising changed everything.

At the time, I was in the ascendancy as a film composer; I was just about to have my name put on the credits for my next film: a first for me and something I was very pleased about. I felt, finally, that I was establishing myself. I had also developed a routine that ensured my enfeebled frame was relatively free from disease; I had found an excellent masseur at the Porchester baths who was willing to give a relatively impoverished Count a discount, and János had managed to wangle me extra ration coupons so that he could make up my beetroot medicine whenever I looked like I was about to fall ill.

Through contacts of János – he was forever writing letters to illustrious Hungarians on my behalf -- I had even made several friends who were members of the Hungarian aristocracy and who weren't remotely like the sinister Magyars who worked in the film industry. We used to play bridge once a week in a delightful Hungarian restaurant in Bayswater and discuss the intricacies of medieval Hungarian history: our ancestors' castles, their battles with the Turks, their family heirlooms. We never talked about the immediate past. This was too dangerous. Even though I could tell that these fellows – who didn't hail from Budapest, so I hadn't come across them – were from excellent stock, I felt that it would be impolite to inquire about what had happened to them in the last year of the war. They all had their own butlers like me. I reasoned that no one who had managed to hold on to a gentleman's assistant during one of the worst wars in human history could be rotten.

Yet I discerned their conduct during the war from their reactions to the startling events of 1956. I'll never forget the day when we all saw the first pictures of the Hungarian students marching over the Chain Bridge. The Hungarian film crew were out on location that day so I didn't observe their reaction to those first famous images, but I returned home to find János in a considerable state of excitement. He said that one of my card-playing friends, István, had phoned to say that we should meet in the Bayswater restaurant immediately.

I found the normally sedate surroundings alive with activity. Just about every Hungarian in the vicinity seemed to have descended upon the place; a television and several wirelesses were placed on top of the counter of the bar and every velvet-ruffled booth was jammed packed, with all heads inclined to the wireless. The television wasn't relaying any pictures at that point, but the radio was spluttering out Hungarian at an alarmingly fast rate. Apparently nearly half a million people had surrounded the Parliament building to listen to a speech by the reformer Imre Nagy. Change was in the air. I could hear the crowd reciting the patriotic poem, 'Arise Hungarians!' in the background.

When I asked Istvan what was going on, he whispered to me, 'We're going to kick all those Jew-boy communists out of the country!'

He kept his voice deliberately low because he knew that there could well have been Jewish Hungarians in the room but it was loud enough so that the 'bridge fraternity' could hear. I coloured. Suddenly I had an idea of how he had behaved during the war. If he hadn't actively connived to put the Jews on the trains, he couldn't have helped any of them. For the first time in a long time I thought about Anna. She had been very much involved in my fantasies of returning to Hungary as a great film composer and screenwriter – I imagined countless times how I would shower her with gifts – but I ceased to think about her as a real person. She was merely the recipient of my imaginary beneficence, a cipher with whom I could do what I wished. She had ceased to live an ordinary life or even to have a history, except the history I had reinvented for her. I chose not to think of Anna as a widow, or a mother with a young child; she was still the Anna who dressed up in wild clothes and danced with me.

In a sense the repressive communist regime had aided and abetted these absurd ideas because so little news had escaped from the country. The 1956 revolution changed all of that. As I listened to the radio over the next two weeks and heard about the thousands of Hungarians fighting against the communist establishment, my thoughts returned to Anna. What was she doing? I just knew that she would probably be entangled in the fighting in some way. She wouldn't have tolerated the hideous repression that was being perpetrated by the regime; she was bound to be helping the revolutionaries. If she was part of the uprising, was she being careful not to get hurt? What had happened to her son? What had happened to her?

Memories of the war flooded my mind as I listened to those reports of the fighting. I remembered Anna running across Budapest in the snow and screaming for her husband on the broken promenade. Had she learnt of his true fate? Did she now know about my involvement? Guilt that I had repressed for years now plagued me.

When the revolutionaries finally expelled the Soviets, disbanded the secret police and established the National Guard, I tried my best to celebrate with the other Hungarians in the Bayswater restaurant, but it was difficult. I knew firstly that many of the ex-pats were jubilant for the wrong reasons: they were ecstatic that the 'Jew boy commies' had been given a hiding and that they might soon be getting their former properties back. I was also very uneasy because I knew that at any minute I would receive some kind of missive from my sister and I would finally know the truth.

When the letter did arrive, it was both a relief and a disappointment. It was delivered at the beginning of November, on the very morning that the Soviet tanks rolled back into Hungary. It was addressed to me

in very childish handwriting. I tore it open only to find the simple
message: 'You must take George now. Look after him. Margaret'.

I was panic-stricken. No one had made any demands of me since
the war but this one seemed particularly unreasonable. Was I expected
to chuck up everything I had established in London and make the
arduous journey to Hungary to rescue her child? Of course, I was
aware that this was needed of me and knew that many other ex-pats
had already motored down to eastern Europe anticipating that the
newly liberated country would be throwing open its borders.

I dithered all day, unable to compose a single note for a new Robin
Hood film that Eli had saddled me with. Eli was now so deaf that he
couldn't hear anything I shouted into his ear. He had just told me that
I was not, after all, going to get a credit for the film, and yet I still was
expected to compose all the music. Why didn't I kick up a fuss and
insist upon recognition? In truth, I was quite happy with my anonymity
at that moment; I felt that Eli was obliged to think kindly of me and
this made me think I was a better person than I was. I could fool myself
that I was hugely magnanimous in the way that aristocrats were in the
days of Corvinus.

But I wasn't. I was a wretched, niggling, selfish coward who was
not willing to rescue his poor sister or defenceless nephew from God
knows what in Hungary. Just about everyone I knew was getting
involved in a collective effort to assist the Magyar people in whatever
way they could. While they were driving back to their mother country
with the vehicles stuffed full of blankets, chocolates and passports, I
was fretting about in the recording studio ruminating upon my bad luck
at being born into the accursed nation. You see, jostling amongst my
patriotic thoughts about Hungary were much darker ones. They were
like icebergs threatening at any minute to rupture the fragile vessel of
my nationalism. There were times when I thought it was a bloody
awful country, full of racists, bigots, depressives and deranged
idealists. What did I care if it tore itself apart? I had my own life now;
I wasn't dependent on it any way. I could walk away if I wanted. I

could stop going to Hungarian restaurants, cancel my annual membership of the Porchester baths and cease playing bridge with the wretched washed-up rural gentry who now lived in Bayswater.

I sought János's advice. He was clearing up the dinner things that night when I broached the subject. He held the silver tray steady as he listened to my muted grumbling.

'A letter, János, a letter has come from Margaret and she's asking me to look after Anna's son. And I know I should be very concerned for her welfare and my nephew's but I just don't know if I'm in good enough health to make the journey on the way back to Hungary only to be confronted with a lot of communists,' I said.

János lifted up his chin and gazed at the window. The lights of London shimmered in the distance. I reflected that I lived in a civilised city. I knew I would never be shot at or assailed in any way in this seat of the empire.

'I have the matter in hand, your Excellency. I should not trouble yourself with it anymore,' he said. With this brief statement, he opened the door and vanished into the kitchen carrying the silver tray.

This stopped me in my jittery tracks. I followed him: an unprecedented event.

'You mean you've dealt with it?' I asked, scrutinising his features closely to see if there were any signs that he was lying.

'Yes, I have taken the necessary actions. The details need not bother you,' he said.

I was aware that he was forever writing letters to all and sundry across the globe – mostly old Hungarians who had settled in foreign climes – and now realised that these missives must have had some purpose beyond the purely social. János had his helpers everywhere. I felt reassured. I didn't have to cogitate upon the business any more. János had dealt with it. He knew best and acted for the best. He was, in fact, by far the best man to ruminate upon such matters. I lifted a glass of my beetroot medicine to my reflection in the window and silently toasted my butler.

As the potion slipped down my addled passageways, I thought a little about János. He was really the person to whom I owed the greatest debt. He had saved my life and effectively rebuilt my whole character. He had taken me from the brink of destruction to a flourishing career in the flicks. He was my saviour.

But what of him? Why did he remain with me? Yes, I knew that he was still deeply attached to those old Magyar values of service and deference, but I felt that it must be more than that now. After all, we were in England, the old Hungary had been ruined and would never be reinstated; he was under no obligation to remain with me. Why did he stay? I knew in my blood why he did but I couldn't articulate the reason. We had something between us that was more profound than any other relationship I had ever had with anyone else; he was my brother, my father, my mother and my valet.

I wiped away a tear. I felt like I was going to cry for a long time when another thought stuck me. How were we surviving in such comfort? Although I didn't like to think about it too much I was cognisant of the fact that János was flush with money. He never asked me for wages and always bought every household article out of his own pocket; he paid for the groceries and bills. How did he manage this? It wasn't as if he had much time to himself; on most days he would accompany me to the film studio in order to see that my needs were catered for.

I contemplated asking him outright about his finances but decided against it when he re-entered the room in his white apron, wearing his plastic gloves and carrying a feather duster and sponge. I watched him clean the table and mantelpiece out of the corner of my eye and saw that his attention to detail hadn't diminished with the passing years.

I cleared my throat as he dug out vagrant specks of dirt with his duster.

'János, I was just wondering if I should think about your wages,' I said. I considered saying that really he deserved to be paid but I couldn't say this; I found such a bold approach was far too embarrassing. And besides, I didn't really have the money with which to remunerate him.

'I shouldn't trouble yourself with that, your Excellency,' he said with his back to me as leant forward and wiped down the silver frame of Anna's photograph – the one with her in the harlequin suit.

My knees joggled as I inquired, 'Why shouldn't I?'

János placed the photo securely back on the mantelpiece and admiring it with narrowed eyes, replied: 'Everything has been taken care of and the less you ask the better.'

He pronounced these last words with such precise formality that I almost felt chided. It wasn't my business to know about sordid money matters. I was a former Count, still 'an Excellency' in his eyes. Like my father before me, I shouldn't have to sully my hands with the whole business.

I took a step backwards. My curiosity had been aroused but so had my conscience. I wasn't sure that I wanted to know how János managed to keep us in such style. I had enough to think about.

25: THE ARRIVAL

I suffered relatively few pangs of conscience over the next few days. Even the news that Imre Nagy had taken refuge from the Soviet army in the Yugoslavian embassy, that most of the revolutionary strongholds had been smashed and that hundreds of thousands of people were fleeing Hungary didn't disconcert me. János had the matter in hand. I didn't have to worry about my sister or my nephew if my butler was supervising their safety, albeit from a great distance. I suppose by this time I had invested him with supernatural powers; he was omniscient and omnipotent. Believing in him was the closest I had ever come to believing in God.

This airy, cloud-covered fantasy toppled to earth with a bump when I returned home one day to find an awfully dirty young boy, dressed in rags, sitting at my dining room table. I couldn't believe it at first; there was a common street urchin slurping soup off my expensive china with one of my best silver spoons. I dropped my leather satchel, which contained the score to the Robin Hood film, and ran into the kitchen before the boy had a chance to look up from his soup.

János was busy frying a steak over the stove but acknowledged me when I entered with a courtly bow of the head.

'János, there's something playing with my cutlery and china in the next room,' I said, trying my best to mask my disgust.

János flipped the steak in the pan. A small hissing plume of smoke arose from the pan, filling the room with the smell of succulent beef.

'Yes, indeed, that would be your nephew, George. I am pleased to report that he arrived in England safely yesterday, having escaped from Hungary with a lorryload of steel-workers. Margaret should certainly be commended for devising his escape and putting him in such good hands. He seems to have had a wonderful time,' my butler said with a broad smile.

I didn't know what to be more surprised by; the fact that János was smiling or that I was now encumbered with the responsibility of looking after a young child. My mouth hung open. I blinked. I sniffed the steak once again. I began to mouth some words but nothing came out. I tottered backwards and propped myself up against the crockery cupboard.

'So, Margaret put George on the lorry? What about Anna? Where does she fit into all of this?'

János lifted the steak onto a plate, drained some peas in a sieve and added some *tarhonya*, Hungarian soft noodles, to the side of the dish. He put the plate on the silver tray and turned to face me.

'There are several letters addressed to your Excellency that George brought with him. I have left them unopened on your bedside table,' János said and then walked out of the kitchen.

He left me trembling by the sink. I could tell he was being evasive. He hadn't looked me in the eye all the time he had been preparing George's food. There was something in those letters.

I gathered my wits together and with my heart thumping, rushed into my bedroom. I switched on the bedside lamp. The large, bony shadows of the four-poster bed fell against the table, casting the letters in relative darkness. There were three. Two addressed to me in Anna's hand and one in Margaret's childish scrawl. It was Margaret's letter that I picked up first.

It was dated November 5th 1956. The paper was crinkled up and tear-stained. Translated without the spelling mistakes replicated, it read: 'Oh master, your sister is dead. She was shot. She was caught in cross-fire near the Corvin cinema. She was a nurse. She was brave. Please look after George. Love Margaret.'

The letter dropped out of my hand and I slumped down on the edge of the bed. I felt a huge weight pressing down on my chest. The room seemed to be shrinking to the size of a postage stamp, crushing me into a minuscule ball. I shut my eyes and suddenly I was out cold. I had ceased to be.

* * *

János woke me. He was lifting me up and offering me a snifter of brandy followed by a chaser of my beetroot medicine. I still didn't quite know where I was. I believed I was back in Budapest. My mind seemed to have locked on the night that Anna visited me in March of 1944 – when she demanded that I get her and her husband passports and money. There had been a similar darkness then; a marshy, pitchy blackness that invaded my very soul.

'I can get the money, János, but you will need to get the passports for them,' I said.

'For whom, your Excellency?' János said.

'For my sister and her husband, of course. You will have to the Ministry of the Interior and fetch them tomorrow. I'll give you letters of recommendation,' I said.

'Yes, yes, I will,' János said softly.

Our conversation continued in a similar vein as my butler supplied me with more brandy and medicine. Eventually I fell asleep. For the first time in over ten years I was afflicted by nightmares. Dracula stalked me through the streets of Budapest and caught me finally in the twisting maze of the Buda caves, only to have his face blown off by a shell. László's grin emerged from the bloody wreckage of the vampire's visage.

* * *

János roused me in the morning. He gave me a cup of coffee and drew back the curtains. The grey autumn light of London spilled onto the carpet, reminding me of how far away I was from the halcyon days of Andrássy Avenue. My sister was dead. My father was dead. My mother didn't want to know me.

Anna was dead.

'Perhaps it would be best if I phoned the recording studio and told them that you are ill, your Excellency?' János asked.

'Yes, it probably would be,' I mumbled.

I took my time getting out of bed. I had a fearful headache and my mouth was parched. I pulled on my dressing gown and made my way to the breakfast room only to find that the young child was in the same position as he had been last night; wearing the same filthy clothes and still eating. He was scoffing a croissant and slurping at a glass of milk. He didn't look up as I entered the room. I retreated to the kitchen where János was preparing my breakfast.

'Has he been there all night?' I inquired.

'No, George has slept but he was up early this morning and very anxious to have a substantial breakfast,' János said.

I paused and then sighed. I felt incredibly tired and could sense something very close to utter despair rippling like the incoming tide in my stomach.

'Does he know?' I said.

János took a moment to absorb this question but it was clear from his furrowed brow that he understood exactly what I was referring to.

'Margaret told him before he came. It was the only way she could persuade him to leave the country. She had to say that the bad men had killed his mother and that they might kill him. That made him join the steel-workers in the lorry. But I fear he is confused. He seems to think that it is the revolutionaries who are his enemies.'

My butler's sudden loquacity bemused me. I watched him take out a baking tray from the oven.

'How do you know all this stuff?' I asked.

János placed my freshly baked brioche on a plate and proceeded to leave the kitchen, saying: 'You'll find that the young gentleman is very talkative when he's finished eating, your Excellency.'

However, George seemed to clam up the moment I entered the room. He had finished all his croissants and drunk all his milk. He eyed me suspiciously as I nibbled at my brioche. I nearly choked with the awkwardness of it all. I had no idea what I should be talking to him about.

'So, George, how would you like to see some of London?' I asked.

There was no reply. I surveyed the boy's features. He was awfully thin. His eyes were so sunken that they seemed to be peering out of black holes. His shirt and trousers were not only very dirty but ripped in several places. His shoes were scuffed and he wasn't wearing any socks.

And his mother was dead. I put down my brioche. I couldn't eat. I rubbed my eyes and tried to stop my whole frame from quivering. I wanted nothing more than to return to bed. My headache was getting worse.

'Perhaps it might be a good idea if we took the young gentleman shopping for some new clothes?' János said, obviously sensing my discomfort and coming to my rescue.

A light kindled in George's tarry eyes. He smiled. I felt winded when I saw that he had the same smile as Anna's. The same smile that she had given me when she was mounted on the horse on the merry-go-round in the City Park. I could still see the sticky, pink crystals of the candyfloss smeared across her cheeks. Those white teeth gleaming; her warm hand in mine.

'Yes, yes. I want a uniform. Just like Uncle Joe's, and a cap. And I'd like to go marching and then shoot some people,' he said, banging the table with his fists.

'A uniform like Uncle Joe's?' I said.

'Of course, Uncle Joe, Uncle Joe, makes it rain, makes it snow, fighting for the good of mankind, and kicks the capitalist's behind!' the boy said gleefully. 'I want a Red Army uniform if they don't have that.'

'Err... I'm not sure that's going to be possible. You see...' I muttered. I had run out of things to say. I would have to explain to him that we weren't on Uncle Joe's side in England and my headache was far too bad for that.

János coughed behind me.

'We will do our best to accommodate the young master's wishes, but while we are searching for those uniforms, will you settle for some civilian clothes? Stalin does often dress casually,' my butler said.

George looked gloomy but conceded with a wordless grunt that civilian clothes would be adequate for the time being.

I couldn't decide what my reaction to the child was. On the one hand, I felt excessively irritated by his surliness, alarmed and bemused by his interest in Stalin and uniforms – but desperately sad at his plight. I watched János curl his hand into the child's and escort him back to the guest bedroom where he was sleeping. I was reminded of how János used to treat me when I was a boy; there was a tenderness in his demeanour back then that he no longer showed towards me.

I sat staring at the window, my mind filling up with the golden light of Andrássy Avenue, drifting among its autumnal leaves; staring at the sphinxes outside the Opera House; wishing I was a boy again. I was jolted out of my day-dreaming when János returned with George. He had been transformed. Somehow János had found a pair of shorts and trousers that just about fitted him, even if they were too big.

He led George to the door. The butler turned to me and asked me if I wanted to accompany them on their shopping expedition. I refused, explaining that my headache was too awful to contemplate Oxford Street. Both man and child looked relieved and sallied forth from the flat.

I retired back to bed. I propped myself with my pillows, watched the crisp, wintry sunlight play on the rose-entwined wallpaper for a while and then took a deep breath. I reached for Anna's letters and opened one. It was dated November 1953.

Dear Zoltán,

They have sent me away to the country. In the end the name of Imre Virág counted for nothing. I am still a Countess in their eyes, despite all the commitment I have shown to the cause. They've been good enough not to incarcerate me in a gulag, but I have to say that this 'place in the country' is not luxurious. I keep thinking what you would make of the lice and rats that infest the hut I have to live in, or the manual labour I have do in the fields; pulling up turnips and suchlike. You wouldn't like it at all and the thought of your reaction is the only thing that makes me laugh at the moment.

Why do you never write?

I think of you all the time. I think of how we used to play in the nursery with the dolls' house and it helps warm me here. I think of running around the zoo and how you thought the camel was a humpy monster that was going to eat me. And I remember rescuing you from Wenceslas! And it helps me smile a little.

My husband is gone. You are not here. My child has been taken away from me; he's staying with Margaret in Budapest. I loved watching him grow but I fear I haven't been a good mother. In the years after the war I worked so hard to help the communists and neglected him, thinking that I was helping everyone and my husband's memory in doing so. But now I can see I was wrong to do that. George hardly knows me. Margaret is more his mother than I am. And when I return from here he will know me even less.

And so when I close my eyes, it is you I think of. Watching you on the subway staring with such amazement at all the people, seeing you laugh as I tickled you, giving you your medicine.

I remember you all the time.
You are my love.

Anna

I put the letter down. My tears threatened to spill off my face and destroy those fragile, precious words. I sank down into my bed and groaned with the agony of it. The pain of knowing how selfish I had been, the ghastly knowledge of her death, all the things I had not done. While she had been 'in the country' I had been swanning around in those film studios, doing absolutely nothing to help her; not even thinking about her properly.

I swallowed a whole bottle of my medicine and tried to sleep but I couldn't. Too many images were flying through my mind: the merry-go-round, Anna's wooden, rat-infested shack, George in a Red Army uniform, Imre's death. I opened my eyes and reached for the other letter. It was dated October 1956 and was much briefer.

Andrássy Avenue
Budapest
Zoltán
You have done nothing to help me here. Nothing. There is fighting now. We are going to get rid of these evil bastards who are posing as communists. The true revolution is about to come to Hungary. Imre is going to be proud of me. I am going out now. Soon you will visit us and see what can be done. Imre was right. It can be done.
Anna.

How different she seemed! I marvelled at her resilience. Despite everything that happened to her she was still willing to fight for the cause of Marxism. What a terrible mistake she had made!

However, I was less inclined to cry for her. The terrible self-pity of the last letter had entirely disappeared as she stepped out onto the war-torn streets of Budapest. She had gone out fighting.

Finally, I was able to sleep and mercifully without dreaming. I was woken in the late afternoon by János who brought me a cup of coffee. He glanced briefly at the letters lying on the bedside table and seemed to pale. He set down the tray quickly and said, 'You mustn't believe everything you read in those letters, you know.'

I sat up and wiped the sleep out of my eyes. I took a sip of coffee and asked him what he was talking about.

János peered uneasily at me and adjusted his black tie, coughing a little: 'I am aware that the Countess was prejudiced against me because of her husband. You mustn't believe everything that you read.'

With this, he turned on his heels and left the room. I gazed at him open-mouthed, trying to figure out why he was telling me this. I finished my pastry, drained my cup and padded in my dressing gown into the next room, where I found János playing chess with young George.

The altered appearance of the boy cheered me a little. His hair was cut short, his face was polished and he was sporting an Eton collar, a bow-tie, a black blazer, and grey trousers. János had done a topping job of preparing him for an English education. I congratulated them both on their obviously successful trip and sat down beside them. János poured me a brandy and continued with the game.

'So, what do you think of London?' I asked George.

No reply. The earnest young chap seemed too engrossed in his game to give me an answer. I persisted in asking him what he thought of his new clothes and the metropolis but the boy had clammed up. He continued looking at the chessboard and playing the game. János was forced to answer the questions for him.

That night, after we had all turned in for bed, I was awoken by a terrible racket. I tumbled out of my room only to find George marching around the dining room in his pyjamas shouting at the top of his voice: 'Uncle Joe, uncle Joe makes it rain, makes it snow, Uncle Joe.'

I tried to rouse the boy out of this noisy stupor but with no luck. I had to wake János who managed, after some serious coaxing, to persuade the boy to return to bed. After half an hour of reading, 'The Enchanted Cat', a Hungarian fairy story to him, George fell asleep. Having poured myself a stiffish drink, I listened to János's deep, crisp voice read about evil fairies and intrepid woodcutters from the dining room. When he tiptoed out of the guest room, I hissed at him to sit down.

'What are we going to do with him?' I said.

János smoothed out the creases in his dressing gown and drew back his white hair with the palm of his head.

'I'm not sure what you mean, your Excellency,' he said.

I poured myself some more brandy.

'It's obvious that he's not enjoying it here. He seems to look at me like I'm the devil incarnate,' I said.

'He just doesn't know you very well, sir.'

I sighed. I could sense that János's feelings for George were quite different from mine. He seemed to have some affection for the surly blighter. I knew that I should have shared his emotions but I felt oddly cold-hearted towards the boy. I had a suspicion that he didn't like his mother at all; the laudatory stuff about Stalin was bound to have antagonised her. But why did my butler seem fond of him?

'I just think he might benefit from a British education rather than being stuck in this flat with two ageing Hungarians,' I said brutally. 'Boarding school would be by far the best option for him.'

My butler's face moved back into the shadows. He crinkled his forehead.

'I thought that the young gentleman might benefit from learning about customs of the old Hungary. I would be more than willing to take responsibility for his education,' he said.

In all my years with János I had never faced such insubordination. He had never contradicted me so flagrantly as he did then. I was tired, I had drunk too much and I wanted the issue of George resolved finally. And I knew I certainly did not want my butler devoting all his energies to a delinquent child. János was an old man. He was mad to think that he could single-handedly bring George up.

'No, János – this will not do at all. Tomorrow I will go and see my mother and discuss with her what provision can be made for George's education.'

I spoke emphatically and then lurched off to bed without waiting for János's reply.

Even though, I had a horrific headache the next morning, János tried to pursue his case over breakfast. We both spoke in English while the child glumly ate slice after slice of brioche, watching us intently.

'Are you sure he can't understand what we're saying?' I asked.

My butler nodded, adding: 'This is all the more reason why he shouldn't be sent to the establishment that you are suggesting. He has no knowledge of English; it would be a terrible shock for him. He's already endured a great deal. Now, I could teach him English during the day as well as Hungarian history and we could find a tutor to prepare him for all the relevant exams. He should be brought up in much the style that you were, your Excellency.'

Suddenly I understood. János wanted to replicate, in some small measure, the conditions of my childhood. He was just as nostalgic for those days as I was, only he needed actual people to fulfil his fantasy. The pair of us were hopeless Hungarian dreamers.

'I appreciate that it might be difficult for him to settle in at first, but I think he'll pick up the language quickly and he'll be much happier being around young boys of his own age than he will with us.'

Realising that he wasn't going to defeat me with this argument, János changed tack. He offered me another slice of brioche and then filled up my coffee cup.

'I'm not sure we will find the funds to carry out such an exercise. Such educational establishments as you are referring to are not cheap.'

'That's exactly why I'm going to see my mother today,' I said, pushing away my brioche and finding that it was immediately snatched from its plate by George.

* * *

I hadn't seen my mother in over ten years despite the fact that she lived only a ten-minute tube ride from me in Mayfair. Her second husband had risen high up in the Government and was very reluctant to have anything about his wife's past revealed in the newspapers. If it had been discovered that his wife had formerly been married to a Count who had played a role in Hungary's pre-war fascist regime, he might have had to resign. So it was made clear to me, in no uncertain terms, that I was not to intrude on their lives in any way.

Still, from the moment George had arrived I knew that I would have to pay her a visit if only to tell her that her daughter was dead and that her grandson was now in this country. As I left the tube station and walked through Berkeley Square, I reflected that I could hardly be criticised for my behaviour when I compared it with my mother's. She had been far more neglectful of her former husband, her children and grandchild than I had ever been to my sister or nephew. I had, at least, been willing to shoulder the responsibility of looking after George; she had simply fled from all of us. I had stuck with my father until his suicide, I had saved my sister from death in the Budapest ghetto, I had taken George in. What had she done? Nothing.

Well, now it was time for her to do her bit, and besides, George would be far better off at boarding school than with us. Despite what János said.

I hit the brass knocker sharply against the door of her beautiful Georgian residence. A maid greeted me and after some explanation allowed me to wait in the hallway of the house. Sickly oil portraits of various English lords were dotted around the lugubrious hall. The lords all looked so boring, so cold, so normal when I compared them, in my mind's eye, with the portraits of the Pongrácz counts that used to hang in the Andrássy apartment.

Eventually, after I heard some furious whispering on the upstairs landing, a very thin woman in an elegant, demure suit and a white shirt descended. Her hair was short and blond and her skin was pulled very tightly across her face. I blinked. Through the heavy make-up, I dimly perceived the features of my mother: she had Anna's brown eyes and would still have had my sister's proud nose if it hadn't been subtly altered. She was a different woman.

I opened my mouth, but no words came out. The tight-faced lady beckoned me with a quick flick of her wrist into a small room next to the dining room. It was a study of some sort; there was a desk, a couple of chairs and a big globe standing in a mahogany corner. The rouged lips didn't speak until the door was closed. Her brown eyes didn't look at me.

'What do you want?' she snapped.

I sat down and took off my hat, bemused by the abrupt manner of this woman. Who was she? Was she really my mother?

'Mother...' I croaked lamely.

'You mustn't call me that,' she said, pinching her lips and sitting behind her desk. 'Mrs Barrington will do.'

But I could see that she was finding it difficult to restrain her emotion. She had given birth to me. I was her only surviving child had she but known it. But she was also desperate to forget her former husband, his infidelities, the hold he once had on her. Her hands played nervously with the blotting paper on her desk.

'Anna is dead,' I said, scrutinising her face for some reaction.

'I know,' she said, looking down at the desk, her eyes refusing to meet mine.

'You know? How do you know?'

'All my affairs are watched very closely,' she said. 'I know all about you and Anna. I know exactly what you have been doing, believe me.'

'You know about your grandson then?' I said.

She stopped fiddling with the blotting paper and touched her face. Gosh, it looked tight. I could also see now that although plastered in make-up there were swollen bags under her eyes. She had been crying.

'Yes, yes. And I want to do anything I can for him,' she said, now surveying me with more optimism.

'Well, despite the protestations of János, I do feel that he should be sent away to boarding school. I can't see that I'm going to do him any good,' I said.

An awkward smile of relief, of concurrence fluttered on my mother's lips.

'You're quite right. Boarding school would be an excellent place. Obviously, he cannot attend one of the more prominent institutions because he would be far too conspicuous there. But there are plenty of lesser public schools which are excellent and will ensure his relative anonymity,' she said softly.

She stood up and handed me a card, indicating that it was time for me to go now.

'You mustn't come here again, Zoltán. I feel dreadful for saying it, but it's true. The press often watch who is coming in and out of this house and we don't want to get their suspicions up, do we? This card contains the name and address of my solicitors. They will deal with George's schooling and send the bills to me,' she said, adding in a very low voice: 'We must all do our duty.'

With that I found myself standing in the hallway of the house again with the portraits of the dour lords staring down upon me. The study door closed behind me. I was alone once again.

I returned home to find János teaching George how to make *Jókai bableves*; a thick bean soup that contains smoked gammon, sausage and small dumplings. This was unprecedented. I had never thought that

I would see the day when my butler would deem it fitting for a young gentleman to learn how to cook. George was chopping up the sausage and laughing as he said, 'Chop, chop, chop, off goes his head!'

He stopped his inane chant the moment he saw that I was in the room.

'What's going on here?' I asked in the most light-hearted voice I could muster.

János turned to me with a meat cleaver in one hand and flour on the other and said, 'I am just teaching the young gentleman the rudiments of Hungarian cooking. I feel it would stand him in good stead.'

I thought this was a ridiculous notion: George would have servants or a wife to do his cooking when he was grown up. But then I considered again. He probably wouldn't have servants – they were certainly a dying breed in England – and looking at him I judged him to be such an eccentric that he almost certainly wasn't going to find a wife. Perhaps János was correct.

'Right...' I said. 'I'll just be waiting for you next door...'

I departed and retired to my bedroom, nursing a small bout of neuralgia. János woke me shortly before dinner time with a rather unexpected but pleasant cocktail.

'It was the young boy's suggestion. Apparently, he's heard a lot about you from Margaret and your sister. He was puzzled as to what a cocktail was and why you liked them and so I made one for you to show him the procedure,' the butler said.

'You're not teaching him to become a valet, are you?' I said as I stepped into my evening wear.

'No, sir. I just have a premonition that he might well benefit from some of my knowledge,' János said, as he helped me with my tie.

I didn't reply to this but proceeded to explain what had happened earlier on in the day with my mother. I stressed in particular that she thought it was an excellent idea that the boy be sent away.

'I would be very sorry to see the young gentleman go, sir. I feel with the right care and attention he could become a very fine gentleman indeed,' János said.

This was too much. Why was János contradicting me? Why was he making me feel so guilty about giving the child a good education? It was unendurable. He was my servant not my conscience.

'He is going away and that's that. I don't want you talking about this anymore; it's going to bring on another attack in me. Do you understand?' I said furiously.

To my surprise, János did not back down. He did not click his heels in that deferential way he had, bow slightly, and say, 'Very well, your Excellency.' Instead he straightened himself up and took a step towards me. His shadow loomed over me. At his full height he was a very tall man. Between the multiplicity of his crow's feet, his eyes seemed moist.

'I have obligations to the boy, sir. Obligations that force me to say in the strongest possible terms that he should remain with us,' he said.

I gulped. I couldn't believe what I was hearing. I had ordered him to drop the subject and he had ignored me.

'Obligations? What obligations? What on earth are you talking about?'

He turned away from me and walked to the window. He remained silent for a long time. This irritated me. I deserved an answer. I repeated my question, moving closer to him. I could see that he was inhaling deeply and putting his hands together as if praying.

'We must not talk about this, sir. I must ask you to respect my privacy,' he said.

I flicked my bow-tie with my fingers. He had no right to privacy in this matter. George was my nephew. He had Pongrácz blood in his veins. I had every right to know about anything that affected his welfare. The memory of my visit to my mother briefly flashed through my mind. My stomach lurched. She had been similarly cagey with me. She hadn't told me why she had ignored me all these years. I knew why but I deserved an explanation, an apology even, from her. And here was János bottling up on me in the same fashion.

'No, János, I won't have it!' I shouted, the repressed rage against my mother, against Hungarians, against my isolated fate suddenly exploding in me. I was like a mortar bomb that has lain buried in the ground for many years and now has had its bed of earth disturbed. 'You must obey me. You must tell what is going on! If I can't even depend on you to tell me the truth, who can I depend on? We have lived through everything together. You have been the one person I have relied on.'

What had initially been anger at János's disobedience now transformed into tears of self-pity. My throat was burning. János was the only person I had left and he was spurning me. These last words made him turn around. The branches of a tree scraped at the window. It was very dark outside. I hadn't noticed until now quite how dark it was. There was sweat beading the whole expanse of János's weathered forehead. But his brown eyes still did not meet mine.

'We have lived through everything together, haven't we?' he said, now raising his eyes to look at me.

I shivered. I had never seen this look from János before. It seemed as if he was almost pleading with me to treat him as an equal, a fellow fallible human being. What was going on?

'We have,' I said, feeling my bluster simmering down. 'And now you must tell me because, because...' I was finding it difficult to grope for the right words until I eventually blurted out, 'because we are friends!'

János bit his lip and reached for his pocket. He dabbed his forehead with his white handkerchief.

'And you will forgive me for whatever I say to you?' he said after he had finished moping his face.

Again, I was knocked off balance. I steadied myself against the four-poster bed and said rather too brusquely, 'Yes, of course. Of course, I'll forgive you.'

János had become deathly calm now. As still as a ghost. He said, 'No, that is not good enough. You must really forgive me.'

I sighed impatiently and then looked at his resolute features. He wasn't going to tell me anything until he was convinced that I was going to be truly understanding.

'How can I forgive you if I don't know what it is you have done?'

János's reply was immediate. 'Because that is what I have done with you.'

His clipped, brutal words hung in the air like a ship at the edge of a waterfall, waiting to plunge into the depths. It occurred to me that he probably had had to forgive a great deal in my behaviour. He had seen me at my very worst. The image of me constantly calling for his attention while Miss Virág lay dying in that cellar sprang to mind.

'Yes, I'll do that,' I croaked, reaching for the cocktail and swallowing all of it in one gulp.

He turned away from me again and pressed his head against the cold, dark windowpane. He placed both of his big hands against the glass. The hairs on the back of his hand were now all white.

'They knew about you all in the apartment. László knew...' he faltered and then seemed to crumple.

I bounded up to him, peering into his face to check that this was what he had really meant to say. He avoided my eyes again and sat down on the bed, looking giddy.

'They wanted your sister's husband and if they didn't get him they were going to kill all of you. I told them where he was,' he said, his face stark, his eyes gazing disconsolately down at the Turkish rug. 'At the time, I knew I had no choice. I didn't want to burden you with the decision so I took it myself. But as we were driving away from there, after all that happened, I realised what I had done. I realised I had obligations to his son and that if I was ever able, in any way, to make some kind of reparation, I would endeavour to do so.'

I don't know when János left the room. Both of us sat in silence trying to absorb the full force of his revelation. The idea of forgiving him didn't enter my mind. I was too busy trying to replay all those events in my mind and comprehend them in this new light. There was now a horrid logic to it all. János must have phoned László that day and told him where Imre was hiding -- so that's how László had caught my brother-in-law.

I didn't go to dinner that night. I sat in my bed and thought, churning over what he had told me. I was incredulous at first. It was he who had betrayed Imre. Both he and I knew what had happened to that poor man and yet, even though we had been inseparable for most of our lives, we had never spoken of it. We had pretended that it hadn't happened. We had known Imre was dead and yet we hadn't told Anna.

János had virtually signed Imre's death warrant.

Had he been in league with László?

How was I going to live with him, knowing this? How could I survive without him?

János was right. He certainly did have obligations to George. He owed that child more than anybody could possibly know except myself. How was he ever going to repay that debt? How was I?

And yet what else could János have done? He had to surrender Imre if the rest of us were going to survive.

And what of George? What should I do now?

I pulled up the covers and curled up into a ball. I didn't want to think about it. I shut my eyes and concentrated upon thinking about Anna playing with the dolls' house in the nursery. I remembered the luxuriance of her hair as she untied it and let it fall from her shoulders. Her hair. Her soft, lovely hair.

I woke to find someone in my room. It was still dark. The tall, stooped silhouette of my butler was haunting the window. The streetlight cast a ghostly glow over his wrinkled features. His moustache was a ghastly white.

'János, what are you doing?' I asked, sitting bolt upright in the bed.

'He liked his dinner, your Excellency. He greatly enjoyed the bean soup, which he made,' he said. 'If he goes away, he'll still come back at weekends, won't he? He'll come back and I'll teach him how to cook in the correct Hungarian fashion.'

I thought about this for a moment.

'Yes, you can teach him how to cook.'

'I will certainly do that. I will carry out that instruction,' János said.

With that, he stepped back from the window and stood still for a few moments. I listened to his breathing slow down to its normal rate. And then with his typical, measured, rhythmical steps he left the room.

The next morning, I found that both George and János served me breakfast. Apparently, the young gentleman had been learning about how to make the perfect omelette; he'd cracked the eggs and whipped them up.

'János says that I'm the best whipper in the business,' George said as he held the steaming plate before me.

It was the first time the boy had ever spoken to me. I could see that János's attention was slowly but surely breaking that shell of reserve that encased the boy. I gazed at János as I ate the omelette – which, I must say, cooked in just the way I like it. The old man showed no signs of tiredness or any indication that he had behaved in a most unusual way during the night.

'George and I are going to inspect schools today and find which one he would most like to go to,' said János.

I narrowed my eyes at the butler, trying to work out what his position on schools was. Still in doubt as to whether he was referring to day or boarding schools, I decided that I had to take matters into my own hands.

'Yes, I have decided that it would be best for you to attend a boarding school. Somewhere where you will receive a good education,' I said.

Not a word more was said until both János and George were about to leave the flat. I asked the butler as he was putting on his coat, 'So we really are going to find a boarding school for him, are we?'

János nodded and then added as he was just leaving, 'If he receives the relevant lessons.'

Over the next few weeks, János and George spent most of their time scouring the south-east of England looking for a suitable school. Apparently, the boy was very particular about what schools he wished to attend. He wanted to be a pupil in an institution that had imposing wrought iron gates and contained a statue of a great soldier in its forecourt.

'But this is ridiculous,' I protested, speaking in English so that George wouldn't understand me. 'You can't let the boy choose his own school, especially when he has such erroneous notions.'

János finished making a dumpling and handed it to the boy who then dropped it into the bubbling pot.

'I entirely understand the young master's wishes; he wants to be part of a great institution. He won't accept anything mediocre,' my butler replied.

But George had Pongrácz blood in him and I felt that I understood better why he had such particular criteria for his school. He was hoping that no school would be adequate. He was enjoying the company of János far too much to want to sit at a dreary desk and learn his three R's.

My intuition was confirmed one night when János returned home, looking positively triumphant. They had found just the right school north of Watford, the Bottomley School for Boys; it had huge, sculptured gates, a magnificent statue of Lord Bottomley on his horse in the forecourt and it would be willing to provide George with English lessons.

I noticed that as János eulogised the school's great historical traditions, its large grounds and cricket pitch that George looked even more solemn than usual. I asked the boy if there was anything the matter and he shook his head. He still wouldn't talk to me at great length but at least he was communicating with me. A few weeks in England had really changed him physically; he seemed taller, had put on some weight and the bags under his eyes had disappeared. Even so, dressed up as he was in his high collar, black jacket and grey trousers, he looked very much the refugee; there was still a hounded, ghostly glint in his eyes and his small hands would often tremble when he was confronted with trouble.

His fingers were quivering now. He put the last of the dumplings in the soup and then ran from the room.

'Are you sure that he wants to go there?' I asked János again.

I think that János didn't understand people who reneged upon their words and he repeated with the utmost confidence that the Bottom (as it was affectionately known by all and sundry) would do a good job. 'Besides which they will let him come home for the weekends,' he added.

A few days before I would have balked at this news but now I realised János would keep the child out of my way, I was less inclined to insist that George was a permanent boarder. Besides, I was also growing rather fond of the child's eccentricities: his singing of Stalinist nursery rhymes, his propensity to march up and down in the dining room before eating his dinner, and his devotion to cooking and to János. I was beginning to notice too that George had definitely inherited something of my father's love of design, engineering and architecture, except that his passion was Soviet military hardware, not bridges. He was often to be found sitting at the dining room table, attempting to draw various guns, rifles, ships and tanks.

I was somewhat disconcerted not to find George doing this when I left the kitchen; trying to perfect a drawing of a Kalashnikov rifle was his customary habit before dinner. Instead I heard a low moaning emanating from his bedroom. Tentatively I entered the darkened room and saw that the boy had thrown his jacket on the floor and was sitting crouched over his drawing pad with his pencil in hand, crying.

'Isn't a bit dark for you to draw in here?' I asked, still standing in the doorway.

He didn't answer at first. He looked up at me, obviously surprised to find me there. He shifted his head to one side in an attempt to see whether János was behind me. When he saw that he wasn't, he turned away from me and plunged his face into the pillow. It was a gesture that I immediately recognised. I used to do it all the time when I was feeling sorry for myself. I didn't know what to do. I wasn't used to dealing with children.

But I hadn't survived the war only to be frightened off by a little child. I walked into the room and sat down beside George, his head still buried in his pillow. He sat up.

'It will work out at the school. You will like it there and you can come back here at weekends,' I said, without much conviction in my voice.

George seemed to think about this. I handed him a tissue, a box of which János had thoughtfully placed by his bed. He took it and wiped his eyes.

'They pulled him down, you know,' the boy said.

This puzzled me. I leant forward and asked him what he meant.

'They got blow torches and separated his body from his feet. Only his boots were left,' he said, the tears beginning to stream down his face again.

I thought about this for a moment and then realised what he was talking about the statue of Stalin that the crowds had pulled down at the onset of the October revolution. He was crying because that evil tyrant's effigy had been destroyed. I cleared my throat.

'George, you do know why those people did that, don't you?'

'Because they were evil capitalists,' he said in a matter-of-fact voice.

I shook my head vigorously.

'Stalin was a bad man, George. He did many bad things, including things against your own mother. That was the reason why she was sent away from you. That was the reason she died,' I said, feeling rage bubbling up in my chest. 'Hasn't János spoken to you about this?'

George considered what I had said and wrinkled his forehead, clearly surprised by this news.

'János would never criticise Uncle Joe,' he said slowly.

'That's because János is a valet; it is not proper for a valet to say that his master's opinions are incorrect.'

'But everyone says that Uncle Joe is your friend. He will look after you if you believe in him. Even Margaret said that. Even Mama said that,' he said. His lip started to tremble.

'That's because she had to. They all had to say Uncle Joe was good.'

'So why are you saying he's bad? You have to say he's good as well.'

'We're in England, and people in England know Uncle Joe was a very bad man.'

'But at home they said he was a good man. Why can't I go home?'

I was hopelessly out of my depth now. I tried to explain that England was a democracy and that people could speak freely here but that in Hungary people had to keep their own views to themselves. George didn't really understand. Trying to explain the differences between communism and capitalism to a nine-year-old wasn't easy. As I fumbled for an explanation, George smiled and said, 'I could report you to my teachers, you know. You could get into a lot of trouble like Mama did.'

I didn't like to dwell too much on this last comment. Feeling a chill, I suddenly wondered why she had been 'sent away to the country'.

I shuddered and hastily suggested that it was time for dinner.

Once George had safely been packed off to bed, I told János about my conversation. Nothing I said seemed to surprise him in the least. He poured me a brandy and together we sat down on the two chairs that faced the windows. This was the first time we had ever sat down side by side in the evening. Normally János would either be in his room reading, ironing clothes or preparing food in the kitchen. But now that I knew the truth about János, oddly there seemed to be more of a sense of us being equals than had ever existed before.

Perhaps it was because János had finally realised, with the arrival of George, that he was living in England, that he would never return to Hungary and would never see restored the social order that he had so loved. Or perhaps it was because he was aware he was George's most reliable protector and that this responsibility gave him social parity with me.

'George is labouring under the delusion that Stalin is like God,' he explained. 'I have been aware of this for some time. I have told him that it is, in fact, our Lord who should enjoy this role in his mind but he refuses to believe me. This is yet another reason why being exposed to the environment of the Bottomley school would benefit George. It has an excellent chapel and a strong religious tradition as well as an army corps, all of which, given time, George would like.'

'I see you've changed your tune about the schools business then,' I said, swallowing my brandy.

János winced. This was the first time he had ever really been forced to change his mind about something.

'I suppose I feel that I can still carry out my obligations to the child if he attends that institution.'

* * *

I'm very glad that I didn't go along on their initial visit to George's school. If I had seen it then I would have probably insisted that he didn't attend it. When I did eventually view its insipid teachers, its sleepy children, its dank corridors, its ivy-infested courtyards, its cramped classrooms, its horrific prison-like dining hall and its green, tarnished statue of Bottomley, I was horrified. It seemed the most sinister, wizened place that I had ever encountered in England. It was positively Hungarian in its gloominess.

Perhaps that's why George loved it so much. János proved uncannily accurate in his assessment of George's character. Within a year, the boy had replaced Stalin with God, his Russian marching songs with English ones and his love of Soviet military hardware with a great enthusiasm for English weaponry. He was now, more importantly, speaking the English language fluently and employing the same brisk, clipped tones that an officer might.

At first, he had been very anxious to return home at weekends but as his English improved he became more reluctant to swap the company of a rowdy group of boys for two fastidious, old-fashioned Hungarians. Eventually he claimed that his commitments to the army corps meant that he couldn't see us as frequently as he wished.

But he did come home for the holidays and it was then that I learnt that his allegiances to the Soviet cause had switched to fighting against the Red Menace. He had a very capable history master who had explained to him what had happened behind the Iron Curtain much better than I ever could. By the end of his first year, he started to curse the evils of communism.

'They killed my mother, you know,' he said to me, looking up from a Biggles storybook. 'They killed her because she was fighting for what was right; she wanted Hungary to be more like Great Britain.'

I found his whole demeanour as he was saying this very curious. He pronounced his words in such military English that he seemed to have no real emotion invested in his mother's death. He had acquired some of the stiff upper lip English manner that I had only seen in films, never in a real person. And it was clear that now his mother was out of the way he could construct an entirely different image of her from how she was. I knew that Anna couldn't stand the English imperialists and that far from wanting to destroy communism she merely wanted to change it for the better.

But I didn't disabuse him of his notions because it obviously brought him a great deal of comfort. 'She was a good egg, my mother,' I would hear him saying to János. 'She liked the British bulldog spirit. And she liked Biggles. She used to read the stories to me before I went to bed, you know.'

'Did she now?' János would say, knowing full well that this was utter codswallop.

'Yes, and she always made me say my prayers. She knew the Our Father and would say it even though she could have been arrested for saying it,' he added.

I was severely tempted to interrupt now because the concept of Anna's saying her prayers was so foreign to me that I couldn't even endure entertaining such an absurd idea. But I resisted. It would create unnecessary friction and besides the boy seemed so happy in labouring under this delusion.

Unfortunately, George's education also had the effect of making him less respectful of the time-honoured Hungarian traditions in which János had been so anxious to school him. He refused to learn any more cooking, insisted that we always spoke English and often would refer disparagingly to the Hungarians' military prowess. Even János's tales of St Stephen's great exploits on the Hungarian Plains, Corvinus's great Renaissance court and battles with the Turks failed to inspire much loyalty in him.

János tried his best to be sanguine about George's lack of interest in things Hungarian, saying that he was now a young English gentleman and that he was quite right to assert British superiority repeatedly in his conversations. However, I could tell he was bitterly disappointed. He had had such great plans for George. He was ready to groom him to be a sophisticated European Count, a dashing charmer who would woo grand ladies and politicians with his impeccable manners, his superb dancing and culinary Magyar delights. Instead it soon transpired that George was more interested in being a coarse English patriot than a debonair socialite.

It was then that I realised that János's first loyalty was to my father. The Count had been all of the things that János hoped George would become. (Of course, the Count was never a great chef but I think János's belief that George should learn to cook was his sole gesture towards modernity.)

János's failure to teach the boy how to waltz properly, to rustle up a masterful goulash, to eat decorously or even to have remotely good manners seemed to draw us more closely together. Failure was a good friend of mine. The list of my aborted projects was long: I had managed to lose my title, my lands, my father, and my sister. I was one of the few people thrown out of the Liszt Academy of Music, I had been rejected by my mother, I had no normal sexual proclivities and, lastly, I had been sacked by Ealing Studios.

Shortly after the crushing of the Hungarian Uprising, Eli Goldstein died of a heart attack. I had expected to be appointed the official composer for the next few films but this was not to be. Frightened that their films weren't modern enough, the studio hired a ghastly American jazz musician to spice up their soundtracks and he, taking one look at my aristocratic features, promptly fired me.

It was just as well because I had lost my appetite for the business. I had persistently failed to turn up for rehearsals of the Robin Hood soundtrack and wasn't interested when they asked me to make some alterations to it. Somehow the things that had happened to me during the Uprising sucked the wind out of my sails and left me frozen in London like a painted ship on a painted ocean.

The knowledge that my sister was dead seemed to demolish a part of my brain. The brightly lit arena of my fantasy world which had crowded many of my waking hours with images of children playing in our Andrássy apartment was shut down. The lights were turned off.

The stage was plunged in darkness. And there was I, sitting in the stalls, waiting for the show resume -- but it never did.

Equally distressing for me was the new relationship that I had with János. His confession to me liberated him but it also imprisoned me. He treated me much more like an equal now; he took much more interest in George and his education than I ever did and would often drink brandy with me in the evenings. He ceased calling me 'your Excellency' and would often avoid calling me anything. If pressed he was settle upon 'sir' but this was rare. He was much more relaxed and seemed determined to enjoy his semi-retirement.

The gradual easing of all these mores depressed me. My social superiority was not stressed to me repeatedly throughout the day anymore. I realised that this was the one thing that had helped me maintain some notion that I was a good person. Once this charade was dropped I found myself dwelling a great deal more on the darker side of my nature. I had no facade to maintain, I was answerable to no code of practice, I wasn't obliged to the old order and I certainly felt no inclination to fit in with the new one.

Quite by accident, I discovered The Jolly Traveller, a pleasant but secluded pub in a mews near where I lived. It was just the place I had been searching for during the ten years I had been living in London. A venue where gentlemen could meet like-minded gentlemen. There were opportunities for this, of course, at the Porchester Baths: I had met a considerable number of like-minded gentlemen during my time there. But it was all dashed awkward at the Porchester. For one thing, it was full of Hungarians and it was never easy to escape their prying eyes and, for another, the police closely watched the Baths. If there was any sign that illicit activities were going on in their cubicles they would have been shut down.

I had no such problems at The Jolly Traveller. The owner of this fine establishment was most sympathetic and offered the most luxurious and convenient facilities that I had come across; the toilets were always kept spotlessly clean and there was a carpeted section by the sinks. Most importantly, you could lock yourself in so there was no worry about being interrupted.

* * *

János survived until George's graduation from Bristol university in the summer of 1969. It turned out that while George was never going to win any awards for his manners, dancing or cooking, he was talented in other ways. He seemed to have inherited my father's technical skills and achieved, as a consequence, a first-class degree in engineering. I was desperately sorry that neither the Count nor János were present when we received the news, several years later, that George had got his first major job working as a construction engineer on the building of the Humber suspension bridge.

But János was dead by then. He was a very elderly man at the time of George's graduation and had barely been able to make the journey to Bristol to attend the ceremony. He suffered from crippling arthritis in those last years and this made even the smallest movement agonisingly painful. In a cruel reversal of roles, I spent the last few years of the 1960s looking after him. Perhaps surprisingly I didn't mind doing this too much. The Jolly Traveller had shut down a few years previously, and the beginnings of old age meant that I had rather lost interest in meeting like-minded gentlemen and really had very little to do. János's ailments kept me occupied. My exploits at The Jolly Traveller had also caused me to lose much of my old squeamishness and I made an adequate nurse.

But mostly it was the way János started talking so freely about the golden days of Andrássy
that meant that I never resented caring for him. His body may have been decaying but his mind was as sharp as a blade. Together we would voyage back to those days, recounting repeatedly that trip to the zoo, talking endlessly about Anna's keen intelligence, my propensity to feel sorry for myself, my father's bridges.

This was what was most interesting for me: hearing János's tales about my father. I was also able to piece together the hitherto buried story of my butler's life while he told me about the great days of my father's youth. János had been taken into service by my father when he was only ten in 1890; he started as a groom in the stables of the great Pongrácz castle in the Transylvanian mountains. However, when he helped my father recover from hunting accidents on several occasions, the older Count, my grandfather, decided to train him as his chief valet. This meant teaching him how to speak English, to cook, to dance, to mend clothes, furniture and anything mechanical.

'Your grandfather saw that his son would need someone to protect him at all times. He saw that your father was a very rash and impulsive person who would need a butler versed in all the relevant skills to look after him. Just before the old Count died he told me that I must ensure, now that I was properly educated, that I carried out my obligations to the young Count,' János would tell me, adding: 'Of course, I tried my best, but when your father married your mother I lost all control of him. Your mother insisted that he listened to her rather than to me. I think this fatally confused the Count in the end and he sought solace in inappropriate ways.'

János never referred explicitly to my father's affairs but it was obvious that this was what he was referring to. Yet this wasn't the only explanation that he had for my father's decline into suicidal depression: the Treaty of Trianon, his unhealthy obsession with bridges, the sacking of Miss Virág and Anna's marriage were all blamed. I realised that my father's death was the single most disturbing event that ever happened in his life. Nothing after that had seemed as terrible.

'You see, I didn't fulfil my obligation to the Count, did I?' he said once as I helped him into bed one night shortly after George's graduation. 'I had made a promise and I reneged on it.'

'I don't see what else you could have done. You carried out your obligations just like you did with George,' I said.

This was the right strategy. A thin, cracked smile spread over his lips as he lay down on the pillow.

'He has done well. I know he hasn't achieved what I thought he would, but I can see now that probably is for the best,' János said. 'Probably for the best.'

Those were the last words anybody heard my butler say. He died in his sleep that night.

A surprising number of people surfaced at his funeral. They were mostly Hungarians from the Bayswater restaurant I used to frequent and several faded luminaries who used to work at Ealing Studios. By the late Sixties, the studio had fallen into serious decline and the three Magyars who had been so puffed up on the set now seemed shrunken and sad.

One of them approached me after the burial -- which took place in the graveyard of a Roman Catholic church in north London. It was a blustery, autumnal day. Golden horse-chestnut leaves swirled around our feet as George and I passed through the iron gates that heralded the entrance to the graveyard.

'Yes, I was jealous of you having such a good butler. I wish I had had such a good man in my employ,' a bald, ageing man with big blue glasses said. I recognised him as the chief set designer for the Robin Hood film for which I composed the music for and several other awful movies.

'He was the best valet I ever encountered,' I said, feeling somewhat choked.

'He certainly was,' the bald man said. 'I have yet to come across a butler who even does his master's blackmailing for him!'

I contemplated this mysterious comment and then asked him what he was talking about.

The bald man laughed contemptuously. 'You don't know? Surely you must know. János was politely asking for money from several rich Hungarians who were living in England and America. He had written statements that implicated them in all manner of dreadful things that had occurred during the war. Not that it all affected me, of course, but I knew people who were. Apparently, he made a packet for many years.'

He dusted off his hands and jumped into a car that was waiting for him outside the gates. George and I stared through the railings at János's freshly inscribed gravestone gleaming in the low, watery light of the afternoon. George blinked.

'They deserved it,' he said and taking me by the arm, he helped me across the slippery pavement into the hearse. I watched the golden leaves swirl before the car window as we drove away, thinking of all the times János and I had together, remembering in particular that last fateful drive out of Hungary. János was my protector, my true parent, and yet I hadn't realised that until now. A sorrow gripped hold of me that went beyond words; I had never truly expressed my gratitude or love to him. I had never appreciated him enough. I had spent too much of life taking him for granted. London became blurry.

'János, you don't have any pálinka, do you?' I whispered to my reflection in the window.

But of course, there was no reply.

Epilogue

5TH MAY 2017

From: KarolinaTarr99@outlook.com
To: BelaPongracz9@gmail.com

Dear Béla,

Poor Zoltan, reaching out for János, for Anna!
And I can feel his guilt at what he did.
And yes, I feel mixed feelings for him – and for János too.
There was a dark side to both of them.
I want to say it's very Hungarian somehow – but maybe it's just human.
At first, I thought your idea about writing a film script was a good one, but then, after finishing it, I went down to the Danube and walked there, and looked at the shoe-sculpture by the steps.
I showed the metal shoes to you when we first got together: you know, the ghostly shoes with no people inside them, just empty shoes leading down to the Danube making you feel that the people are still there somehow, stepping into the water.
The memorial to all the Jews that were exterminated in Hungary. I felt guilty about the thought of exploiting the Count's words for our own personal gain.
If we do write a script, we need to do it in the right frame of mind.
We should be professional about it. Take it seriously. Do you understand me? If we're just going to do this because it's a good way of getting back together again, then I don't think we should do it.

Do you understand me?

You've got to be honest with me. Do you really believe in the Count's words? Are they the truth? Or are they just an excuse, a diversion, a way of furthering your own career, your own romantic interests?

We need to respect his words. We need to work hard on something. Let's talk!

Yours sincerely,

Karolina.

10TH MAY 2017

From: BelaPongracz9@gmail.com
To: Magda1119@hotmail.com

Dear Mum,

I'm sorry that I am not answering your calls at the moment.

I am writing to tell you that I am not coming home. I am going to stay in Budapest for a while longer. Spring is here and it's gorgeous on the promenade: blossoms blowing into your face, the sparkling sunlight on the Danube, the smell of pastries and perfumed trees, the sounds of klezmer music and boats taking tourists underneath the great bridges.

I've found a job as a production assistant at the Korda Studios -- you know, the film studios I told you about. The pay is not great, but it's enough for me to live here. I've moved out of the centre and I'm living very cheaply in a small flat on the outskirts in an old Soviet council complex. It's very basic, but the people are friendly. I'm learning Hungarian, and I've met someone, Karolina. I'm not sure you'd like her; she's very opinionated. She works at the studios too. Together, we are working on a script based on Zoltan's story.

I know you'd hate that idea, but I am finding it is really helping me to think things through. I am Hungarian, and I never knew it until read the Count's story and I came here. I can feel your grandmother, Anna, inside me. Her resistance.

And it feels this is her speaking as I write to you.

I don't want to discuss washing my underwear with you anymore. Let's talk about something else.

Let's talk about your father. I am beginning to realise now why he was such an angry man. He lost his mother and father to the Communists and the Nazis, and then he was packed off to a horrible boarding school. The only person who really cared for him was János.

And János! I never knew about him. I can feel him inside me now. I have learnt from him. It's important to serve this story faithfully. I am learning this in my job as a production assistant: you've got to pay attention to the details, to the director, the camera person, the lighting, the temperature of the coffee, the air conditioning in the actors' dressing rooms.

You've got to listen patiently, and say, yes, I will make sure that happens. I feel János inside me as I carry out the orders of the guys at the film studios, and I feel my grandfather, Imre, in me as I write the script with Karolina.

I'm gripped by a desire to learn more. I have been reading a lot about Hungarian history, reading amazing authors like Sandor Marai, Imre Kertész. Péter Esterházy and George Szirtes.

I am beginning to understand more about where your anger comes from, Mum. The anger that pulses through you as you suck on your cigarettes and jab your criticisms at me. There have been times when I wish I could speak to my great-uncle again, but I am beginning to realise that I am speaking to him all the time.

He is inside me now. His funny, prolix cadences. His music! I am listening to Bartók, to Debussy, and I've even found some of the Count's own music on the internet. It's amazing that I didn't look before this, but it's there on YouTube! Crazy! His horror movie music from the 1950s -- his name is there on the credits. He wasn't lying. It was all true.

Here's the opening of our film:

The camera swoops down upon a black and white photograph of Budapest in 1919, an aerial view of Andrássy Avenue. It is empty. Street vendors tie black ribbons around bouquets of flowers; inside an apartment, an archduke puts on a black suit and thrums his fingers on a gold-tasselled armrest. There is no traffic on the streets. In the depot, the trams sit motionless. Cut to a tram driver with a child on his knee staring into space: both are dressed in black. A priest hoists a black flag so that it flies on a church tower. Cut to the camera observing the flag fluttering in the wind.

VOICE OVER: Hungary wore black on the day of my birth…

I realise that this script will probably never get made because it would be far too expensive to film, but Karolina and I want to write the script that does justice to the Count's words.

You may scoff, Mum, and think we're wasting our time, but I hope you in time you'll come to see that we're not. I am finding it so healing to get inside my great-uncle's words, to feel them, to work with them, to re-imagine them. To work with someone who cares about them too. Karolina cares.

Your ever-faithful son,

Béla.

ABOUT THE AUTHOR

Francis Gilbert is a Lecturer in Education at Goldsmiths, University of London, being course leader for the PGCE Secondary English programme and the Head of the MA in Creative Writing and Education. Previously, he worked for a quarter of a century in various English state schools teaching English and Media Studies to 11-18 year olds. He has also moonlighted as a journalist, novelist and social commentator both in the UK and international media. He is the author of *Who Do You Love, Teacher On The Run, Yob Nation, Parent Power, Working The System -- How To Get The Very Best State Education for Your Child*, and a novel about school, *The Last Day Of Term*. His first book, *I'm A Teacher, Get Me Out of Here* was a big hit, becoming a bestseller and being serialised on Radio 4. He has appeared numerous times on radio and TV, including Newsnight, the Today Programme, Woman's Hour and the Russell Brand Show. In June 2015, he was awarded a PhD in Creative Writing and Education by the University of London.

Also published by Blue Door Press

WHO DO YOU LOVE BY FRANCIS GILBERT

'I enjoyed *Who Do You Love* a lot. It's beautifully-written, very funny about sex and the excruciating confusion of being young and single then middle aged and trapped. I think you've captured something about a generation in a way that will touch a lot of readers.... Really, a terrific novel.' Amanda Craig, literary journalist, and author of *A Vicious Circle* and *Hearts and Minds*.

Nick is cracking up. In his mid-forties, he has just been sacked as an arts journalist, with little prospect of getting such a well-paid, prestigious job again. Even more worrying for him is his suspicion that his wife, a Deputy Head at a school, is having an affair with a much more successful person: does she want to trade in Nick for a better model?

But most devastating of all is the fact that he learns that a former lover, Ellida, has died. Unable to find a new job, Nick miserably fails, despite his best attempts, to be pro-active and positive, and retreats into memories of the past.

By turns comic, tragic and romantic, *Who Do You Love* is a stirring novel which explores the big issues of passion, death and grief; a fast-paced contemporary love story but also moving exploration of what it means to be alive today, which should appeal to fans of writers like David Nichols, Ann Tyler and Nick Hornby.

TAKING IN WATER BY PAMELA JOHNSON

"An absorbing story of how tragedy continues to shape a lifelong after the headlines are forgotten *Taking In Water* is thoughtful, sensuous. I was completely caught up in it." Helen Dunmore.

Lydia has found a way to live with her past. Or so she thinks. It's 2002, almost fifty years since the sea smashed through Lydia's grandmother's front door, sweeping away her family. Lydia survived the flood of 1953 but was left holding a terrible secret. In the solitude of her remote beach-hut studio overlooking the North Sea, Lydia survives but when art historian Martin arrives to research her years in the art world of 1960s New York, she's forced to decide: is it more dangerous to reveal her past or to keep on hiding?

About the author: Pamela Johnson has published two previous novels, *Under Construction* and *Deep Blue Silence*, both with Sceptre. She's a writing tutor with a reputation for nurturing talent. Teaching fiction on the MA in Creative & Life Writing, Goldsmiths, among her ex-students are Evie Wyld, and Ross Raisin.